S0-AXU-474

THUS SPAKE
BELLAVISTA

Luciano De Crescenzo

THUS SPAKE
BELLAVISTA

NAPLES, LOVE, AND
LIBERTY

Translated from the Italian by
Avril Bardoni

GROVE PRESS
New York

Copyright © 1977 by Arnoldo Mondadori Editore S.p.A., Milano
Translation copyright © 1988 by Pan Books Ltd.

All rights reserved.

No part of this book may be reproduced, stored in a retrieval system, or
transmitted in any form, by any means, including mechanical, electronic,
photocopying, recording or otherwise, without prior written permission of
the publisher.

The name Grove Press and the colophon printed on the title page and the
outside of this book are trademarks registered in the U.S. Patent and
Trademark Office and in other countries.

Published by Grove Press, Inc.
841 Broadway
New York, N.Y. 10003

First published by Arnoldo Mondadori Editore, Milano

Library of Congress Cataloging-in-Publication Data

De Crescenzo, Luciano, 1928–
[Così parlò Bellavista. English]
Thus spake Bellavista: Naples, love, and liberty/Luciano de
Crescenzo: translated from the Italian by Avril Bardoni.—1st ed.
p.   cm.
Translation of: Così parlò Bellavista.
ISBN 0-8021-1077-0
I. Title.
PQ4864.E2394C6613 1988   88-11184
853'.914—dc19   CIP

Designed by Irving Perkins Associates

Manufactured in the United States of America

This book is printed on acid-free paper.

First Edition 1989

10 9 8 7 6 5 4 3 2 1

I should like to possess a blanket
so long and so wide
that it would cover
every single handsbreadth
of my city all at once.

PO CHU-I (A.D. 772–846)

CONTENTS

A BRIEF WORD OF INTRODUCTION

PHILOSOPHICAL ESSAYS or short stories? Let's say both, because while the chapters with odd numbers aspire to the first category, though their style is purely conversational, the even-numbered chapters belong to the second, being simply anecdotes of everyday Neapolitan life, some derived from personal experience, others from reports in the media. Marotta and Plato are the book's twin guides and mentors: Marotta for the anecdotal pieces, Plato for the dialogues between Professor Bellavista—our Socrates—and his group of more or less unemployed student philosophers. May God and the reader forgive me the comparison; I allude, of course, only to the kind, not the quality, of the undertaking.

Although the reader is naturally at liberty to select only the chapters with even numbers or, if so disposed, only those with odd numbers, the plan of the book is not unlike that of an old-fashioned geometry textbook where the setting out of each theorem is followed by a practical example of its application: here, the Neapolitan anecdotes provide, as it were, a QED to some of the philosophical theories expounded by the Professor in the course of his dialogues on Love and Liberty.

The idea for the book came to me one day in Milan when a colleague of mine, born and bred in the north and with no experience of life beyond the industrial triangle, decided to take himself and his whole family to Naples for Easter. Concerned—not without due cause—about what he would make of my native city at his first encounter with it, I held, throughout Holy Week, a series of briefing sessions designed to prepare this Lombard expedition for its foray into Parthenopean territory. I showed my friends photographs of backstreet Naples, described the occupations unique to the city, explained the concept of non-privacy, and finally found myself providing a rundown on the whole Neapolitan ethic summarized by *penzamm' a salute* and *è pate 'e figlie.** When my friends returned, I found that some of this information had indeed proved useful and that a certain benevolence, possibly due to my efforts, had predisposed them to a better and more sympathetic understanding of the real Naples.

I am aware of the fact that by choosing to write such a book I have made myself an immediate target for the reigning Neapolitan intelligentsia, who regard native idiosyncrasy and the *"cielo azzurro"* type of anecdote as Naples' worst enemies, but it is precisely in order to avoid incurring such criticism that I would ask the impatient reader to continue beyond the first four or five chapters of the book and to read it (always supposing that he is enjoying it) to the end; and at the end, in the very last pages, he will find, as he would in any self-respecting detective novel, a complete and exhaustive denouement.

Contemporary Neapolitan literature has moved in alternating phases: the period from the second half of the nineteenth century to the 1940s was rich in poets, musicians, and painters who gave the world that image of Naples we all know so well: *"Chist'è 'o paese d' 'o sole,"* in the words of the song, *"chist'è 'o paese d' 'o mare, chist'è 'o paese addò tutt' 'e pparole, sò ddoce o sò amare, sò ssempe parole d'ammore."*† In this consort of mandolins, the only false note was struck by Matilde Serao, in her marvelous little book *Il ventre di Napoli* ("The Belly of Naples"), a book I never tire of recommending to anyone who sincerely wishes to understand Naples. Since the end of the war, however, the literary scene has been stood on its head. Woe to any writer who dares mention the sea, the sun, or the Neapolitan heart! Malaparte, Luigi Compagnone, Anna Maria Ortese, Domenico Rea,

---

*"One must think of one's health" and "He has a family to provide for"; the latter furnishes a global justification for any and every infringement of the property laws.—*L. D. C.*

†"This is the land of sunshine, the land lapped by the sea, this is the land where every word, bitter or sweet, speaks of love."

Raffaele La Capria, Vittorio Viviani, and all the rest of them were determined to strip away the cosmetics that had embellished the face of our city for so long, and perhaps in so doing they also removed a layer of the skin itself; but the people, even deprived of their mandolins and guitars, continued nevertheless to possess a characteristic physiognomy. True, the advent of the consumer society in the postwar period gave increasing scope to the exercise of bad taste on the part of the masses, so that while the barefoot fisherman of the eighteenth-century Neapolitan oleographs was quite rightly beloved by the poets, it was an unfortunate fact that his jeans-clad successor sporting pointy boots, shoulder bag, and transistor radio at full volume never inspired a similar consensus of approval. But in this period, again, we find a lone voice singing in a different key: Peppino Marotta, word-painter extraordinary, continued to produce poetic descriptions of his native city, of Materdei and the Pallonetto of Santa Lucia, with all the tenderness of former times.

Now, at this point I should like to make something clear. I have a concept of Naples that is not so much of a city per se but rather an ingredient of the human spirit that I detect in everyone, Neapolitan or not. The idea that "Neapolitanism" and mass ignorance are somehow indissolubly linked is one that I am prepared to fight with all the strength I have. Quite simply, I refuse to believe that the living conditions of a population can only be improved at the cost of annihilating everything human in their way of life. Indeed, there are times when I think that Naples represents the last remaining hope for the human race.

All the writers I have cited, from Serao to Ortese, from Rea to Compagnone, obviously had—and still have—a wholehearted love for Naples, but to wish away a dialect in the hope that such an exorcism will serve to integrate the Neapolitans more fully into the national life of the country as a whole is to my way of thinking equivalent to genocide, however laudable the motives. Following such a line of thought to its logical conclusion, one might ask why, seeing that the context of all political and economic discussion is no longer Italian but European, we should not adopt the English language without further ado. In this connection I should like to quote a few marvelous lines of Sicilian poetry by Ignazio Buttitta that were read to me a few days ago by my friend Salvatore Palomba, himself a Neapolitan poet of great sensitivity.

> *Un populu*
> *mittitulu a catina*
> *spugghiatilu*
> *attuppatici a vucca*
> *è ancora libiru*
>
> *Livatici u travagghiu*
> *u passaportu*
> *a tavula unni mancia*
> *u lettu unni dormi*
> *è ancora riccu*
>
> *Un populu*
> *diventa poviru e servu*
> *quannu ci arrobbanu a lingua*
> *addutata di patri:*
> *è persu pi sempi.* *

Wishing to use dialect wherever possible but at the same time minimize the difficulties for my non-Neapolitan friends, I adopted the stratagem of reciting the relevant text into a tape recorder and then patiently translating, word by word, the Neapolitan sounds into their Italian equivalents. Thus, the dialogue retains something of its original dialectical flavor. The reader

---

*"Bind a people in chains, deprive it, muzzle it, it remains free. / Take from it work, passports, food on the table, and beds to sleep in, it remains rich. / A people becomes poor and servile when robbed of the tongue of its fathers; then it is lost forever."

who wishes to savor the local atmosphere as much as possible should try to imitate the Neapolitan accent in his mind while reading the texts. *

So now I leave the stage to Professor Bellavista, Salvatore the assistant deputy porter, and Saverio, whose real name is Gennarino Auriemma, who has no regular employment, and who is, as he would say, *"sempre a disposizione"*—always available.

L. D. C.
Rome, October 1976

---

*Much of the Neapolitan dialect was unavoidably lost in translation, but it has been retained where possible.

TRANSLATOR'S NOTE

EVERY ITALIAN academic or professional qualification generates a title: *dottore* (a graduate in any field whatsoever, including those that carry, in addition, a specialized title such as *architetto,* architect, and *ingegnere,* a graduate in engineering); *professore* (a teacher, not necessarily at university level); *avvocato* (lawyer, legal consultant), etc. Nonprofessional titles include *cavaliere* (formerly a member of the minor nobility, now the recipient of an award of merit, e.g., in the arts or industry), and *don* (in Italy in general an ecclesiastic, or denoting landed gentry, though in Neapolitan usage often no more than an alternative to *signor,* Mr.). These titles are a constant feature in conversation, and I have retained them—frequently in the shortened Neapolitan forms and capitalized, as they form part of the name—because there is no English equivalent to this excellent gambit, which avoids both servility on the one hand and familiarity on the other.

Thus Spake
Bellavista

I

SALVATORE

In Naples everyone lives in a state of drunken self-
forgetfulness. The same is happening to me; I hardly
recognize myself, I seem to have become a different
person altogether. Yesterday I thought: "Either I was
mad before, or I have now become mad."

GOETHE, *An Italian Journey*

THE PORTER'S LODGE of 58 Via Petrarca. We were sitting around a table, myself, the assistant deputy porter Salvatore Coppola, Dottor Passalacqua (third floor, first door on the left), and a stranger who, having arrived a little while ago to inquire about an apartment to rent, decided to stay for a while.

"Well, then, in that case you obviously don't understand the first thing about politics!" exclaimed Salvatore Coppola, assistant deputy porter. "And you a man of learning, too!"

"Learning's got nothing to do with it," I protested. "Every man's entitled to his own opinion where politics is concerned, and there's nothing wrong with that provided he also respects the opinions of others."

"But don't you see, *carissimo Ingegnere,* that this is not a matter of opinion but a matter of international politics!" Salvatore continued. "The essential thing is that all Neapolitans vote as one man for the Italian Communist Party, and then we must leave NATO immediately and sign a treaty of friendship with Russia."

3

"But what makes you think, Salvatò, that the Russians are stronger than the Americans?" asked Passalacqua.

"Americans, Russians, what does it matter who's stronger? I don't care about that, Dottò. But just think for a moment. What would happen to us if a third world war broke out and we were all captured?" His hands went up in a gesture of surrender. "Imagine. War comes, we're on the side of the Americans, now who's actually going to intern us? The Russians, of course. Correct me if I'm wrong. Well, I'm telling you that we as Neapolitans could never survive as Russian prisoners of war. Not in a million years. In the first place, we're not used to a hard climate like Siberia, which is cold, but I mean really cold, and in the second place, we wouldn't have the right gear. To put it simply, Dottò, we'd freeze our butts off in a few weeks. On the other hand, if we were on the Russian side, things would be completely different. In that case, we'd be taken prisoner by the Americans and packed off to America immediately, where, with the help of the Lord and a nose for business, a man could learn the language, and then, seeing as one thing leads to another, what's to keep him from doing just fine for himself, especially while the war lasts?"

"And suppose we were captured by the Chinese?" inquired the gentleman who came to see about the apartment.

"Then we'd be in a real pickle, my friend! Chinese food is disgusting anyway, and just imagine what they'd dish out to us poor wretched prisoners: one riceball a day, with luck. Ugh! And how do you think that I, Salvatore Coppola, with the sort of appetite I've got, could exist on one riceball a day?"

Salvatore Coppola is the assistant deputy porter by virtue of the fact that 58 Via Petrarca already has a porter, Don Armando, and a deputy porter in the person of Ferdinando Amodio, a mythological being half man, half chair. To preempt any misunderstanding, I should explain that Ferdinando enjoys the best of health, and yet I cannot recall ever having seen him stand up. He does not even stand up at Christmas to ask for his tip. He summons you.

Don Armando, on the other hand, likes to describe himself simply as a gentleman who happens to live rent-free at 58 Via Petrarca, Apartment 1, ground floor. And he explains his particular situation to all the new tenants as soon as they move in:

"You see, I both am and am not the porter for this block of apartments. I will explain. My life, unhappily, has never been an easy one. Mine was a genteel family (my grandfather was, modestly speaking, a gentleman of leisure, and my father a clerk with the Water Board), and we lived respectably, owning three properties in Borgo Loreto. Until the black day when my grandfather struck up a friendship with a trial-happy lawyer and all at once the house was awash with legal documents and, to cut a long story short, I soon had to wave goodbye to father, grandfather, and all three properties. So what happened was this: I'd always had one ambition in life—to live in Via Petrarca with a nice view from the window. But tell me, how could a poor devil like me, without a lira to bless himself, ever hope to achieve such a goal? I was resigned to eking out a miserable existence in two rooms at 17 Via Nuova Bagnoli, subjected night and day to the stench from the Ilva factory, when suddenly this chance in a million comes along: the job of porter at 58 Via Petrarca, with salary, free accommodation, and windows overlooking the sea! But, you might object, it means working as a porter. No matter, I reply: if that's what it takes, so be it. But, you say, it means stepping down the social scale. So what? My friend, I don't give a damn for your social scale! When I sit at my window looking out over Capri and Vesuvius, I feel like a company director—no, President of the Republic is more like it! Now, as far as the actual office of porter is concerned, I have voluntarily made over part of my salary to Ferdinando Amodio, who acts as my deputy. Professionally speaking, Ferdinando is the best porter in Naples; he never leaves his post beside the main entrance; whatever happens, you can always count on Ferdinando being there, on duty and immovable."

Given the static constitution of Ferdinando, the dynamic

duties of the post are delegated to the assistant deputy porter, Salvatore Coppola, who thereby shares in a share of Don Armando's salary. It was Ferdinando himself who, with the air of one seeking to forestall serious misunderstandings, explained the situation:

"You see, Ingegnè, I'm a bachelor, and with no wife to do it, who would clean the stairs for me?"

Let us not, at this point, fall into the error of asking how on earth three grown men, two with families to support, manage to live on one porter's salary. For a hundred years, over a million Neapolitans have survived on a few thousand salaries plus additional incomes of a variable nature that can be earned daily through services conjured up out of the air.

Our three porters, for example, enjoy a kind of fiscal right in anything that goes on in the block they supervise. Whether it's replacing a maid, arranging for work to be carried out by third parties, buying and selling property, secondhand cars, wives, or motorboats, or providing information of a confidential or financial nature, it all serves to put money into the pockets of three breadwinners, and, it must be noted, every contribution is amply earned because their competence is exceptional.

To give some idea of how this works, Ferdinando receives a fixed monthly remuneration from the architect Scalese for pretending to be asleep whenever Scalese's shy mistress pays him a visit.

"Very well, then," said Dottor Passalacqua, "so as to keep Salvatore happy we all vote Communist; then, if war comes, Salvatore can go off to Miami Beach as a prisoner."

"That's not the point, I was only joking. The fact is that you, my dear Dottor Passalacqua, are a trifle allergic to the very word 'Communist,' and you fly off the handle as soon as it's mentioned. And that's the sober truth: as soon as someone mentions Communism you're up in arms."

"Salvatò, I've already told you that I refuse to discuss politics with you," Passalacqua replied.

"Naturally, because you're a liberal aristocrat and I represent the people, and you don't want to talk to the people."

"But you, on the other hand, are a lover of the people, right, Salvatò?"

"I admit I'm not crazy about them, but I certainly respect them a lot more than you Liberals do."

"My dear Salvatore, the truth is that you Communists claim to love the people, but as far as I can see, all you really do is hate the rich."

"Ah, no, forgive me for contradicting you, my dear Dottor, but I'm far too busy working from morning till night every day earning a crust of bread to spare the time for hating anybody."

"There's demagogy for you, pure demagogy!"

"Where?" asked Salvatore, looking around. Salvatore knows perfectly well what demagogy is, but it amuses him to pretend not to.

"Where's what?" Passalacqua asked.

"The thing you were talking about."

"I said demagogy, Salvatò, because all you Communists ever talk about is bread, a crust of bread, bread and work, and so on interminably."

"What should I say, then? That I wash five flights of stairs every day to earn a plate of lobster?"

"Salvatò, leaving aside the fact that you never wash the stairs, not even once a month, and that you don't even know what the fifth floor looks like, the point I was making is that the Communists are always singing the same old song about the people dying of starvation. In this day and age, Salvatò, let's be honest, people in Italy no longer die for lack of food."

"It must be a great disappointment to you Liberals."

"Come on, Salvatò, be serious for a moment. I'm a technical man, and I have faith in numbers, in statistics. Do you know what statistics are?"

"Only approximately, since my education was somewhat neglected. I presume—correct me if I'm wrong, Dottò—that if

they put my ass in an oven and my head in a fridge, I could be said
to be statistically comfortable."

General laughter. The company had now increased. Crowds in
Naples appear out of nowhere, and invitations are unnecessary.
Participation is impartial, and people tend to agree not with the
best argument but with the best orator. Salvatore is a Communist
and claims to have taken part in the famous four-day Naples
uprising despite the fact that he was only eight at the time.
Passalacqua, on the other hand, describes himself as a Liberal,
unaware that he is actually a Monarchist and Fascist—in the
best possible sense.

"Salvatò, you're a good man, but you must try to understand
what I'm saying," said Passalacqua impatiently. "We're trying to
have a constructive discussion, and all you do is interrupt with
witticisms."

"So what about these statistics, Dottò?" asked the man who
came about the apartment.

"Now, the statistics, the statistics show that the annual
income per capita, that is, per person, in Italy is one million one
hundred thousand lire for every inhabitant, which makes Italy
one of the richest nations in the world."

"Most revered Dottore," said Salvatore, standing to attention
and bowing respectfully, "I am most grateful to you for the
information that I, as an Italian citizen, am one of the richest
men in the world, a fact that had, I assure you, totally escaped my
attention, largely owing to the fact that at this moment in time, in
my capacity as assistant deputy porter, I earn only thirty thousand lire a month courtesy of my employer, Ferdinando Amodio,
who is sitting just outside and can hear every word I say. However, you are certainly right to remind me that to make up for
this, Don Giovannino Agnelli has an income of a little more than
a billion a month, so that statistically we're all fine, me, Agnelli,
and Ferdinando."

"Splendid! Just what I wanted to hear!" cried Dottor Passalacqua triumphantly. "I knew that you were bound to bring up the

question of inequality of income. But have patience, my dear Salvatore, and in the end you'll see that I'm right. The statistics, then, the statistics prove that the daily consumption of food in Italy amounts to thirty-two hundred calories per person, while the total number of calories necessary to live and live well is twenty-seven hundred a day. And don't try to tell me that Giovannino Agnelli sits down at his table every day and gorges himself on eight or nine hundred thousand calories. I grant you he may be eating lobster, caviar, or whatever shit you like, but he only has a stomach the same size as yours to fill. You must agree that if statistics prove that the number of calories consumed is thirty-two hundred per person, somebody must be eating them and therefore nobody in Italy can be dying of hunger."

"Listen, Dottò, you've studied at the university, and you know much more than I do about all these statistics. I would never dream of suggesting that you might have invented them on the spur of the moment, but so what? If you're right, it can only mean that the thirty-two hundred calories that I consume every day are the most worthless calories in the whole of Italy. They must be, because otherwise how can you explain the fact that every night I go to bed with a slightly empty feeling?"

"The statistics," continued Passalacqua doggedly, "the statistics show that there are nearly fifteen million cars on the road in Italy, and that therefore every family in Italy, on average, owns one."

"And I, on average, do not," replied Salvatore.

"Even so, you still can't argue that Don Giovannino Agnelli, when he runs to the store to buy the nine hundred thousand calories he needs for his lunchtime snack, does so with a fleet of ten thousand cars."

"The problem is, most learned Dottore, that you measure everything in terms of cars and pizzas."

"The problem is, most esteemed Salvatore, that it suits you to wail like the cats on the rooftops, who, as we all know, wail and make love at the same time."

"Okay, okay, from now on I'll wail no longer. I'll be an assistant deputy porter minus any right to wail."

"God give me strength! Every time I get into a discussion with a Communist I break out in hives," said Dottor Passalacqua, appealing to the rest of the company for support. "How I should like to be God for just five minutes. I would say, 'Tell me, Salvatore Coppola, do I understand that you approve of Communism? Does Russia really appeal to you? Or China? Then I will give you your heart's desire. I will send you to live in China, and I will simply remove one Chinese who has had enough of China and send him to Naples in your place.' "

"That's all we need, a Chinese assistant deputy porter!"

"I'd like to say just one thing more. Before shouting 'Long live Mao! Hurrah for Communism!' it would be just as well to see what Communism is really like," said Passalacqua.

"I agree," replied Salvatore. "We've already tried Fascism and Christian Democracy, so let's try Communism for a while, and then we can talk about it again."

"The problem is that if we find we don't like it, we can hardly say, 'Sorry, but we were only joking, and now we want to go back to democracy,' " said Passalacqua. "But listen, just imagine for a moment that I haven't been born; I'm a nine-month fetus, and my mother is about to give birth to me when an angel comes along and says, 'Doctor Passalacqua, God the Father would like to see you for a moment.' "

"What? Were you a doctor before you were born?"

"God the Father looks at me and says, 'My dear Passalacqua, you are about to be born, and because I like you, you may choose whichever country of the world you please and I'll see that you're born there,' and I'm delighted and start to think what a wonderful opportunity, now I can choose a country with all the comforts of home. So let's see: we'll forget about Asia, there's always some war going on there, and the Middle East, the Far East, Korea, and Vietnam are forever in turmoil: they're either being invaded or, what's worse, liberated."

"Agreed," said Salvatore. "We have to admit that Asia has a rough time of it."

"Then how about Africa, that mysterious and fascinating continent, which nevertheless has, when you come to think of it, one fatal flaw."

"And what's that? The heat?"

"No, independence. Ah, yes, because what's happened? It used to be divided up into colonies, then along came all these democratically minded people and said what a crime it was to have colonies, down with the colonialists, independence for the blacks! So they were given independence. And ever since, the poor wretched blacks have been at each other's throats with God knows how many civil wars and coups d'état. It's like my saying to my four-year-old son, Lucariello, 'Lucariè, you're a free man, so do whatever you like,' and then being surprised if he runs out into the road and ends up under the wheels of a car."

"All right, then," said one of the bystanders, "we'd better forget about Africa."

"So what about America?" Passalacqua continued. "The United States of America! The richest country in the world, so rich that it can help the poorer nations, and not only with money but with arms too, so that in the event of a Communist invasion, in jumps America all ready to fight a lovely war of liberation. The Americans have become the official defenders of Planet Earth. So, if you all agree, I think we ought to drop the idea of America too."

"There you're absolutely right," interrupted Salvatore. "It's time the Americans started to mind their own business."

"Now, having rejected all these places, it seems we've only got Europe left to consider. Let's start with Communist Europe. Where Russia's concerned, no one really knows what it's like to live there; some people say one thing and some another, but in my humble opinion, it can't be all that wonderful."

"And why not?"

"In the first place, everybody has to get up early in the morning to stand in rows and watch parades, and you see all the poor wretches marching through Red Square carrying enormous placards weighing God knows how much with photographs of Lenin and Karl Marx. And then, whenever their leaders meet they have to kiss each other, man to man, on the mouth—a custom that, as far as I'm concerned, would prove a grave hindrance to any political career."

"Disgusting!" The comment came from Ferdinando, who, although seated some distance from us, had not missed a word of the conversation.

"So now we are only left with Western Europe: England, Sweden, Germany, France. Out of these, as much for the sake of the climate as anything else, I would choose Italy, and to avoid the risk of ending up in Milan, I would specify southern Italy. Finally, to be on the safe side, and provided it was no great trouble to anybody, I would ask to be born in Naples. And since the Lord has granted my wish and allowed me to be born in Naples, what should I do? Complain?"

Applause from the audience. The man who came about the apartment went over to Dottor Passalacqua and shook his hand.

"Okay, okay," said Salvatore. "You've convinced me that Italy is a fine place to live and that Naples is the best city in the world. I'm relieved, too, to learn that everyone in Italy gets plenty of food. But allow me to make just one observation. Yes, in Naples we do get a decent meal every day, but the problem is that we're never really sure about it until the last moment, and it's the uncertainty that bothers us."

II

SLEEPING BEAUTY

CAVALIERE SGUEGLIA is a man of regular habits, a bachelor of forty-six. He and his sister Rosa (married name Gallucci) run a hardware store at 282 Via Torretta, not far from the Mergellina railroad station. As I said, Cavaliere Sgueglia is a man of regular habits: for the last twenty years, ever since his father died, he has left home at eight-twenty, breakfasted on a cup of coffee and a brioche at the Caffè Fontana, and raised the shutters of the shop in Via Torretta at precisely nine o'clock. Donna Rosa arrives somewhat later owing to the fact that she has to get her husband off to work at the city offices, and their children, three unruly adolescents, off to school.

As soon as she enters the shop, Donna Rosa parks herself behind the cash register and stays there, keeping one eye on the customers and the other on the street boys, the *guagliuni,* to make sure they get no chance to clean the place out. Her brother, she complains, is too soft and hasn't come to terms with the fact that in these days of skyrocketing prices, the theft of one adjustable spanner makes an appreciable difference to the day's receipts. The Cavaliere never goes out to lunch. At one o'clock he just lowers the shutters almost to the ground, and Donna Rosa prepares him a snack on a little stove in the stockroom before rushing home to feed her starving brood while the Cavaliere, *puveriello,* snatches a thirty-minute nap on a cot among the cans of paint, bathroom fittings, and rolls of chicken wire.

At precisely eight o'clock every evening the Cavaliere

closes the shop and sets off in the stream of traffic crawling down Via Posillipo; after about twenty minutes he turns off into a shady cul-de-sac where he parks his car, a two-tone Fiat 1100 with reclining seats that has scarcely logged ten thousand kilometers in the three years since he bought it, and enters his apartment. A frugal supper (nearly always the same and naturally prepared by himself), a little television, and then to bed: *Madonna mia,* thank you for all you've done for me today, I trust you will do the same tomorrow, Father, Son, and Holy Ghost, Amen.

So, you may be saying, what kind of story is this? What does it matter whether Cavaliere Sgueglia is a man of regular habits or not? Ah, I reply, indeed it matters, because the regular habits of the Cavaliere are crucial to the incident I am about to relate. I must insist on the point that the routine I have described has been repeated, without variation, over nearly twenty years. Never, as far as I know, has he been to see a film or a friend or a relation; he never entertains, never pays a social call. Except on Sunday, that is. Every Sunday, at one o'clock, he dines with his sister. Mass, cakes from Caffè Fontana (two rum babas, one custard tart, one Danish pastry, two cream horns), *Il Mattino,* three hands of *scopa* with his brother-in-law while Donna Rosa prepares the meal, and then home again for the second half of the soccer match, *Carosello,* and the Sunday sports.

Now we come to the interesting part. Last Thursday, at around half past one in the morning when our Cavaliere was in his first deep sleep, he was awakened by the continuous shrilling of the telephone. Wondering who on earth it could be at that time of night, he got up and went to lift the receiver, already convinced that it must be bad news. And indeed he was right: it was his brother-in-law calling to tell him that Donna Rosa was ill: she had had severe abdominal pains, and her husband had taken her to the hospital, from where he was now calling and where Donna Rosa would, in all probability, be operated on for appendicitis as soon as the surgeon arrived.

Muttering only, "I'll dress and come over," the Cavaliere, still half asleep, threw some clothes on, stumbled downstairs, and went out to the little street where his car was parked. But it wasn't there. To be more precise, there was a different car, covered with a dark tarpaulin, in the very place where he always left his own. Still not in full possession of his logical faculties, the Cavaliere walked around it and cautiously raised a corner of the tarpaulin, and then, to his utter amazement, he discovered—*Gesù*, could he be dreaming?—that not only was the car his but there was a man sleeping peacefully inside it! For nearly three years Gennaro Esposito, unemployed, had "retired" to the Fiat 1100 belonging to Cavaliere Sgueglia every evening at half past eleven. Taking advantage of the unswerving regularity of the Cavaliere's routine, he had not merely put the seats down to a comfortable reclining position but, opening a large suitcase that he later stowed in the trunk, had taken from it everything he needed to make his "bed": pillow, blankets, sheets, and an alarm clock for the ledge over the dashboard. An early riser, Gennaro had set the alarm for half past six, when he would get up and set about tidying the car. He had even equipped himself with a whisk broom to remove every trace of his nocturnal occupation. Truth to tell, there was one thing he could not remove, and that was the odor of his own body, but after all these years the Cavaliere had grown used to it and from the start had taken it for *essence de Fiat*.

But to return to the night in question, we left the Cavaliere standing dumbfounded, staring in disbelief at Gennaro Esposito, unemployed and of no fixed abode—though that is, perhaps, a moot point, because in actual fact Gennaro did have one, his fixed abode being the Fiat 1100 belonging to Cavaliere Sgueglia and bearing the license plate NA294082. When the Cavaliere finally grasped the situation, he woke Gennaro with a yell, and Gennaro, even more astonished than the Cavaliere, asked him, quite reasonably:

"Cavaliè, what on earth are you doing in the middle of the street at this hour?"

"My sister's ill, she's been rushed to the Loreto hospital."

"Oh, dear! Donna Rosa? What's the matter with her?"

"Who are you? What the hell are you doing in my car? And who told you . . ."

"Cavaliè, don't you worry about who I am. Tell me more about Donna Rosa. I'm worried. What's the matter with her?"

"I'm not sure, I think they said something about appendicitis, but who the hell are you, and who gave you permission to . . ."

"My dear Cavaliè, don't waste time on details like that! Don't worry about me, I have merely benefited from your hospitality a few times, that's all; it's much more important for us to think about poor Donna Rosa. Where did you say they took her?"

"Loreto hospital."

"Fine. I'll come with you."

"What do you mean, come with me?"

"Cavaliè, you're not thinking very clearly at the moment. I understand. It's the shock and being woken up in the middle of the night, and of course you're worried. But cheer up, Gennaro's here and he'll stick by you. I hope you don't mind my saying so, but I feel like one of the family."

"What do you mean, one of the family?"

"That's settled then, Cavaliè, it's my *duty* to come with you!"

The Cavaliere and Gennaro passed the night together at the hospital. Gennaro was most helpful, and the Cavaliere introduced him as "a fellow tenant." Together they chose the surgeon to be entrusted with Donna Rosa's appendectomy, and together they awaited its successful outcome. When they separated, the Cavaliere made Gennaro swear on all the mythical children that he, Gennaro, claimed to be supporting that he would never again use his car as a bedroom. However, despite the solemn oath, rumor has it that the Cavaliere has since sold his Fiat 1100 and bought himself a coupe.

III

SAVERIO

A city, an area, from afar
are but a city or an area;
but as we draw nearer they become
houses, trees, roof-tiles, leaves, grass,
ants, the feet of ants, down to infinity.
All this is contained
within the word area.

BLAISE PASCAL, *Pensées,* no. 60

"OF COURSE you know Professor Bellavista?"

"No, I've never met him."

"*Gesù, Gesù!* To think that anyone so devoted to Naples should never have met Professor Bellavista! The Professor knows Naples inside out! He can describe it down to the ground! He knows every wrinkle! My friend, I'm not suggesting you don't know a thing or two yourself, but when he hasn't had a drop too much, Professor Bellavista can tell you anything you want to know about the city and its history. We did try once to get him on *Lascia o Raddoppia,** but he refused because he hates television."

"What is he a professor of ?"

"He used to teach philosophy, but he's retired now, and he owns three small apartments at Riviera di Chiaia as well as the house on the slopes of Sant'Antonio, where he lives with his wife, Signora Maria, and his daughter, Signorina Patrizia, whose real name is Aspasia, although nobody except the Professor ever calls her that because Signorina Patrizia doesn't like the name."

*A television quiz game.

17

"Ah, so he's married?"

"In a manner of speaking, Ingegnè, because the Professor doesn't have much to do with his family. They all live in the same house but never speak to each other because he's a man and they're women. The Professor says he can't cope with the language of females."

"He must be quite an interesting character."

"He certainly is, and Saverio here will back me up. Savè, tell our friend whether Professor Bellavista is an interesting character or not."

"Saverio Santopezzullo at your service," announced the newcomer. "If you were saying that Professor Bellavista's an interesting character, you haven't said the half of it. The Professor's a mine of information, and when he says something it's gospel. With no disrespect to you, Ingegnè, the Professor talks like a printed book, and it's a pleasure to listen to him. To tell the honest truth, I can listen to him for hours on end, though I admit that I don't always follow what he's saying, but that doesn't matter because I've only got myself to blame if I didn't learn anything at school, though my papà warned me often enough, so of course the conversation tends to be over my head."

"The truth is," Salvatore elaborated, "that Don Saverio's rather partial to a glass of *vino e' Lettere,** and the Professor's always very liberal with it."

"And apart from that, when the weather's hot it's very nice to get a bit of cool breeze on the veranda, with the sea at your feet and the scent of cyclamen in the air."

"That's right, because when we go to see the Professor in the summer we always talk out on the veranda, that is, he talks while we drink and eat slices of *percuoco*† dipped in wine."

"The Professor says that Socrates used to do the same a hundred years ago."

---

*A red wine from the district of Gragnano, its name, Lettere—"Arts"—providing Salvatore with a neat pun.

†Succulent yellow peach.

"Shut up, Savè."

"When can I meet this Professor?"

"Whenever you like, but not today, because it's Thursday. On Thursdays the Signora plays canasta and the Professor shuts himself in the bathroom all day."

"He stays in the bathroom all day?"

"It's not the kind of bathroom you're thinking of, Ingegnè. Not even His Blessed Majesty Vittorio Emanuele III ever had a bathroom like this! The Professor lives in one of those old Neapolitan houses built like they used to be with great big rooms. So, since he likes to spend a lot of time in the toilet, if you'll pardon the expression, the Professor decided to convert one of these rooms and had them put in the pipes and the toilet, if you'll pardon the expression, bath and bidet. The idea was, in the Professor's words, to create a room for cleansing the body and the soul. He even installed a stereo, because he always listens to music even when he's sitting on the toilet, if you'll pardon the expression."

"And the pictures, Ingegnè!" added Saverio. "Original paintings with the name of the artist on little brass plates underneath. And he hangs them in the can! That bathroom is so magnificent that several times I've told the Professor he ought to give a dinner party there someday."

"The Professor says that people are divided into those who take a shower and those who take a bath."

"Don't forget," Saverio interrupted, "that there are some people who don't take either."

"Shut up, Savè. As I was saying, the Professor maintains that productive men, like the Milanese, prefer to shower: it uses less water and less time, and they get themselves cleaner. Neapolitans, on the other hand, when they can be bothered, prefer baths: they have a good soak and lie back and mull things over in peace, and that's logical if you think about it, because if you want to ponder something, what you need is comfort and solitude, but in a house there's always someone bothering you and wanting to chat about this or that. Not in the bathroom, though. You can lock the door, stretch yourself out in the tub, and stay there till the water's cold."

"The more you tell me, the more anxious I am to meet the Professor. How shall we arrange it? Can we call him?"

"That wouldn't be any good because the Professor never answers the phone, and if it was up to his wife we wouldn't be allowed to darken his doorstep."

"I'll tell you what we'll do, Ingegnè," said Saverio. "We'll just show up. We'll go by the day after tomorrow, Saturday, because then Luigino will be there too, our poet in residence, as the Professor calls him."

"And who is Luigino?"

"Luigino," explained Salvatore, "is librarian to the Baron of Sanmarzano and lives in his house. Actually, the Baron hasn't got a library anymore because when he needed money he sold it to some rich people from Turin, but he'd grown so fond of Luigino by then that he asked him to stay on, and Luigino keeps him company every day except Sunday, when the Baron goes to see his mother, the Baroness."

"The Baron," said Saverio, "has no children, and we're all hoping he'll remember us when the time comes."

"But why do you call him a poet?"

"Because," replied Salvatore, "when Luigino speaks he makes you forget all your troubles."

"As for me," said Saverio, "Luigino's way of speaking always makes me think of my first love, Assuntina Del Vecchio at eighteen, the one and only cause of my present status of unemployed employee—I say unemployed employee because my boss is Don Alfonso of Barra, house carpenter, and he's unemployed. I swear upon the eyes of my children, and may I not see them tonight if I lie, that if it wasn't for Assuntina Del Vecchio aged eighteen I would now be in a very different position. You see, Ingegnè, Zio Ferdinando, my mother's brother, wanted to take me to London as an assistant pizza maker because he said that when it came to making pizzas there was absolutely nothing to it, but damn stupid idiot that I was, I went and fell head over heels for Assuntina Del Vecchio aged eighteen, and a young man's fancy being what it is, Zio Ferdinando had to go and make all the pizzas by himself."

"And what happened to Assuntina Del Vecchio?"

"What do you think happened? She became my wife, but she's nothing like the Assuntina Del Vecchio aged eighteen who got me into fistfights with all the men, civilian and military, who turned around to stare at her every time we walked down Via Caracciolo."

"The Professor says," added Salvatore, "that Saverio ought to claim damages on grounds of false pretenses."

"And I would win, my friend. All I'd have to do is show them a photograph of Assuntina Del Vecchio aged eighteen."

"Pay no attention to him, Ingegnè. Saverio's still in love with his wife, and she has him under her thumb. He denies it to please the Professor, but the truth of the matter is that with three children, if it wasn't for the fact that Signora Assuntina does some dressmaking at home, heaven only knows how they'd manage."

"Ah, that's just about it: a dressmaker and three children. What a life!" Saverio sighed. "But can you imagine what might have happened if I had gone to London with Zio Ferdinando? I'd have learned English, and all the English signorinas would have fallen in love with me, because with all respect to the present company, I have to admit modestly that where the girls are concerned I've never been backward in being forward, so it might have happened that some rich English *miss* would have noticed me and made a habit of coming to Zio Ferdinando's for a pizza, and what with a pizza today and a pizza tomorrow, the *miss* would have fallen in love with me. Saverio dear, Saverio here, Saverio there, and she would have married me. And as soon as I had my hands on the loot I'd have taken up acting and gone to *Olliud*, and Naples would never have seen me again except on movie posters: *Last Tango in Paris* starring Saverio Santopezzullo and Maria Scenaidèr."

"Savè," interrupted Salvatore, "what a crock! The only part they would have given you in *Last Tango* was stand-in for Maria *Scenaidèr* in the big scene."

"Have either of you ever seen *Last Tango*?"

"No, but we've heard people talking about it."

IV

A Misdemeanor

"Dottò, we're in for a fine!" said the cab driver resignedly.

"What do you mean, we're in for a fine? That I'm liable too?"

"Absolutely."

"I can't for the life of me see how. Or is it normal practice, according to you, that when a driver commits a traffic violation his passenger pays the fine?"

"Hold on, Dottò, excuse me, but that's hardly the whole story. Let's get things straight. First you tell me to step on it, and now you refuse to pay for the consequences."

"When did I tell you to step on it? And what's that got to do with it anyway?"

"It makes all the difference! When I picked you up from the station, what did you say? 'The Capri hydrofoil—and step on it.' Am I right or not?"

"Listen. Leaving aside the fact that I only said, 'The Capri hydrofoil,' even if I had asked you to 'step on it,' you, as I understand it, are the only person responsible for driving the vehicle."

"Of course, but why would it have been in my interests to drive through a red light? I did that only as a favor to you, to get you to the hydrofoil as quickly as possible. How can I make a living if instead of earning money when I work, I have to pay it out?"

"Then don't drive through a red light next time."

"Actually, the light I went through was yellow. I don't know about you. But here comes the policeman, and we'll see what he has to say."

"What do you expect him to say, for heaven's sake? That if a driver goes through a red light his passenger's license will be revoked?"

"I don't know. We'll soon see."

The officer approached at a leisurely pace and saluted.

"Driver's license and public service vehicle license."

"Forgive me, officer, sir," began my driver as he pulled out the documents, "but you're a working man yourself, aren't you, here all day, come rain or shine, directing traffic. I'm working too, but this gentleman's off to Capri. Tell me, who do you think should pay the fine?"

The officer laughed. "If the gentleman wishes to make a voluntary contribution, I'm sure no one would object."

"Contribution? What good's that going to do? I'm not about to pay a cent of it!"

"Actually," said one of the crowd of spectators clustered around the cab, "the gentleman's in the right. It's up to the driver to pay the fine. However, his passenger must realize that he's got to tip him enough afterward to cover the cost."

"*È padre di figli!* The man's got a family to support!" added a little old lady, sticking her head through the window of the cab. "There he is trying to earn a few lire, and he can't spend it all paying fines for gentlemen who want to go to Capri."

"Officer, sir," said the cab driver, climbing out onto the road in order to converse more comfortably with the law, "do you know, I was waiting at the stand in Piazza Garibaldi for three hours before getting a fare, and when I saw this gentleman I took him for a foreigner. If I'd known he was a Neapolitan, and a little cheap as well, I would have refused to take him . . ."

"Listen," I said, looking at my watch, "either you take me to my destination or I get out. If I stay here any longer I'll miss the hydrofoil."

"There!" said the cab driver triumphantly. "Now you admit you're in a hurry!"

"Okay, okay," said the policeman. "This time I'll let you off.

But remember, if I catch you again it'll mean a fine. People who are going off to enjoy themselves should never be in a hurry: it takes all the pleasure out of it."

My cab pulled away through a crowd of smiling, satisfied faces.

"Thank goodness it turned out all right, Dottò," said the cabbie as he drew up on the quay. "Believe me, if they'd made you pay that fine I'd have been really upset."

"How much?" I asked laconically as I got out.

"You decide."

V

THE PROFESSOR

Viene suonno da lo cielo
viene e adduorme sto Nennillo
pe pietà ca è piccerillo
viene suonno e non tardà.

Gioia bella de sto core
vorria suonno addeventare
doce doce pe te fare
st'uocchie belle addormentà. *

S. ALFONSO DE' LIGUORI,
Pastorale

"HERE WE ARE, Professor! How are you today?" said Salvatore, entering the Bellavista residence. "We've brought along our friend De Crescenzo the Ingegnere, a famous Neapolitan scientist. They say he invented the American electronic brain."

"Where did you get that idea?" I said, trying to stem the tide of Salvatore's introduction. "I'm not a scientist, and I've never invented anything in my life."

"Pay no attention, Professò," chipped in Saverio, brushing my disclaimer aside. "Our Ingegnere is too modest. I heard that as soon as he graduated, strict instructions came from America to snap him up at any price before an unfriendly country got hold of him."

*"Come, slumber, from the skies, /bring sleep to this Child, I pray, /for he is but a babe; /come, slumber, do not tarry. /Sweet darling, my heart's treasure, /may slumber come upon thee /softly, softly, /and close these pretty eyes."

26

"God almighty!" I protested. "How do you manage to invent so much nonsense all at once?"

"Just let them have their say, Ingegnè," said the Professor, smiling as he shook my hand. "Just let them get it over with. This is only their way of showing their admiration for you. And you yourself are partly to blame. Oh, yes, because had you been content to be a surveyor, they would have been quite happy to promote you to the rank of engineer, but as you are an engineer already, how else can a poor devil express affection and esteem except by introducing you as a scientist at the very least?"

"Professò, while the rest of you are settling down, shall I go and get the wine?"

"Good idea, Saverio, you know where it is. And ask the signora to give you some glasses. But wait a moment: perhaps our friend would prefer coffee?"

"No, thank you, I would really like to try some of this Lettere that Saverio speaks so highly of."

"You've made a wise choice, because to tell the truth, the coffee my wife makes has never been anything to brag about."

"To be fair, coffee made at home is never as good as the coffee you get in a bar."

"That's not always true," the Professor objected. "When coffee is prepared by a loving hand it can be excellent. You can tell by the quality of the coffee in the pot whether or not there is a loving relationship between the one who has made it and the one for whom it was made."

"Assuntina's coffee is revolting!" announced Saverio, returning with wine and glasses.

"You must remember, my friend, that coffee is not simply a liquid but something that is, so to speak, halfway between liquid and air; a concoction that, as soon as it touches the palate, is sublimated and instead of going down goes up and up until it enters the brain, where it nestles in a companionable sort of way so that for hours on end a man can be working and thinking, What a wonderful cup of coffee I had this morning!"

"In our office," I said, "we hardly ever go out for a cup of coffee because we have automatic vending machines on every floor. You put a coin in, press a button, and get whatever kind of coffee you like, espresso or cappuccino, with sugar or without."

"American machines, are they, Ingegnè?" asked Salvatore.

"No," I replied, laughing, "they're probably made in Milan."

"The Milanese and the Americans," said the Professor disapprovingly, "are two of a kind, namely the kind who believe that coffee is a beverage to be drunk. My God, do you realize how serious a matter it is, this business of automatic machines for dispensing coffee? It's an offense to the sensibility of the individual, it should be referred to the Civil Rights Commission."

"That's going a bit too far."

"Not at all. It is your duty, my esteemed Ingegnere, to explain to your superiors that when a civilized man requires a cup of coffee, it's not because he needs to drink coffee but because he has felt the urge to renew his connection with humanity; he is therefore obliged to interrupt whatever work he happens to be doing, invite one or two colleagues to join him, stroll in the sunshine to his favorite bar, win a minor altercation about who is going to pay, say something complimentary to the girl at the cash register, and exchange a few comments on the sporting scene with the bartender, all without giving the slightest hint about how he likes his coffee, because a proper bartender knows his customers' tastes already. This is a ritual, a religion, and no one is going to persuade me that it can be replaced by a machine that swallows a coin and spits out some anonymous liquid with no taste and no smell! Imagine what it would be like if the Vatican decided to replace the Communion service with vending machines in every office. The worshiper approaches, kneels, inserts a coin, and makes his confession into a tape recorder, then he gets up and kneels on the other side, inserts another coin, and a mechanical hand places a wafer on his tongue while a built-in jukebox that he programmed at the start plays a Gregorian chant or Schubert's *Ave Maria*."

"The Professor's right," said Salvatore. "You have to drink

coffee in a spirit of respect, of devotion. I remember the bartender at my local bar in Materdei giving me a good piece of his mind one day when he saw me reading the sports page and drinking coffee at the same time. 'What do you think you're doing?' he said. 'Why aren't you paying attention?' "

"Someone at the door," said Saverio as a bell rang. "That'll be Luigino. I'll go let him in."

Luigino entered the room, introductions were made and greetings exchanged, then Saverio went to get a chair for Luigino and a glass of wine for himself.

"Luigino, my friend, how are you?" said the Professor. "We haven't seen you for a whole week."

"I know, we've been very busy this week, and on Tuesday we had a visit from Professor Buonanno, the teacher from the Conservatory who plays the violin. Professor Buonanno is an old friend of the Baron's, and every now and then he comes to play for us, but this time, I promise you, he excelled himself. One of the pieces he played was by Bach, I don't remember the name of it, but it was beautiful, really beautiful. The fact is that now that we've sold off nearly all the furniture, the Baron's place has become, so to speak, bigger and bigger and more and more like a church, and this made the tone of the violin sound extraordinarily clear. There were times when the music seemed to fill the entire house, and other times when the sound spun out so fine that we were afraid to breathe for fear of breaking it, and it even made our scalps prickle."

"Luigino," asked Saverio, "would this Professor come here sometime to play for us?"

"I don't know, but I could ask him."

"Do that, but make it soon, because the Ingegnere is only staying in Naples over Christmas."

"Speaking of Christmas, the Baron and I have begun to set up the *presepe** as we do every year, and it's taken us two whole days

*Manger scene.

just to unpack the shepherds from their boxes, clean them, and fix all the broken arms and legs with fish glue."

"The *presepe*," said the Professor, "is a matter of great importance to us here in Naples. Forgive my curiosity, Ingegnere, but which do you prefer, the *presepe* or the Christmas tree?"

"The *presepe*, naturally."

"I'm glad to hear it!" said the Professor, shaking my hand. "Humanity, you see, is divided into two camps, the *presepisti*, those who favor the manger, and the *alberisti*, those who prefer the Christmas tree, and the reason is that the world at large is divided into the world of love and the world of liberty. But it would take too long to go into that now; today I would rather talk about the manger."

"Yes, do, Professò," said Salvatore. "Talk about the manger. We're all ears."

"Well, as I was saying, the division of humanity into *presepisti* and *alberisti* is so important that in my opinion it should appear on one's identification papers alongside sex and blood type. Oh, yes, because otherwise an engaged couple could well find out too late that they have incompatible ideas about Christmas. You may think that I'm exaggerating, but I'm not: *alberisti* and *presepisti* each have a completely different set of values. The former place great emphasis upon Style, Money, and Power, while the latter give precedence to Love and Poetry."

"In this house," said Saverio, "we're all *presepisti*, right, Professò?"

"Not quite. My wife and daughter are *alberisti*, like most women."

"Assuntina likes Christmas trees," muttered Saverio.

"The gulf between the two groups is so wide that they simply cannot communicate with each other. The wife watches her husband setting up the manger and asks, 'Why don't you just go and buy a ready-made set from UPIM* instead of making the

---

*A large chain of department stores.

whole house reek of fish glue?' No reply. Because how does one explain that a Christmas tree, which is only beautiful when you've covered it with baubles and lit the candles, might just as well come from UPIM but a manger is different because the beauty lies in the preparation and even in your anticipation of it, when you say to yourself, 'Christmas is nearly here, now I can set up the manger.' Those who like Christmas trees are consumers, but he who loves the manger is a creator, good, bad, or indifferent, and his essential gospel is contained in *Natale in casa Cupiello.*"*

"I've seen that, Professò, and I can still remember the place where Eduardo says, 'I set up the *presebbio* all by myself and against the wishes of the family.'"

"The shepherds," continued Bellavista, "must be handmade and rather crude, and most important of all, they must have been born in San Gregorio Armeno, in the heart of Naples, not like those plastic figurines sold by UPIM that look so artificial. The same shepherds must be used year after year; it doesn't matter if they're a bit battered, the important thing is for the head of the family to know each one by name and to be able to tell a little story about him—'This is Benito, who hated working and wanted to sleep all the time, and this is Benito's father, who watched over the sheep up in the mountains, and this is the shepherd who witnessed the miracle'—so that as each is taken out of the box he is properly presented. And each year Father introduces the shepherds to the youngest children, and every year when Christmas comes around the little ones recognize them and love them as if they were members of the family, real people, even those that happen to be historically inaccurate, such as the Monk and the Hunter with His Gun."

"Then, Professò, there's the Cook, the Couple Sitting at Their Table, the Watermelon Man, the Greengrocer, the Chestnut Seller, the Innkeeper, the Butcher . . ."

---

*A play by Eduardo De Filippo, set around a Christmas manger.

"I suppose," said Salvatore, "they had to work long hours even then to make a living."

". . . and the Washerwoman," Saverio continued, "and the Shepherd Carrying the Hens, and the Fisherman who's actually fishing in the water trickling down from an enema bag rigged up behind the manger."

"My father," said Luigino, "always used to arrange the damaged ones so cleverly that you couldn't see they were missing the odd arm or leg. 'Luigì,' he used to say, 'now Papà is going to find a strategic position for this poor old shepherd with only one leg,' and he would prop him up behind a hedge or a wall. I remember one shepherd who shed bits of himself every year until only the head was left, and then Papà put him inside one of the little houses, at the window. Papà made the houses out of old medicine boxes and put lights inside, and all year, whenever I had to take some medicine, some awful-tasting syrup, for example, he would hold up the box it came in and say, 'Luigì, we can keep this box for Christmas, it'll make such a pretty little house for the manger, but first you must drink the medicine, otherwise how can Papà make the house?' "

"And then, at midnight," continued Salvatore, "we used to form a procession and walk through the house singing *Tu scendi dalle stelle*,"* the youngest leading with Baby Jesus and everyone else carrying lighted candles."

"*O' presepe! L'addore d'a colla 'e pesce, 'o suvero pe fa 'e muntagne, 'a farina pe fa 'a neve . . .*"†

---

*"Thou descendest from the stars," a carol traditionally played by shepherds on their bagpipes.

†"The Manger! The smell of fish glue, the cork used for the mountains, the flour scattered for snow . . ."

VI

ZORRO

"ANTONIO CARAMANNA at your service. No complimentary tickets available. The director is out, and I don't know when he'll be back."

"Thanks," I said, "but I didn't come for a complimentary ticket. I came for some information about the Naples fans; I hear you've been involved with them for some years, so I was hoping you might be able to tell me something about them—if you can spare half an hour."

"Some years, you say? My dear sir, I have had the honor of serving the Naples Soccer Club since the old days of the Arenaccia: Sentimenti, Pretto, and Berra, Milano, Fabbro, and Gramaglia, Busani, Cappellini, Barrera, Quario, and Rosellini. Then, after the war, we transferred to Vomero, to the Stadio della Liberazione, as the Stadio Collana used to be called, and finally, as you see, to San Paolo, where my function is to deal with *portoghesi,** hoodlums, and teddy boys."

"Do you have many gate-crashers?"

"At the really important matches there may be as many as eleven thousand coming in without paying. Of course, that includes not only the actual gate-crashers, those who get in by strictly illicit means, but also those with passes or complimentary tickets. However, if you're interested, I can break that figure down for you. At every match there will be four thousand spectators with complimentaries and various forms of passes, three thousand with forged tickets, and four thousand

*Gate-crashers.

33

gate-crashers. And it is against this army of eleven thousand that I, Antonio Caramanna, at the head of a small band of stalwarts, wage merciless war every other Sunday."

"But why do you give away so many comps?"

"In Naples a complimentary ticket is a status symbol, a sign of belonging to a superior race. You should stand by the entrance and watch the expression of superiority on the faces of the holders of complimentary tickets when they show them to the stadium officials. A Neapolitan will tell you that he has never paid to watch a soccer match with as much pride as if he were telling you, for instance, that his ancestors fought in the Crusades. If, on the other hand, anyone in Naples finds himself having to pay for a ticket, it means he's a failure, he knows nobody and counts for nothing."

"Tell me about the actual *portoghesi*."

"Well, they come in two varieties: those who try to barge their way in and those who use their wits. The first kind don't worry us too much—we just have to put police officers in the right places, set up double barriers at the gates, and watch the walls around the stadium. The others are the dangerous ones; they've got a hundred tricks up their sleeves. If you come to next Sunday's game, I'll show you one who's worth a hundred of the rest: Zorro."

"Zorro?"

"Yes, sir, that's what we call him, because he always manages to get in free, and after the match he comes up to me clenching one fist and holding his arm with the other hand, and flips me, to put it politely, the 'sign of Zorro.' "

"And how does he get in?" I asked, laughing.

"A different ploy every time, Dottò. I think he must spend the rest of the week plotting how to get in gratis on Sunday. He says that if Papillon was a master at breaking out, he is a master at breaking in."

"Tell me about some of his exploits."

"Zorro's skill is inherited. His father was a big hit with Neapolitans on the occasion of a dramatic game at the Stadio della Liberazione: Naples against Bologna, three to three. Fans invade the field, and a forfeit is declared: Bologna two, Naples zero. Naples would have won if it hadn't been for a referee sent from Milan expressly to make Naples lose, and I must explain that although I'm completely objective about it, all Italian referees have it in for Naples, and that's why we've never won the championship, though we're hoping that next year things will be different, but as I was saying, right at the end the referee declares a forfeit against Naples. All hell breaks loose. The fans go wild, fights break out, and the field is pretty well wrecked. Referee and linesmen flee to the dressing room, protected strenuously by the police and stadium guards, but the mood of the fans becomes increasingly menacing and a crowd collects outside the dressing room, shouting and hurling abuse at the three officials. At this point Zorro's father appears, allies himself with the forces of law and order, helps to push back the angry crowd, soothes the most agitated ones with fine words and repeated appeals for calm, gains the confidence of the officials, gets into the dressing room, and beats up the referee. We got a three-match suspension and a heavy fine."

"And Zorro, what does he do?"

"I hardly know where to begin, Dottò. Zorro is the bane of my existence. Before the start of every match I go around checking all the entrances and thinking, Where is he this time, the bastard? Once he made a hole in the wall by taking out several of the tufa blocks and then charged admission—adults five hundred lire, children one hundred—and afterward he carefully closed the hole so that he could repeat the operation for several weeks running. When he and his gang come to a match they look like a medieval raiding party, with their ladders, ropes, hooks, and a whole assortment of jimmies and wire cutters."

"And haven't you ever caught him?"

"Only once. We found him and one of his pals in the freezer of an Algida ice-cream truck, nearly frozen to death. We had to lay them out in the sun for half an hour to defrost them."

"What other tricks has he tried?"

"Everything you can imagine, Dottò, everything. For example, when we used to let disabled people in for nothing, he turned up in a wheelchair, very cunningly disguised in a beard and moustache, and on that same occasion he rented wheelchairs for a thousand each to twenty other 'disabled' people. On another occasion he met the referee at the station, came into the stadium with him posing as the official escort, and was absolutely livid when he wasn't allowed to sit in the VIP box. So you see what I'm up against, Dottò. An ambulance comes and goes with its siren screaming full blast. Do you think someone's been hurt? Not a chance. That's Zorro bringing his family to the game."

"So, Cavaliè, from what you've told me I assume you've admitted defeat."

"Never, Dottò. A few minutes ago I learned that twelve policemen's uniforms have been stolen. You can bet Zorro's behind that. But I'm ready for him. Antonio Caramanna never admits defeat. Come see the match on Sunday and you could be in at the kill. Incidentally, Dottò, now that I come to think of it, I've still got one complimentary ticket left. You take it, because the match on Sunday is a very important one. We're playing Fiorentina, but we're not too worried because the trainer said that this year Naples would be the best team in Italy. Up with Naples, Dottò!"

VII

THE THEORY OF LOVE AND LIBERTY

> "Put that cigarette out!" shouted the bus conductor.
> "But I've only just had coffee."
> "Ah, that's different."
>
> A. SAVIGNANO

"PROFESSÒ, I have to confess that I'm almost schizophrenic about Naples. Sometimes I love the place and sometimes I loathe it. I can't explain why, but anywhere else in the world I'm tortured by nostalgia, and when I return to Naples I can't wait to get away."

"My dear friend," Bellavista replied, "that is perfectly normal. Most émigré Neapolitans, particularly those with a certain level of education, find that once they have lost their Neapolitan 'muscles,' life in their native city becomes physically unbearable for anything over a meager span of two or three days at a time."

"I find this very sad," I continued, "because, you know, when I'm away from Naples, I defend the place for all I'm worth. And with all sincerity I do believe that this is the only city in the world where I can hope to understand others and be understood myself. There are times when I even feel sorry for those of my friends who are not Neapolitan and who, however sensitive they may be, can never really enter into the spirit of our culture. And by 'culture' I obviously don't mean only the writings of poets like Di Giacomo, Viviani, and De Filippo but also the native wisdom of our old people, their sense of proportion, their manner of speech, indeed everything that people who want to be offensive call 'the Neapolitan mentality.' "

"But why do you consider that offensive?"

"Because it generally assumes a debased mentality compounded of political apathy, social indifference, and parasitic incompetence."

"*Mamma mia!* That certainly is a low opinion of the Neapolitan mentality!"

"What do you expect, Professor? Unless one has an extraordinary affection for Naples, it can be unbearable at times. Take my arrival at the central station last Saturday, for example. I was hardly out of the train when I was accosted by a man selling bottles of whiskey, pornographic pictures, and watches, then another who wanted to carry my suitcase and tried to grab it from me without even asking if I wanted it carried. There must have been a hundred people around me eventually, offering everything from illegal cabs to hotels, and one man simply asking for the train fare to visit his sick mother at the Aversa mental hospital. And outside the station it was utter chaos: the traffic, the continual and mindless blasting of car horns, the pushing and shoving, people butting into lines, everyone shouting at the tops of their voices, the understaffed restaurants serving the worst food in the world, the dirty sugar bowls on the bar tables, the squalor of the metro, the hubbub of the streets, radios blaring at full volume, noise everywhere."

"Is that all?" asked Bellavista calmly. "Listening to you, I was reminded of my very dear friend Dottor Vittorio Palluotto. Do you know him?"

"I can't say that I do."

"Dottor Palluotto moved to Milan for business reasons some five or six years ago and is now a high-powered director of some high-powered firm of consultants whose name escapes me. However, since he moved to Milan, Vittorio has become, so to speak, spoiled, and the very things that used to be the stuff of his daily life in Naples have now become unbearable to him. The truth is that Vittorio has lost the built-in silencer that muffles the noise of the world of love, and as a result his whole scale of values has changed. Nowadays, Vittorio Palluotto sees efficiency and productivity as the cardinal virtues and is in danger of forgetting the secondary negative effects that these presumed virtues entail."

"Dottor Vittorio always comes to see the Professor around Christmas," said Salvatore.

"In fact, he should be here any day now," said the Professor, turning toward me, "and if you do me the honor of visiting me again sometime . . ."

"I'd be delighted."

"Then I shall have the pleasure of introducing you to my friend and foe Dottor Palluotto."

"Friend and foe! The Professor's right about that," Saverio broke in. "They go at each other like cats and dogs, and I'm telling you, they'd argue the hind leg off a donkey. Want to bet that one of these days they'll go too far and really come to blows? As I keep telling them, What's the big deal? Naples is what it is, and there's nothing anybody can do about it. If Dottor Palluotto likes Milan so much, why doesn't he stay there instead of coming here and getting all hot under the collar?"

"I went up north just once," said Salvatore. "I did my military service at Peschiera on Lake Garda, and believe me, it was quiet beside that lake—so quiet that I went to bed with a headache every night. There's the fog, too. I think God must have said to Himself, Where shall I put all this fog? I know, I'll put it in the Po Valley, because the people who live around there, the northerners, are so gloomy anyway they won't even notice it."

"In suggesting this theory," added the Professor, "Salvatore has an illustrious predecessor, Oscar Wilde, who said that it wasn't the fog that brought about the will to work but the will to work that brought about the fog."

"Isn't our Professor wonderful?" said Saverio. "He knows everything!"

"But to get back to Naples," continued the Professor, "in my opinion, the very fact that life in Naples goes to extremes, that it is essentially hyperbolic, should make us pause and think. I believe that a stranger finding himself confronted by Naples for the first time should refrain from judging it overhastily by his own standards and writing it off as uncivilized; on the contrary, seeing that such an uninhabitable place is not only inhabited but even quite famous, he should realize immediately that there must be another side to the coin, some compensating factor."

"Professò, we're all ears," said Salvatore. "Tell us about the compensations."

"My friends, they are all around us every day of our lives, but to understand this you must first let me summarize my theory of Love and Liberty, because otherwise we will find it very difficult to weigh the pros and cons of Neapolitan life."

"If I'm not mistaken, you mentioned such a theory once before," I said. "Would you care to explain it to us?"

"Are you pressed for time?" the Professor asked. "Do you have to leave soon?"

"Not really."

"As if anyone would budge!" said Salvatore. "I've heard this before, when the Professor explained it to Dottor Vittorio, but I admit I didn't catch every last detail, so I'd be grateful if the Professor would go over it again."

"With pleasure. I would ask you one favor, however. Because the theory is complicated by the difficulty of defining its key words, Love and Liberty, please listen carefully right from the start."

"How could we not, Professò!" exclaimed Saverio. "Not only are your conversations of the greatest interest, but we are honored that you take such trouble with us. In fact, I have an idea. Wait a minute while I get another bottle of wine so I won't have to go out again and risk missing some vital point."

"Anything fascinates Saverio when there's wine around," said Salvatore mischievously. "But don't you worry, Professò; just take your time, because we've got nothing else to do, seeing that nearly all of us are, so to speak, on vacation."

"Is this your own theory, Professor?" I asked.

"Actually, the first person to talk to me about Love and Liberty was a friend of mine in Milan, Giancarlo Galli. Later, using his ideas as a starting point, I expanded them and combined them with Epicurean philosophy. Now, once Saverio opens the bottle and sits down, I shall begin. And the first thing I must do is to clarify what we mean by the desire for love."

"The desire for that certain something," said Saverio promptly.

"No, Savè, just this once, that certain something, the something that's always on your mind, is not the issue. By love, in this context, I mean the instinctive desire that a man feels for the company and affection of other men."

"You mean pansies, Professò?" Saverio again intervened.

"Really, Savè! I've already told you that sex is not the issue where this theory is concerned. Just drink your wine and try to listen! Honestly! If you keep on interrupting I shall forget where I am. The explanation is complicated enough without your putting your two cents' worth in every other minute!"

"Don't you worry, Professò," said Salvatore. "I'll make Saverio behave himself."

"Love, then, as I was saying, is the feeling that impels us to seek the companionship of our fellows, and the acts of love are all the things we do in the attempt to share our joys and griefs with others. This reaching out to our fellow men is instinctive. Anthropologists would probably see it as a defense mechanism of primitive man, whose chances of survival would have been increased by alliance with other men. Obviously the capacity to love varies from man to man, so we have the egocentric who is unable to love anyone, the family type who loves only his own kin, the patriot who loves only his countrymen, the philanthropist who loves all humanity, and finally St. Francis, who loved the whole world in all its manifestations with equal intensity."

"I too feel a love for all humanity, Professò," said Saverio, "and I just can't understand how any nation can go to war with another. If a man only stopped and thought for a moment, he'd realize that the people he's fighting are human beings like himself, that they too must have mothers and wives and children waiting for them at home, and if he knows all this, how can he drop bombs on their houses? *Gesù, Gesù,* sometimes when I think about these things, I feel like I'm going nuts!"

"So you, Saverio, make no distinction between, say, Italians and Americans, or even between Italians and Chinese?"

"None at all. As far as I'm concerned, they're all human beings, and I love them all in the same way."

"Even if they're Neapolitan?"

"That's another story! Neapolitans are our own flesh and blood, and if I met one anywhere else in the world, I'd give my right arm for him. But I was talking about humanity, not Neapolitans."

"But you see, my dear Saverio," the Professor continued, "it's easy to love humanity but difficult to love our neighbors. Christ didn't say, 'Love humanity as thyself,' but 'Love thy neighbor as thyself,' and do you know why? Because your neighbor, by definition, is the person nearby, the man sitting next to you in the metro who smells, perhaps, the man next to you in line who maybe tries to barge ahead of you—in short, your neighbor is the person who threatens your own liberty."

"So what you're saying, Professò," said Salvatore, "is that someone who wants to be a good person and love his neighbor has to put up with the smell."

"Exactly, Salvatò, and if you don't like the smell, that means you are not a man of love but a man of liberty."

"And what's that?" asked Salvatore.

"I'll explain. To desire liberty in this context is to desire to protect one's *intimità.* The term is not, perhaps, ideal, being generally used in connection with aspects of life we quite rightly prefer to keep to ourselves, while the personal sphere we try to defend is actually much larger and extends from freedom of action to freedom of thought. There is probably no word in the Italian language that can encompass this—a fact that sheds a good deal of light on the Italian character—but the English language can supply the deficiency with the term 'privacy,' and by adopting this word, which expresses not merely a sentiment but a way of life, we arrive at the conclusion that the desire for liberty is a desire to protect our own privacy and at the same time a readiness to respect the privacy of others."

"Following this line of reasoning," I said, "we all possess, albeit in different proportions, both these natural tendencies, for love and for liberty; but although both, as you define them, are desirable, they are nevertheless in permanent conflict with each other. So when he's alone a man will try desperately to find companionship, but at other times, when he feels tied down by a relationship, he will long to be left in peace."

"Precisely," said the Professor.

"How right you are, Professò," interrupted Saverio. "There are times when Assuntina really gets on my nerves. She knows perfectly well that after dinner I like my forty winks out on the balcony, but what happens? She always chooses just that moment to start pestering me with 'Savè, have you done this? Savè, have you done that?' Yackety-yack-yack, right in my ear! But when she took the children to Procida to stay with a cousin who had a house near the sea and was always saying why don't you come stay for a few days and let the poor little darlings splash around in the water we've even got an inflatable canoe, and then wanted her own children taken care of from morning till night . . . Well, believe me, when I was home all alone I nearly went crazy. I was wandering around the empty rooms like a zombie, and when Assuntina came back I went to meet the steamer an hour and a half before it was due."

"Saverio, my friend, that is a perfect example of what I was trying to say. In your case, liberty was defeated by love."

"Can I say something, Professò?" asked Salvatore. "If love and liberty are both good, then surely any decent man will want them both. What I'm trying to say is that we should be lovers of love and lovers of liberty at the same time, if you see what I mean."

"Quite right. In fact, this should be the hallmark of human

excellence. In practice, however, the two ideals are always at loggerheads and tend to get in each other's way. Perhaps we should try to establish which of the two, love or liberty, a man ought to strive for."

"Which would you say, Professò?" asked Saverio.

"There are two very different schools of thought on this matter, within both Western and Chinese philosophy."

"Tell us more."

"Mo Tse-ti, a Chinese philosopher of whom you have probably never heard, said . . ."

"Oh, yes, we have!" intervened Saverio. "In Neapolitan we call him Mao Ze-tung."

"He's got nothing to do with it," retorted the Professor. "They're two completely different people."

"But they both belong to the Ze family," insisted Saverio. "This Mo Ze-ti you're talking about might be an ancestor of Mao Ze-tung."

"In Chinese, *tse* means 'master,' explained the Professor. "So Mao is the surname, *tse* the professional title, and Tung the first name. If I were Chinese I would be called Bellavista Tse-Gennaro."

"So what did this Mo Ze-ti have to say, Professò?"

"He taught that one should love the whole world. He said that one should love another person's parents in just the same way that one loves one's own. In fact, he preached universal love and traced the source of evil in the world to what he called 'discrimination.' "

"Which means?"

"It means to make a distinction between family and strangers, between countrymen and foreigners, and so on."

"It sounds to me like this Mo went a little overboard," said Salvatore. "According to him, I ought to feel the same love for my wife and, say, the Minister for Foreign Affairs?"

"*Mamma mia!*" exclaimed Saverio. "That's going too far! What nerve! I'll tell you one thing, Professò, if this Mo Ze-ti had come to Naples and said anything like that here, they'd have taken him for a raving lunatic and shut him up in Aversa!"

"In opposition to these ideas," continued the Professor, disregarding the interruptions, "another school of philosophy developed: Taoism. Yang Chu, the first philosopher of the Taoist school, said, 'If you want to live the good life, you must think of nobody but yourself and shun all other company.' And having said this, he went up a mountain and never came down again."

"Those weren't philosophers at all!" said Saverio. "I'd call them a couple of con men."

"Not so fast. Mo Tse-ti and Yang Chu were simply exponents of the opposite extremes of love and liberty, but their radicalism was later qualified by other philosophers. One of these was Mencius, who subdivided love into three types: love for inanimate things, love for living beings in general, and family love. And among the Taoists Lao-tse and Chuang-tse transformed the individualism of Yang Chu into its opposite, that is, into a human spiritualism."

"Maybe, Professò, but if I had to choose between these two Chinese, I'd take the first one's philosophy," said Saverio.

"Mo Tse-ti, you mean?" said Bellavista. "But his wasn't necessarily better. It was Taoism that eventually produced the more practical system, that of Chuang-tse, or the philosophy of the middle way."

"That's just fine, Professò, but let's not bother too much about these people. They're Chinese, they're so different from us!" said Salvatore. "Professò, the Chinese live on one bowl of rice a day without a peep!"

"As a matter of fact," the Professor continued, "we don't even have to look as far as China to find a philosophical dualism between love and liberty: in the West we have the German sociologist Tönnies, for example, who published a very important work on the subject during the nineteenth century called *Gemeinschaft und Gesellschaft*."

"*Mamma bella d'o Carmine!*"*

"Don't be frightened, I'm about to explain it to you in very

**Madonna bella del Carmine*, an expression indicating fear.—*L.D.C.*

simple language," continued the Professor. "Tönnies used the term *Gemeinschaft* to describe all those communities where relationships are determined by friendship, and *Gesellschaft* to describe social systems dependent upon laws, that is, on principles that theoretically guarantee equal treatment for all. Now, these two systems will obviously each have a different type of infrastructure: the first, *Gemeinschaft,* will be structured vertically like a pyramid, having a godfather at the top and well-defined descending gradations of authority; this type of society requires an attitude of obsequiousness on the part of the weaker members toward the stronger and at the same time calls on everyone to collaborate. A *Gemeinschaft* society operates by recommendations, by such phrases as 'I can count on him,' 'Anything for you,' 'A pleasure, I assure you,' 'I would take it as a personal favor if you would do so-and-so for him,' et cetera, et cetera."

"Professò, in this whatever-it-is you're talking about . . ."

"*Gemeinschaft?*"

"That's right, in this whatever-it-is, I don't think life would be too pleasant," said Salvatore, "because if an individual didn't happen to have friends in high places he'd never get anywhere. I'll give you an example. If Saverio happened to be the only friend I had and I was his only friend, and if we couldn't scrape up even the price of a meal between us, we'd both starve. '*Tieneme ca te tengo,*'* as we say in Naples. If you see what I mean."

"I understand what you're saying, Salvatore, but bear in mind that Tönnies never claimed that the quality of life in a *Gemeinschaft* was superior to that in a *Gesellschaft,* he only pointed out that the very problems raised by the *Gemeinschaft* type of society favor the keeping up of friendly relationships. But to continue my explanation of Tönnies' work, he observed that *Gesellschaft,* unlike *Gemeinschaft,* has a decidedly horizontal structure characteristic of the Anglo-Saxon type of democracy.

---

*A case of the blind leading the blind.

And strangely enough, despite his German nationality, Tönnies made no attempt to conceal a certain predilection for *Gemeinschaft,* the society founded upon love. This becomes apparent by his reference, for instance, to 'the warm impulses of the heart' and 'cold intellectualism.' "

"Tell me, Professor," I said, "would you consider the Mafia an association based on love?"

"That, I think, is self-evident. It's an association based upon both love and power. However, the Mafia represents *Gemeinschaft* at its worst just as bureaucracy represents *Gesellschaft* at its worst."

"And which would you say are the nations of love and the nations of liberty?" I asked.

"No nation is based entirely on love or entirely on liberty. The two are mingled in the spirit of every nation, so if we were to call them black and white and color them in on a map, there would be no pure black and no pure white, but we would have every conceivable shade of gray. However, we would be able to distinguish two zones, one darker, which we could define as the Kingdom of Love, and one lighter, which we could call the Republic of Liberty."

"I bet," said Saverio, "that we would be in the Kingdom of Love. Am I right, Professò?"

"Quite right, Savè," said the Professor. "In fact, Naples would be the capital of the Kingdom of Love, with vast territories extending over the major part of southern Italy and outposts in northern Europe too, for example, Ireland and several parts of Soviet Russia."

"And where would the capital of the Republic be, Professò?"

"I have always thought it would be London."

"Where I was supposed to go and make pizzas with Zio Ferdinando," said Saverio. "Just as well I didn't!"

"When I think of London," continued Bellavista, "I always remember the time I saw a man in line at a bus stop, in the dark, all alone."

"What? I don't understand," said Saverio. "In line all alone? How could you tell that he was in line?"

"I could tell by the way he was standing by the signpost, quite still, facing left so that other passengers, of which, however, there were none, could line up behind him."

"*Gesù!*"

"But there you are. The English have made respect for other people into a religion. Your typical English home has a gate, a path leading through a small garden to a front door, some rooms on the ground floor, and bedrooms upstairs. Next door there will be a house identical to the one I have described, and beyond that another just the same. It may be cheaper to build a large house with one front door and a communal staircase and several apartments, but that isn't their way. Everyone wants his own front door, his own garden, and his own private staircase so that he need never even know his neighbor's name, let alone who he is, what he does, or anything else about him. Moreover, there's nothing he wants more than to be left alone and completely ignored by his neighbors in return."

"I," said Saverio, "know everything that goes on in my part of town."

"Naturally, because all the houses in Naples are linked by clotheslines, and news runs along these lines and becomes common knowledge," said Bellavista. "And if you think about it for a moment, you can see why. If a lady on the third floor of one house wants to run a line to the third floor of the house across the street, then she and her opposite number must get together and make some mutually acceptable arrangement. One will go to the other and say, 'Signò, I've had a wonderful idea. Let's put up a line between our two apartments so that we can both put our wash out to dry. When do you want to do your laundry? Tuesday? Good, then I'll do mine on Thursday so we won't get in each other's way.' Thus a contact is made and a friendship begun."

"I love to see wash drying in the sun," said Luigino, who had been silent until now. "When I was little I used to think it had been put there to celebrate something, like flags. And even now the sight of it makes me feel happy. I have never understood why they ban outside lines in some upper-class areas. And these lines connecting every house to every other house are an important part of Neapolitan life, don't you agree? Just imagine, if God decided to transport one house from Naples to Heaven, He would soon notice, to His utter amazement, that as He lifted it up all the houses in Naples were rising after it, one after the other like a vast line of bunting, houses and clotheslines and wash and all the singing, the shouting, the girls, and the *guaglione.*"

"Bravo, Luigino! You should write a poem about all the houses going up into the sky!" exclaimed Saverio.

"When the first line has been put up," continued the Professor, "the ladies start to get to know each other, they quarrel and make up, then they quarrel with the ladies on the floor beneath and make friends with them too. Of course, the system has its drawbacks, there is a price to pay, namely that everyone gets to know everything about everyone else and nothing can be kept secret. Loves and hopes, birthdays, infidelities, wins in the lottery, and cases of diarrhea all become public property. It's love that runs along the clotheslines communicating joy and sorrow. No one is free, but no one is alone, and the warm climate favors this sharing of news by keeping doors and windows open all the time."

"What the Professor says is absolutely true!" said Salvatore. "We're not like the English. We have to stick our noses into everyone else's business, we have to know what's going on, we're just plain curious."

"No, Salvatore, what you call curiosity is the need for love, the need to communicate," the Professor replied. "If you were to go to a little Italian village or to one of the islands where tourism is still relatively unknown, such as Ventotene, you would notice the kindliness of the people immediately; when they see you in the street, they call out a greeting, when they meet you, they wish you good day. However, at the very same moment, in Milan, maybe two strangers have found themselves obliged to share an elevator, and these few seconds of enforced proximity, with no glance exchanged, no word spoken, stretch out into endless minutes of embarrassment. Such are the drawbacks of civilized society. I notice this, too, when I call out good morning to someone I don't know in a 'civilized' place and this person, because he's used to a society where behavior is regulated according to a set of precise rules, is immediately suspicious and wonders why on earth I should have said good morning to him. We used to have third-class cars on the trains, and naturally it was the poorer people who used them most—poorer from the financial point of view, that is, but certainly not poorer in love. Well, believe me, it was impossible to travel any distance, however short, without having to recite the story of one's life to everyone in the compartment, beginning with name, surname, domestic arrangements, and reason for traveling. Of course, one learned all about the lives of a dozen other people in return, and even if the compartment was a trifle malodorous, by the end of the journey one left one's new friends and their family photographs and half-finished stories, of which one would now never hear the endings, with a real sense of regret. Now, as far as my theory is concerned, the smell of those third-class cars represents an important factor, because such smells recur regularly in all those places with the highest concentrations of love. You couldn't, for instance, ever hope to find it on board one of these new, aseptic airplanes: and furthermore, when one of these machines crashes, its passengers more often than not die without knowing the name of the person next to them, clutching his hand, maybe, at the last moment, but having no idea who he is."

"*Madonna mia,* keep me from such a fate!" exclaimed Salvatore.

"Just a few days ago, on the metro," said Saverio, "I met a carpenter from San Giovanni a Teduccio who must have been at least eighty, but I swear he looked like a *guaglione* playing hooky from school! I got on at Mergellina as usual, on my way to Via

Firenze to meet my sister Rachele because she's involved in a lawsuit with her landlord, who's the biggest jerk you ever saw, and Rachele always wants me with her when she goes to see her lawyer, so anyway, as I was saying, this carpenter I met on the train, Don Ernesto, took only four stops to tell me about his three wives. Almost one wife per stop! He met his first wife when he was a soldier in the First World War. He said he was wounded in the leg and she was a Red Cross nurse. He made love to her immediately, on his bed at the military hospital with his leg in a cast, and then he had to marry her; but apparently, although she was a strapping girl from Friuli, she died of pneumonia in Naples five years later. His second wife was Neapolitan, and according to him as beautiful as a movie star, but she too came to an unhappy end, crushed under falling masonry during the bombing of August 4, 1943, which I expect the Professor still remembers. Don Ernesto, however, was not to be discouraged so easily, and after a couple of years he married again. It seems this third wife is all skin and bones and has a rather uncertain temper, but nevertheless he says the marriage has worked out splendidly and they're very happy together. And after three marriages he's got seven children and sixteen grandchildren."

"World of love, world of love!" exclaimed the Professor.

"Professò, there was something I wanted to ask you before. Is it really true that if some poor devil gets sick and collapses on the sidewalk in London, no one tries to help him?"

"That's perfectly true, Salvatò, but before you condemn you should understand why this happens. In such circumstances a true Londoner will reason something like this: Here's a man I don't know lying on the sidewalk at my feet; he may be ill, or perhaps he simply likes sleeping on the ground, but either way it's none of my business and I have neither the right nor the duty to do anything about it, and in any case the authorities have no doubt provided for just such an eventuality. After which he steps over him and the man dies."

"*Mamma mia,* Londoners must be the pits!"

"Bear in mind, however, that the outcome would be exactly the same here in Naples, because one passerby would start shouting, '*Madonna!* Here's a gentleman who's been taken ill! Get him a chair, a glass of water!' And in no time at all a hundred chairs and a hundred glasses of water and a thousand people appear, and the poor fellow dies of suffocation, though he does at least have the consolation of knowing that he is being killed by kindness."

"Isn't that a slight exaggeration?"

"I would concede that the situations I have described are paradoxical. But remember that the word 'exaggeration' does not exist in the vocabulary of love. Even the theft of a wallet could be classified as an act of love since it involves taking an interest in someone else's affairs."

"I see," said Saverio. "You're saying people steal because they're curious: 'I wonder what this gentleman is carrying in his wallet.' "

"In my opinion," said Salvatore, "it may be partly curiosity, but it's also partly poverty."

"The moral, my friends, is that we have to make a choice in life," said the Professor. "Do we want law and order and a nice clean city? Then we must do without love. If the hubbub of the city is more than we can bear, then we can always go live in Switzerland. Good idea! Let's all take ourselves off to Berne. But be warned: Berne, so the saying goes, is twice the size of the cemetery in Vienna but only half as amusing."

"Professor," I said, "how do you explain this quite remarkable difference in temperament between the peoples of the north and those of the south? Is it simply a matter of race, or should we attribute the relatively emotional nature of southerners to the warmer climate?"

"I doubt climate has much to do with it. As I mentioned earlier, love reigns in the coldest parts of the world. Take the Irish, for example: emotional, hot-tempered, always ready to help their fellows. Or the Russians, as described by Chekhov and Dostoyevsky. Do you remember Marmeladov in *Crime and Pun-*

ishment telling the story of his life to the people at the inn and saying that everyone should have one place where he can count on being understood?"

"But Marmeladov was a drunkard!"

"Indeed he was. But now that the subject of drink has been mentioned, let's explore it further. The reason a person drinks to excess is that he wants to escape from a state of liberty to a state of love, and the need to drink will be stronger the further he is from that state of love which is natural to him. It is generally recognized that Neapolitans, despite their various defects, are not given to drinking to excess. The only explanation for this is that the people of Naples, living as they do in the world of love, do not require the help of alcohol."

"But it's a fact that Saverio is Neapolitan," said Salvatore, "and he'll polish off a liter of wine whenever he gets the chance."

"He drinks because he enjoys it and because he doesn't have to pay for it, but not to get drunk, not in order to overcome inhibitions in his relations with other people."

"Whereas the Americans . . . ," I said.

"The Americans have a psychological need to relieve the tensions of a day spent in the pursuit of efficiency, productivity, and the cult of power. So we have to conclude that the roots of these differences lie deeper in the past. It is, for example, a fact that while love societies are generally Catholic, liberty societies are predominantly Protestant, and one would dearly like to know which was the cause and which the effect."

"In my opinion," I said, "the differentiation of character predated the Reformation."

"That would be difficult to establish, because the Reformation accelerated the development of civilization in some countries, while in others it impeded the rise of an indigenous culture. The Reformation authorized the faithful to approach God directly, without the intercession of a priest, and above all without having to buy dispensations at the current price quoted by the Roman Catholic Church. Now, in order to effect this change, Luther encouraged people to read Holy Scripture, the interpretation of which had until then been the monopoly of experts, and this entailed, above all, an immediate improvement in the standard of education and consequently a rise in what we now refer to as civilization. The peoples of passionate temperament, however, remained practicing Catholics: they were the ones who loved Mystery, Dogma, the Faith, and hence Love. In other words, we might say that the road to progress and liberty requires the payment of a toll of love."

"So if I've understood you correctly, Professor, you believe that there is a direct link between love and ignorance, and you would therefore claim that men of liberty are of relatively superior quality . . ."

"Nothing of the sort, my friend; don't put words in my mouth that are completely at variance with my convictions. Education and quality are two different things. And it is by no means true that all the men of love are to be found in the less educated strata of society. On the contrary, I would say that from my point of view men of liberty, the rationalists, generally occupy a middle ground between an emotive majority, at the lower cultural levels, and an elite who, besides possessing the attributes of liberty, have also rediscovered in love the true significance of life."

"So it is possible to be at one and the same time a man of love and a man of liberty?"

"Certainly, and while the ratio between one quality and the other gives us a clear indication of the type of man we are dealing with, the sum of these qualities gives us an idea of his worth."

"Returning to the subject of Naples, you would classify the vast majority of Neapolitans as men of love?"

"Without hesitation. Especially the *popolino,* the common folk. When speaking of Naples, we must forget about the hundred or two hundred thousand people similar to ourselves who live in the area between the Via dei Mille and Posillipo. The real Naples, the authentic Naples, is still the Naples of the Quartieri Spagnoli, the Pendino, Borgo St. Antonio Abate, the Mercato

. . . the Naples of the street vendors, the Naples of religious processions and back-street squalor. . . . I often remember the lady in the Sanità district who made suits for us boys—now, what was her name? Rachelina . . . yes, that was it, Rachelina. Anyway, this Rachelina had a four-year-old child whom she absolutely refused to have vaccinated against polio. We eventually had to get hold of a woman police officer to make her change her mind. It was an epic undertaking: Rachelina insisted that the child was under the direct protection of San Vincenzo, the famous monk, undisputed patron of the whole Sanità district. She said that when the child was three he had had an attack of bronchitis with a fever of forty degrees* and that one night, when she had fallen asleep in a chair beside the child's bed, San Vincenzo had appeared in person and said, 'Rachelì, go to bed and sleep easy, I will care for the child.' And in the morning the child's temperature was normal and he was running all over the house. Now, this San Vincenzo, so popular in Sanità, actually has no connection with Naples at all. San Vincenzo Ferreri was in fact a Spanish Dominican who never set foot in these parts, and his only conceivable claim on the popular imagination is that he once made a spectacular recovery from some serious illness after dispensing with all professional medical attention. However, to continue my story about Rachelina, I remember that it was on that very occasion that I saw the *festa* in celebration of the monk for the first time in my life. I'm talking about how it used to be a long time ago, when the *festa* was still a religious occasion and involved half of Naples, from the Stella district to the Piazza del Reclusorio. Nowadays it has been commercialized: most of the interest is centered on an open-air music festival to which all the best-known performers of Italian song are 'cordially invited' by the area's overlords. But at that time—how well I remember it—they still had the church procession. Rachelina's little boy was dressed up as a Dominican friar and had to wait, with about

*40° C = 104° F.

twenty other children who had all been 'miraculously' cured by the *monacone,* outside the church of Santa Maria. Ice creams all around and slaps delivered at regular intervals by the respective mothers did nothing to enhance either the mystic moment or the sanctity of the little friars. When the saint arrived, accompanied by a milling throng of people, the children were lifted up in their mothers' arms, and while everyone clapped and shouted and wept tears of gratitude, each one offered a candle to San Vincenzo and received a benediction and a scapular in exchange. I walked away with a heavy heart, unable to make a logical distinction between a scene such as I had witnessed and some mumbo jumbo performed in the depths of a tropical rain forest, and just as I was wondering if the time would ever come when my beloved fellow citizens would be able to free themselves from all this superstitious nonsense and evolve a more rational social awareness, I found myself near the church attached to the Fontanelle cemetery. I had often heard about this cemetery but had never seen it for myself, so I asked one of the locals where the entrance was, and he suggested I ask one of the priests. I did so, and he offered to accompany me. There were bones and skulls strewn all over the place, a cold clamminess oozed from the rough walls, and by the flickering light of hundreds of tapers I saw a dozen or so women kneeling in silent prayer. The priest told me that these women, some out of simple devotion, some because their sons or husbands had been lost in the war, search through the heaps of bones and gather what they need to reconstruct a complete skeleton they can call their own and make the focus of their care and their prayers. 'Many a time,' said my guide, 'I have had to correct serious anatomical errors, a thighbone used for a tibia, half a pelvis for a shoulder blade, but this is unimportant: what matters is their faith. If you are a materialist, consider well: all that will remain is here before you.'"

VIII

L'ARTE DELLA COMMEDIA

"SIGNORA, another fare, please."

"Why do you want another fare?"

"For the young man."

"What young man?"

"That one, the one beside you."

"You call him a young man? He's not even nine yet, he's a baby!"

"Signora, he may be a baby, but since he's a baby more than a meter tall, he can't ride the bus without a ticket."

"A meter, a meter indeed! He's not even seventy centimeters!"

"I see, Signora, today we're in the mood for joking. That young man—boy, child, baby, call him whatever you like—is a good head taller than the bar expressly installed for this purpose at a height of exactly one meter, and that means he has to have a ticket."

"*Gesù, Gesù!* As if there weren't problems enough in the world! That bar is always less than a meter high! And anyway, can't you see that the child only looks taller because he's standing on tiptoe?" And the signora placed her hand firmly on the child's head, forcing it beneath the level of the bar. "Get down, Ciccì!"

"Enough's enough, Signora. This is ridiculous! We can't stand around chatting all day. Either you pay the child's fare or he gets off the bus, do I make myself clear?"

"So you'd have the heart to leave a baby all alone in the middle of the street?"

57

"The baby's none of my business, for heaven's sake! All I can suggest is that you get off with him."

"Me! I've paid for my ticket!"

Throughout the conversation the bus had remained stationary, waiting with its door open until such time as the matter of the child's fare had been resolved.

"What kind of service is this?" protested a gentleman with a noticeably northern accent. "Are you or are you not going to proceed?" he demanded of the driver. "And you, Signora, are you aware that some of us here have to work? We can't wait forever while you make up your mind to pay fifty lire for a ticket. I'll tell you what: here's the fifty lire, now pay your son's fare and sit down!"

"Who does he think he is!" the signora exclaimed, pointing an indignant finger at the Milanese gentleman. "Pay my son's fare indeed!" she snorted to the company at large. "What nerve! I'll buy a sackful of tickets for my son if I have a mind to!" Then, turning again to the man from Milan: "You're lucky my husband's not here to defend me and I'm only one poor woman alone against all these men, otherwise I'd tell you where to stuff your fifty lire! *Gesù Santa Anna e Maria!* What a body has to go through just for the sake of one stupid little ticket!"

"All right, Signora, have it your own way," shouted the driver, now at his place behind the wheel, "but as soon as I see a policeman we'll see whether you get off the bus or not, like it or lump it!"

And so saying, the driver shut the doors and was preparing to pull away when he was stopped by a chorus of protest in which nearly every passenger joined.

"Stop, stop!"

"Now what's the matter?" inquired the driver.

"We only got in to listen!"

IX

FIXED PRICE

> Men of affairs pride themselves upon being astute and
> capable, but in matters of philosophy they are like little
> children. While they congratulate themselves upon the
> success of their predatory ventures, they forget to
> meditate upon the final destiny of the flesh and will
> never know the great Master who sees the whole world
> in a cup of jade.
>
> CH'EN TZU-ANG (A.D. 656–698)

"I BOUGHT a new television today at the Duchesca," announced
Saverio triumphantly. "Twenty-three-inch stereoscopic screen
and eight channels!"

"Then you got a very bad deal, Savè," said the Professor.

"You must be joking, Professò! I managed to wangle a fifty-five
percent discount plus five on top of that, and installments repay-
able over three years with only the bank interest!"

"You mean you got a loan?" gasped Salvatore.

"No, I mean they all know we haven't got any money and if they
don't arrange it like that we won't be able to buy."

"I wasn't referring to the price, Savè, but to the harm that
television may do to you and to your wife and children."

"But that's beside the point, Professò, because we've already
got a set, only it doesn't work on Channel Two. Signora Bottazzi
gave it to us when she won a prize in the lottery with the numbers
her dear departed Uncle Rafele gave her in a dream. You all
remember Uncle Rafele, don't you? The one who died at seventy-

five making love over at the Pensione Emilia. But as I was saying, that set didn't work properly anymore. It kept making *'e cape 'a cucuzziello,* and the sound was almost completely shot."

"I'm sorry, it did what?" I asked.

"Saverio was saying," translated the Professor, "that his television set distorted heads into the shape of zucchini. Am I right, Savè?"

"It made *'e cape 'a cucuzziello,* Professò."

"So you got this set at a good price?"

"The best, Professò, but what a fight! Let's see, the opening rounds were fought around the middle of last month. I strolled past the shop a few times, and then, without letting on that I was interested in the set, I asked how much it was, and he said casually two hundred thousand but seeing it was for me and since my cousin once worked as a packer with his sister he would let it go for a hundred and thirty in cash. Without batting an eyelash I told him he could keep it at that price but I could take it off his hands for fifty thousand, and he said that for fifty thousand I might as well wait for Signora Bottazzi to win the lottery again and spend it on a nice outdoor antenna. So we were pretty far apart at the beginning, but one of the things you've taught me is that patience pays off, so every time I passed by the Duchesca he came down a thousand and I went up five hundred until finally, toward the end of November, when we'd arrived at a hundred and five thousand on his side and seventy thousand on mine, the shameless crook refused to budge. He wouldn't come down another lira. Somehow he'd found out that I was planning a big surprise for my wife at Christmas, and he was pretty sure he'd get his hundred thousand. But if I say so myself, Saverio Santopezzullo's no fool, so I immediately began to close in and shifted my ground to inside the shop, right in front of a secondhand set, one of those big old-fashioned ones. And today I delivered the knockout punch: I took along a tape measure and measured the old set, and then I said out loud, 'Exactly the right size for the table in the living room!' And when he was least expecting it,

I said point-blank from the other side of the shop, 'Eighty thousand and we've got a deal!' and he immediately said, 'Eighty-five and five hundred for the kid.' Professò, tomorrow evening, for the first time in the Santopezzullo household, we'll be watching Channel Two. Will you do us the honor of stopping by?"

"It's very kind of you, Savè, but you know I never watch television. In my opinion, the only interesting thing about your deal was the bargaining. Just think how dreadful it would have been if you had been born in Switzerland and had to buy your television set in Zurich. There would have been no two ways about it: the price would have been such-and-such, and you would have had to pay it."

"Yes, but the fixed price in Switzerland is lower than the list price in Naples."

"That's neither here nor there. The fixed price is another invention of the world of liberty. Tell me, don't you think it's fairer if everyone pays the same price? Few would deny it, but at the end of the day one pays for such a privilege with another slice of love."

"What do you mean by a slice of love, Professò?"

"Listen, Salvatò. You can go into a supermarket today and pick up the most outlandish thing you like—let's say a can of scarlet paint—and no one will think of asking you what you're going to do with scarlet paint or why you want scarlet instead of blue, say. So you leave the store without having uttered a single word, you stop at the checkout counter, the girl rings up the price, you hand over your money and walk out."

"But what would you expect the girl to say?"

"Savè, I'm surprised at you! Imagine me, for example, going to buy a can of scarlet paint at Cavaliere Sgueglia's, the little hardware store down at Mergellina. First, the Cavaliere and I spend a quarter of an hour chatting about our health and that of our respective families. Then, eventually, the Cavaliere says 'How can I help you, Professò?' and I say, 'Cavaliè, would you be so good as to let me have a five-liter can of scarlet paint?' and he says, 'Scarlet paint?! What on earth for?' and I say, 'One of my tenants has decided to paint a whole room in scarlet,' and he says, 'Forgive me, Professò, but is the man a little queer by any chance?' and I say, 'Good heavens, no! He's an extremely nice person, his brother works at the Banco di Napoli!' 'Ah, that's different.' So, chatting about this and that, we eventually get around to the subject of price, and this is where the real meat of the conversation lies, because it combines personal affairs and international economic policy: rising prices, taxation, the war in the Middle East, my tenant, who actually is a trifle eccentric . . . and every subject serves to pull the price a little bit this way or a little bit that way. And when people start chatting like this, they end up developing a liking for each other."

"But these days," I said, "in the big stores, even food is sold at fixed prices. If you go to buy pears or apples or oranges, first they weigh them, then they put them in little plastic bags, and they label them with the weight and price so you don't even have to go to the trouble of saying, 'May I have a kilo and a half of oranges, and all nice juicy ones, please.'"

"What is the world coming to!" said Saverio. "When Assuntina goes to buy fruit she turns every apple over, and sometimes that peasant Carmeniello loses his temper and tips all the ones she's selected back into the box and says she can't pick and choose like that but must take the apples as they come, bruised and unbruised."

"I've got a friend in Milan," interposed Luigino, "who has been known to ask for a discount even at Rinascente."*

"At Rinascente? Is he crazy?"

"No, he's Giovanni Pennino, a Neapolitan who's been living in Milan for five years. He told me this story himself. He said he went into Rinascente and found what he wanted, an electric toaster, priced at ten thousand five hundred. So he approached the salesgirl and said quite casually, 'Signorina, I'd like to buy

*A chain of very large department stores.

this electric toaster, but I don't want to spend more than ten thousand lire.' 'I'm sorry, sir, we don't give discounts,' she replied, but he persisted: 'Yes, I know, but just for once let's make it a round figure.' 'Excuse me, sir, but round figures are out of the question: everything at Rinascente is sold at a fixed price.' ' "

"*Gesù*, that's wild! And what happened then?"

"My friend asked to see the department manager," continued Luigino, who was doing a good imitation of a female voice every time he played the part of the salesgirl. 'But sir, it would be a complete waste of time to call the manager, because our prices are fixed and that's that.' But Giovanni still persisted, and when the manager arrived he had his story down pat: 'You see, Signorina, I already have a toaster at home very similar to this one, but it's broken, and when I took it to an electrician this morning, he told me that the repairs would cost five thousand lire. What, I thought, five thousand lire when a new one would only cost me ten thousand? So I decided to come to Rinascente and buy a new one, but now what's happened? I find the price has gone up to ten thousand five hundred! So I ask you, what am I supposed to do? Should I buy the new toaster for ten thousand five hundred, or should I pay five thousand to have the old one repaired?' 'My dear sir, how can I possibly advise you? You must do as you think fit! Have your old toaster repaired, by all means, but here at Rinascente, because all our goods are sold at the fixed price, we never give discounts.' And my friend said, 'I feel I should tell you, Signorina, that I am a personal friend of Signora Rinascente.' And she said, 'There is no such person as Signora Rinascente.' 'Indeed there is, Signorina, indeed there is; you just don't know her.' "

"So what happened in the end?" asked Salvatore.

"He bought the toaster for ten thousand five hundred."

"Forgive my asking, Luigì, but what did he actually gain?"

"Every time he goes into Rinascente they all recognize him. They call him 'Signora Rinascente's friend,' and they always greet him with a smile."

X

My Mother

My mother was born in 1883, less than twenty years after the unification of Italy. In our family my parents and especially my grandparents spoke nothing but Neapolitan, and to travel in an airplane, for example, was considered a deliberate attempt at suicide. I mention this so that the reader can understand the problems I faced when, having taken a degree in engineering, I opted to work in the computer field. My first problem was to communicate the fact to my mother.

"Mammà, I've found a job!"

"Well done, my son, well done! You see? Sant'Antonio was watching over you! I have been praying to Sant'Antonio for years. I said, Sant'Antò, this child is studying because he wants a degree, but I am so afraid that after he graduates no one will employ him. And secretly I thought, We have made a mistake with this engineering, we should have made him study accounting, then he would have found a job in a bank, something nice and safe, and we would never have had to worry again. But Sant'Antonio has blessed us. Now you must go and make a nice communion to thank Sant'Antonio, do you hear me? But first tell me where you found this job."

"With IBM."

"But is it secure? I've never heard that name before."

"Giulia," interrupted my aunt, who is younger than my mother and therefore much better informed, "you really are ignorant! Electric appliances are all the rage today. Look at

Signora Sparano's husband, he set up a piddling little shop and made a fortune. They've got a Mercedes and a housekeeper, and they spend their holidays in Ischia!"

"For heaven's sake, I'm not talking about electric appliances! I work with computers! Mammà, computers are not electric appliances like washing machines and fridges, they're very advanced and very powerful machines capable of doing thousands of calculations in a single second!"

"You might get hurt."

"Why should I get hurt, Mammà? I'm in marketing, the department that deals with selling and leasing these computers."

"My son, I don't want to discourage you, but who do you think will buy these computers when there is nothing in Naples that needs computing?"

"All the big companies need computers."

"What for?"

"What do you mean, what for? For their day-to-day transactions! Think of all the accounting that has to be done by the banks, all the salaries that have to be paid out, the wages in industry, city finances . . ."

"How can you imagine that with all the unemployment we've got in Naples people will want to buy your machines? I'll tell you how I think the big companies should go about doing their arithmetic: they should round up all the unemployed people in Naples and give each of them one multiplication problem, and you'd soon see that unemployed Neapolitans can do accounts quicker than your computers. It would have been better if you'd found a job at the Banco di Napoli."

"Don't worry, Mammà. I'll be fine, you'll see."

"What's the price of these computers you sell?"

"There are lots of different models, but they're usually leased rather than bought."

"Leased? And how much is that?"

"Again, it varies depending on the model, but anything from a million lire a month, say, to ten million."

"Ten million a month! Blessed souls in Purgatory, who can you possibly think will want these machines, my poor child? Just remember always to be honest. Never forget that Our Lord is above and He sees and knows everything. He sits up there in Heaven and watches and judges us all."

So it was under the patronage of Sant'Antonio and the guiding eye of the Lord that I began to work in Naples. It was particularly difficult at the start, for this was 1961 and the Neapolitan clientele was in a state of innocence as far as the possibilities of computerized accounting were concerned. The term "information technology" had not even been invented.

"I don't understand, Ingegnè," one prospective customer said to me. "You say that for every article we sell we have to punch a card. But who punches this card? Do you come along to punch it for us?"

"No, sir! You will be supplied with a punch-card machine, and one of your own employees, to whom we will have given the proper training, will take care of the punching of the cards."

"I see. But forgive me, Ingegnè, if we punch a card for every article we sell, by the end of the year our offices will be overflowing with punch cards. And where do we put all these punch cards? We haven't got the space! No, I don't think these are the right machines for us. They're fine for people who manufacture cars in places like Milan and Turin, but we make pasta, customers come and buy their pasta and pay for it then and there, so we never write an invoice, we just pay the workers and the overhead, and whatever's left over by the grace of God we divide among ourselves, me and my brothers."

So as I say, it was difficult at the start. But gradually, as the years passed, even the Neapolitan industries came to terms with the new technology. Today's Neapolitan technicians lag not a whit behind their northern counterparts—indeed, in certain fields they are even ahead of the rest of the country.

But not my mother. She always maintained a certain reserve toward her son's chosen profession and the monstrous machines that cost ten million a month.

There was a point when it all became even more complicated, and that was when I was transferred from Naples to Milan, changing my job in the process from sales representative to PRO, public relations officer. Explaining the concept of public relations to my mother was a doomed enterprise from the start.

"But I don't understand," she said. "You go to work at nine o'clock in the morning, you open the shop, and then what do you do?"

"Mammà, I don't open any shop. All I do is facilitate and improve relations between the company and the public. Now do you understand?"

"No."

"Giulia, listen to me," said my aunt, intervening as usual. "This boy of yours"—the boy being me—"has to be kind and polite to people."

"Do they pay him for that?"

"Of course they do! Public relations is a very important American invention. No sooner does the boy spot a customer than he takes him aside and says, What a nice person you are! Let's go have some coffee . . ."

"And how many cups of coffee does he have to drink every day?"

"He doesn't have to drink the coffee, he only has to entertain his customer. The most important thing is for him to be kind and polite to people."

"Are you saying he wasn't kind and polite before?"

"Of course he was, but now he has to pile it on."

To be brief, gentle reader, I never managed to explain the job of public relations in Naples, and that is hardly surprising in a city where every individual conducts his own PR entirely gratis. So accepting that "no man is a prophet in his own country," I gave up all hope of ever enjoying the respect due my new profession. Even today, when I return to Naples, I find explaining what I do for a living fraught with difficulty. For example, just the other day I was with Don Pasqualino, barber (house calls), dealer in antiques, and plumber by the grace of God, and as he lathered my face he asked, "Ingegnè, tell me, are you the kind of engineer who works on buildings?"

"No, Don Pasqualì, my job is computers, I work at IBM."

A short pause, and then he said cheerfully:

"Never mind, sir, don't worry about it, *pensate 'a salute!* After all, health is the most important thing!"

XI

Epicurus

Honor beauty and virtue and all such things provided
they give pleasure; if they don't, steer clear of them.

EPICURUS, Athen. XII

"GENNÀ, what's your opinion of the current Italian economic
situation?" asked Dottor Palluotto of Professor Bellavista.

"Booming."

"Good God! You really are exasperating sometimes!" Dottor
Palluotto exploded. "How can you say such a thing? A booming
economy? It's impossible to hold a serious conversation with you
when you always insist on making fun of everything. The trouble
is you can't resist playing to the gallery."

"Just a minute, Dottò," said Saverio, "what are you getting so
worked up about? What did the Professor say, after all? Only that
there are some people in Italy who are still enjoying a bit of an
economic boom."

"No, Savè, that's not what I said at all, and Dottor Palluotto
understood exactly what I meant. I said the economy was booming, and I stand by my statement. Italy and the Italian people
have never enjoyed a higher standard of living. From what I have
observed over this holiday period, there are about fifty million
multimillionaires in Italy."

"All right, then," said Dottor Palluotto, sitting down, "let's
hear Professor Bellavista's new economic theory."

"My dear Vittorio, you're too young to remember what life was

69

like before the war, but if your father, God rest his soul, was present, explanations would be superfluous. Now, before the war all Italians, and I mean all, were obliged to live very sparingly indeed. Italy was a poor nation, and we knew this and conducted ourselves accordingly. I'll give you some examples. The rich had meat once or at the most twice a week, and for the rest of the week they made do with eggs, vegetables, and cheese. There were hardly any restaurants, all meals were prepared at home by one's mother or by one of those exemplars of a now extinct species, the live-in domestic servant, old women who used to stay with one family all their lives."

"The last exemplars of slavery in the modern age!"

"Don't be abusive, Vittorio! The old live-in domestics of my youth were the pillars of Neapolitan family life. They were the custodians of the household! They didn't have social security, but they had lots of children instead, all the children who had grown up in the household dividing their love between these women and their real mothers."

"When I was a boy," said Luigino, "we had a maid called Concettina. Concettina must have been about forty when I was born, and I believe that at least half of those forty years had been spent with our family. Concettina was there when I was born and she was there as I grew up, and they tell me that when I had typhoid as a baby, she stayed by my bed for four days and four nights running, four days and four nights without sleep! Whenever I needed money, for the cinema, maybe, or to buy chestnut pie, it was always Concettina who supplied it. Between my brothers and myself, I guess practically all the money Concettina ever earned must have ended up back in our pockets. You see, she had no relatives in the district, and when she died not one lira was found in her room. What we did find, in a drawer, was a photograph taken when she was about twenty, arm in arm with a sailor. And on the photograph was written, 'To my great Neapolitan love, Gustavo.' And there were lots of other little things besides: drawings that I'd done at school, photographs of me and my brothers when we made our first communion, and so many little icons of St. George. Concettina was particularly devoted to St. George, the one who slew the dragon, and every now and then she would make a vow to him. For example, when my father went off to fight in the war, she made a vow to St. George that if he came back safe and sound she would never touch fruit again for the rest of her life."

"And you repaid her by withholding her social security," said Dottor Palluotto.

"That I don't know, Dottò, but we loved Concettina, and I suspect that if we had paid into her social security, she wouldn't have been very happy about it."

"That's sheer sophistry, Luigino! Even allowing that in this case Concettina had probably become a member of the family, the fact is that love, to use an expression dear to the heart of our Professor, very often provides a convenient excuse for exploiting the people's ignorance."

"Vittorio, how differently our minds work!" said the Professor sadly.

"What I don't see," said Salvatore, "is what Concettina has got to do with the booming Italian economy."

"Salvatore is quite right," said the Professor. "The old Neapolitan domestics have been sidetracking us. I was saying that before the war, in Italy, even the rich lived extremely thriftily and only bought things that were absolutely indispensable. For example, as a child I was only once given a toy, and then only because I was ill; it was a little rocking horse that I had set my heart on for a long time, and even then my father didn't decide to buy it for me until the doctor assured him that my life was really in danger. On traditional occasions such as Twelfth Night and name days, we were lucky to get some trifle, birthdays were never celebrated, and no one had even heard of Father Christmas."

"However," said Luigino, "there was one kind of present that's completely gone out of fashion now."

"What's that?"

" 'Something nice!' When children used to go visit a grandmother or an aunt, it was always 'Come here, pet, Auntie's got something for you! Something nice!' And she gave the child a cookie maybe, or a candy. . . . If an aunt were to offer a child a cookie or a candy today, I imagine that all she'd get is a 'No, thanks, and so long.' "

"All in all," said Bellavista, "life was simpler in those days. Certain commodities didn't even exist—vacations, for example, were only for the very rich, and no one, but no one, 'weekended.' Even the word was unknown! My parents went to Capri once in their lives, on the occasion of their silver wedding anniversary. They sent us a postcard with the message 'Greetings from Capri, Mammà and Papà.' "

"And what has *that* got to do with the economic boom?" asked Dottor Vittorio.

"A great deal, in point of fact, because despite the national and international crisis, the population as a whole has totally refused to cut down its spending on luxuries: the theaters, the cinemas, the stadiums, the holiday resorts are as crowded today as if the Arabs had never opened their mouths."

"You're deluding yourself, Gennà; I assure you that this year the population—which, don't forget, is largely made up of factory workers and farmers—has suffered a drastic reduction in its standard of living, and places like Capri and St. Moritz are atypical of the rest of the country because only those who are cushioned against the effects of the economic crisis frequent them."

"I don't agree with you, at least not about the extent of the phenomenon to which you allude. The farmer and the factory worker show no signs of relinquishing the Fiat 500 and meat on the table."

"But why should they relinquish them?"

"That's another matter. I was merely saying that the economic crisis is still only something one reads about in the newspapers and has not yet become a moral issue in the public mind."

"But Professò," said Salvatore, "I don't understand. What should we be doing about it?"

"Epicurus once said, 'If you want to increase Pitocles' wealth, instead of increasing his income curtail his expenses!' "

"And what did he mean, Professò?"

"He meant that if we were all a bit more modest in our pretensions we should never have an economic crisis."

"The Professor has always been a devotee of St. Epicurus," explained Saverio.

"Savè, Epicurus was never a saint, even if, in my opinion, he deserved to be."

"Why didn't they make him a saint, Professò?"

"Primarily because he was born in the fourth century B.C., but also because nearly everyone has always spoken badly of him."

"In fact," said Dottor Vittorio, "the adjective 'Epicurean' is applied to a person who thinks of nothing but eating, drinking, and enjoying life."

"That sounds okay to me!" exclaimed Saverio with a wink. "I assume, Dottor, that by enjoying life you do mean the total satisfaction of the senses?"

"Here we go again!" the Professor protested. "That is exactly how Epicurus' name gets dragged in the mud."

"But the Dottore did say that Epicurus was a man of the world."

"You've completely misunderstood. Now, if you'll allow me just five minutes, I'll explain the Epicurean ethic, to which we Neapolitans, for good or ill, owe much of our character."

"Really? Why's that?"

"Because one of the main followers of Epicurus was a certain Philodemus of Gadara, who lived in the first century B.C. Philodemus moved to Naples—to Herculaneum, to be precise—and founded an extremely important Epicurean school on the lines of the Garden, or Academy, of Athens. In this school Philodemus taught the people of Naples to classify pleasures and to despise power."

"Actually, Professò, you might say the Neapolitans have always been philosophical," said Saverio.

"So," continued Bellavista, "Epicurus said that there are three kinds of pleasures: primary pleasures that are natural and necessary; secondary pleasures that are natural but not necessary; and vain pleasures that are neither natural nor necessary."

"I don't understand, Professò. Which pleasures are you talking about?"

"Pay attention and I shall explain further. The primary pleasures, those that are natural and necessary, are eating, drinking, sleeping, and friendship."

"Is that all? Just eating, drinking, sleeping, and friendship?" asked Saverio. "Are you sure you haven't left out something really important, Professò?"

"No, Savè. As far as Epicurus was concerned, sex was a secondary pleasure, natural but not necessary."

"Well, I don't agree with this friend of yours," said Saverio disappointedly.

"That's just too bad! Now, I was explaining that when Epicurus said that eating and drinking were important, he was not implying that people should stuff themselves; on the contrary, he held that they should limit themselves only to the barest necessities, and thus, by primary pleasures, he meant water to drink, bread to eat, and a mattress of straw to sleep on."

"What a dull life this Epicurus must have had!"

"But you see, there were compensations: these pleasures were primary because life itself depended upon them, but once a man had provided himself with them, he could evaluate with a much clearer mind any opportunity of sampling some of the secondary pleasures."

"For example?"

"For example, cheese. Obviously bread and cheese are more palatable than bread on its own, but equally obviously, cheese is not indispensable. So what does a man do? He asks the price of the cheese. If he can afford it, he buys it, if not, he says, 'Thanks all the same, but I've already eaten.' "

"Epicurus said that?"

"Indeed. In other words, all the secondary pleasures, such as eating better, drinking better, and having a better bed, or such as art, sexual love, music, et cetera, et cetera, have to be evaluated singly, moment by moment, so that we can weigh up their eventual advantages and disadvantages. Now do you understand?"

"Yes, Professò, but it would be easier if you gave us some more examples."

"Certainly. Let's imagine that Saverio meets a very beautiful lady today and that this lady tells Saverio that she would like him to make love to her . . ."

"Your lips to God's ears, Professò!" exclaimed Saverio. "As long as there's no money involved!"

"There you are, you see, Saverio has already set a condition: the lady can be as beautiful as Venus herself, but if she asks, say, a hundred thousand lire, Saverio will lose interest."

"A hundred thousand! What do you take me for! If it was a matter of five thousand and the lady put her heart into it, then maybe, maybe."

"Let us also suppose that this lady is the mistress of a *guappo** and that Saverio knows that if this *guappo* finds out, he's a dead man—what, I ask you, will Saverio do then?"

"Wet his pants, Professò," said Salvatore, "and tell the lady in question that actually he doesn't like women anyway."

"Hey, just a moment, Salvatò! Yours truly has never been afraid of anyone. But I don't see why, with all the women there are in the world, I should have to wind up with the mistress of a *guappo*!"

"So what has Saverio done? He has evaluated the pros and cons of this secondary pleasure and has decided, on balance, that it's not in his interests. That is precisely the philosophy of Epicurus."

"But to be honest, Professò, this philosophy doesn't strike me as particularly original," commented Saverio.

"Hold on. Let's examine it a bit more closely. We said at the

*A member of the Camorra, a Neapolitan criminal association.

start that every time I find myself wanting a secondary pleasure, I must first decide how appropriate it is, so now we will apply this concept to the working life of our friend here, the Ingegnere."

"To me?" I said. "To me as an engineer?"

"Exactly, to you as a working man. Now, you earn a salary that, by and large, we can assume is adequate for all your needs. But there comes a time when you decide you would like to rent a *villetta* by the sea. A liking for the sea is natural, so we are obviously dealing here with a secondary pleasure, natural but not necessary. But you realize that in order to lay your hands on the money to rent this place you must seek a promotion, and this means that you have to make a series of sacrifices, such as working late in the evening, agreeing with your superior even when he is wrong, leaving Naples and going to work in Milan, and so on. Now, how would Epicurus react in such a situation? He would say, Listen, I'm happy enough as I am, and all things considered, I don't give a hoot for your seaside villa."

"My dear Gennaro, the Epicurus you describe is even worse than the popular conception of him," said Dottor Palluotto. "This is not philosophy but superficiality, and I'll tell you why. In the first place, if our friend had always reasoned in the style of Epicurus, he would never have become an engineer and would never have got to his present well-paid position. In the second place, if our friend is working and seeking a promotion, he is doing so not only in order to buy villas and motorboats but because there are other objectives in life of which you may be ignorant but which are called moral satisfactions. Third and last, why should you assume that our friend finds work a sacrifice? Suppose he actually enjoys his work? If that is the case, then you tell me why he should renounce this pleasure."

"Epicurus' philosophy is not superficial, but you are, my dear Vittorio, if you cannot understand what I tell you. I'll take your objections point by point, starting with the third, your hypothesis that our friend enjoys his work. It's an unlikely hypothesis but not impossible. In that case, we simply remove the inconvenience of working all day long from the list of cons and add it to the pros, but this does not invalidate the Epicurean method, which requires us, before deciding to pursue a particular pleasure, to make a global assessment of the problem. Working all day long means that we have to neglect other aspects of life, such as the affection of a wife, spending more time with the children, reading, exercising, and many other possibilities. Now, clearly the individual is in charge, and it is entirely up to him to decide between one secondary pleasure and another; what he may not do, however, is neglect a primary pleasure in favor of a vain pleasure."

"How do you mean?"

"I refer to friendship, to spiritual nourishment. And by friendship in this context we mean love for our neighbor. Work, unfortunately, when it goes beyond a certain point, deprives us of the time needed to cultivate our friends and therefore deprives us of the enjoyment of a primary pleasure."

"But no one's saying that our friend, in seeking a promotion, needs to abandon his family or live like a hermit!"

"So you must admit that it's a simple matter of proportion. And that is exactly the point I was making. You say that our friend, had he reasoned like Epicurus, would not be in his present comfortable position, he wouldn't have studied, he wouldn't have qualified, and he wouldn't have obtained his present post. But I say that that does not necessarily follow. Epicurus does not say that a man should spend his life flat on his back doing nothing at all, because such a choice would put his very survival in jeopardy and would not safeguard his primary pleasures. So what would Epicurus do in this case? He would say to our friend, If you have the time, study and work by all means, but try to divide your time among all the things that are important in life. And so, at last, we arrive at your main point, the moral satisfactions connected with work. Now, I can understand the shoemaker caressing the sole of the shoe he has just made. I can understand the carpenter conjuring a piece of furniture out of living wood and the artist gazing at his canvas with half-closed eyes to see his work better. But I cannot understand the satisfaction of the employee who wants to be manager. I cannot understand the member of Parliament who wants to be minister, the deputy director who wants to be director. I do not understand the man who wants power not for the sake of what power can do but because of what it represents. Contempt for power is at the root of all Epicurean philosophy. Power is vain pleasure par excellence. Remember that 'vain' pleasures are all those that are neither natural nor necessary, so that to be a magistrate or a manager, to wear a piece of stone on one's finger that costs a king's ransom merely because it's called a diamond, are so-called benefits that any sane individual, even if he is offered them as presents, should always refuse for the sake of his own self-respect."

"But there's one thing I still don't understand," said Dottor Palluotto. "If some poor devil wants to be a magistrate, what does it matter to you? What harm does it do you?"

"It does no harm to me but a great deal to him, and the reason is that once this unfortunate soul has opted for a vain pleasure, he immediately becomes involved in competitive activity. All vain pleasures, being the conventional goals of the mindless, are also competitive. In fact, all such pleasures, because they are not natural, survive only thanks to the conditioning of society. So what happens in a typical instance? A company has a managerial post vacant and says that it will promote one of its present employees, and from that moment all the employees, because they are now all aspiring managers, become rivals unable to work together in friendship. Whereas I, for example, frequently take a little stroll down to Mergellina after midnight, and it often happens that I bump into a friend. In fact, very often I bump into Luigino. Isn't that so, Luigino?"

"Indeed it is!" replied Luigino. "Sometimes we go on chatting until two, three o'clock in the morning. For instance, the Professor might say, 'Come on, Luigino, I'll walk you home,' and we walk to my place and then, because I don't like to leave him all alone, I say, 'Come on, Professor, now I'll walk you home,' and we return to his place. And so it goes, I walk him home and he walks me home, and meanwhile we talk and talk and talk . . ."

"Streets are made for walking and talking," commented Bellavista.

"But what's that got to do with the subject?" asked Dottor Palluotto.

"A lot. It illustrates my point perfectly! I mentioned my nocturnal strolls in order to point out that no man of power, no Kissinger or Brezhnev or Carli or Cefis, could permit himself the luxury of strolling with a friend at night, and for two reasons: first, he would not have the time, and second, he probably doesn't have a friend."

"Forgive me, Gennà, but what a ludicrous example!" protested Dottor Palluotto. "You're talking about two people who do nothing practical from morning till night. For all the material contribution that you and Luigino make to society, you might as well spend the whole night strolling, since it is demonstrably true that you have nothing to do the following morning. But for myself, and I'm sorry about your Epicurus, I quite categorically refuse to subscribe to a totally hedonistic view of life."

"Now you're being downright offensive, Vittò!" exclaimed Professor Bellavista. "And you're confusing Epicurean moderation with the hedonism of the Cyrenaics."

"Dottò, I'm surprised at you!" said Saverio, giving the doctor a look of disapproval.

"To live for the moment and to grasp at pleasure whenever and wherever possible has never been part of the Epicurean credo! It was Aristippus of Cyrene who preached the search for pleasure."

"Agreed," said Palluotto, "but even a life based upon total disengagement is unacceptable. The hippie, dressed in rags and trailing from one country to another, living at the expense of the very society he condemns, is to me an object of disgust."

"But hippies are not Epicureans, they're Cynics! Now you're confusing Epicurus with Diogenes!"

"Dottò," said Saverio, "this just isn't your day: you haven't scored once."

"Epicurus, the great Epicurus, the apostle of the right choice, held that the prime virtue was moderation, measure! And Naples is the land of things done up to a certain point. Productivity can be as fatal as sloth!"

"If I'm not mistaken," I said, "you mentioned a few days ago that this theory of the middle way was also found in Chinese philosophy."

"Not only Chinese but also in Indian philosophy and in the works of other great thinkers within Greek philosophy itself. The first of the Chinese philosophers to speak of the 'doctrine of the middle way' was Confucius' nephew, called Tse-szu or something like that, but the world had to wait another two centuries for a real exposition of the ideology of moderation, and we eventually got, in the works of Chuang-tse, the great Taoist philosopher, the theory of the 'middle path' and the concept of 'relative happiness.'"

"I'm completely lost," said Saverio, "what with all these Chuangs and Sik Siks the Professor knows."

"But I can't let you leave without mentioning the greatest of all these philosophers of the middle way, Aristotle," Professor Bellavista continued, unperturbed. "The Aristotelian principle of the golden mean referred back to a doctrine expounded by Plato and defined virtue as a point equidistant between two extremes."

"I don't understand a word you're saying, Professò," protested Saverio, "and I doubt any of the others do either."

"And let us not forget the modern father of the philosophy of common sense, John Locke," the Professor persisted, by now unstoppable. "Locke was the philosopher who said that true liberty consists in the regulation of the passions. Unfortunately, the philosophers of pleasure have always been boycotted by the Utopians, who, in the history of philosophy, have always prevailed in the end, not, in my opinion, because their ideas were superior but because their numbers were. We need only consider the fact that Germany, toward the end of the eighteenth century, was producing nothing but idealist philosophers: Kant, Fichte, Hegel, all German by birth and by cast of mind. They talked a lot and wrote even more, with the result that the poor philosophers of pleasure in moderation, the Benthams and the Mills, couldn't even make themselves heard above the din . . ."

"Professò, Professò, we don't understand any of this!"

"And where did it all end? With the arrival on the scene of Karl Marx and Friedrich Nietzsche. Ye gods and little fishes! Mention prudence to Nietzsche and the least you can expect is that he spits in your face!"

"Professò, we don't understand you at all," said Salvatore. "Who's this Freddie what's-his-name who spits in people's faces?"

"Friedrich Nietzsche. The man who said, 'It is not your sins that cry to heaven for vengeance but your moderation, the miserliness you show even in your very sinning!' "

"Professò! . . . Professò, we really don't understand a single word you're saying," said Saverio.

"I accept your reproof, Savè. And by way of apology I shall tell you a story, a very simple little story, about Chuang-tse. Chuang-tse said that one day, on the way to visit his uncle . . ."

"Uncle Confucius?"

"No, Saverio, Confucius' nephew was another philosopher. This was Chuang-tse, the Taoist philosopher. So, as I was saying, Chuang was going to see his uncle, and his way led through a big wood. At one point, feeling tired, he sat down under an oak tree that was hundreds of years old. He had hardly been there ten minutes when a band of woodcutters arrived and began chopping down some poplars growing near the oak tree. Now, while the woodcutters were going about their business, the oak tree spoke to Chuang . . ."

"The oak tree? The oak tree spoke?" said Saverio. "Professò, I think this must be some more Chinese baloney!"

"Shut up, Savè!" said Salvatore. "This is an allegory. Don't mind him, Professò, just tell us what the oak tree said to your friend."

"The oak tree said, 'As you see, Chuang, they have come to cut down the more useful trees, and now you understand why I have spent five hundred years learning how to make my wood good for nothing.' Chuang then resumed his journey, deciding that when he got home he would write a book on the usefulness of being unuseful. Meanwhile, however, he arrived at his uncle's house, and his uncle was so pleased to see him that he ordered a servant to go and kill a goose to celebrate his nephew's visit, but the servant, before going into the courtyard to kill the goose, asked his master which goose he should take, the one sitting on a clutch of eggs or the one who never laid any eggs at all. Naturally, the uncle told the servant to kill the goose·that was less useful. And that was why Chuang, when the time came for him to return home, chose to travel along the middle path."

XII

SPEEDING

"BUT YOU SEE, DOTTÒ," the cab driver said as we sat in yet another traffic jam, "it's not the streets that are to blame. The problem is that every Neapolitan uses the car even to go around the corner for a pack of cigarettes. I figure he says to himself, I've sweated blood to buy this car, and now that I've got it I'm going to use it! You're not going to believe me, but do you know what the average Neapolitan does every Sunday afternoon around five or five-thirty? He takes the whole family for a drive along the Caracciolo. No kidding. His route is Mergellina, Via Caracciolo, Via dei Mille, Via Crispi, and then down again to Mergellina. Three times around the circuit means he's home just in time for *Carosello*. He just enjoys driving in traffic!"

"Still, I think the traffic police are also to blame for not enforcing the law strictly enough. Take horns, for example. Everyone in Naples uses them constantly and most of the time quite needlessly . . ."

"Don't worry about the horns, Dottò; drivers use them just to keep from feeling lonely. The real problem is that everyone considers himself a racing driver. . . . Look at that!" he shouted suddenly as a Fiat 500 sped in front of him. "Did you see how that idiot cut me off? I've got to see who that damn son of a bitch is! God almighty, it's a woman! Heaven help us! Women! Stay in your own homes instead of prowling the streets like whores on the make! You saw what happened: if I hadn't jammed on the brakes I'd have been in a real mess!"

83

"But in point of fact, you had turned around to speak to me, remember?"

"Oh, come on, Dottò, are you joking? I've been driving for twenty-two years, and not once have I hit another car. It's always been the other car that hit me. Hardly a single fine— apart from a few parking tickets lately, due to the fact that an uncle on my mother's side used to work at City Hall and always got my tickets torn up but now he's gone to his reward in heaven and I have to be a little more careful where I park. Speaking of fines, I can tell you that yours truly is the only driver in the world who ever got caught speeding in a funeral procession."

"What?" I exclaimed, laughing. "In a funeral procession?"

"That's right, sir," he confirmed, turning around again, "actually in a funeral procession. I was following right behind the hearse with the widow and two nephews of the dead man when suddenly, in Via Foria, the widow stopped crying, opened the rear door on the right, and after yelling, 'Giovanni, I want to die too!' tried to hurl herself under the wheels of a trolley car just behind us. You know what it's like in Naples, tragedy makes us light-headed, and there are times when we do the nuttiest things. Luckily, however, the nephew sitting beside her managed to grab her clothing, and after a lot of shrieking and wailing, I, the nephews, and the trolley passengers eventually succeeded in calming the distraught widow. Naturally, while all this hullabaloo was going on, the hearse with the coffin on board had disappeared, so I had to begin my first car chase of the day. And as bad luck would have it, a car with a Naples registration that must have had a foreigner at the wheel, because it stopped at every red light, cost me so much time that I only managed to catch up with the hearse in Piazza Carlo III. Well, I was crawling along at the usual funeral pace again when the nephew sitting next to me suddenly yelled out, 'But that's not Uncle Giovanni!' I was following the wrong hearse! This was a completely different funeral! The widow was shrieking, '*Giovanni mio*, don't leave me!' The nephews were shrieking, 'Auntie, calm down!' All hell was breaking loose in the cab, and meanwhile I had spotted another hearse going up the hill toward Capodichino, so I passed the false hearse and was really stepping on the gas when lo and behold, I found myself being flagged down by a motorcycle policeman. What could I do? I stopped and got out to explain the dramatic situation, and everything was just about sorted out when suddenly the widow, taking advantage of a moment's distraction on the part of her family, leapt out and tried to throw herself over the bridge by the road leading up to the cemetery. And then what happened was that in my efforts to stop the widow from killing herself, I accidentally knocked the policeman for a loop and fell down myself and hurt my knee. In fact, everyone got hurt one way or another except the widow, who came through without a scratch."

XIII

IL BASSO

The bird a nest
the spider a web
man friendship.

WILLIAM BLAKE

"MY DEAR GENNARO, if our discussions never reach any definite conclusion, the fault, perhaps, is entirely mine. You have the typically Neapolitan taste for paradox and anecdote, while I, after years in Milan, have become used to rationalizing problems. So you know what happens. There always comes a point when I fly off the handle and start shouting and you find it amusing. Today, however, I've made up my mind to observe the utmost self-control, because I am determined, utterly determined, that our discussion shall achieve a practical result."

"And what practical result might you have in mind?"

"Your admission that the Epicurean-Neapolitan concept of life, which you describe so vividly, can never lead to any material progress."

"Then we don't even need to discuss the matter, because I'm already convinced that the Epicurean-Neapolitan philosophy will never lead to the kind of progress you have in mind."

"What do you mean?"

"That the problem lies not so much with the way of life as with the purpose one wishes to achieve. It all depends on what you mean by 'progress.'

"In your opinion, is Naples, with its *bassi*,* its polluted sea, its unemployment, cholera, and so on, an example of material progress?"

"Not so fast. For thousands of years humanity has been asking itself the true purpose of life, and now you want me to come up with an answer in two minutes flat!"

"Very well," retorted Dottor Vittorio sarcastically, "excuse me while I make arrangements for a year's sabbatical so that you can take all the time you need to enlighten me."

"I'll tell you one thing: I prefer your outbursts to your sarcasm."

"Forgive me, Gennà, I was forgetting that within these walls you have a monopoly on wit."

"Here we go," said Salvatore. "They're at it again!"

"No, not at all," said the Professor. "Let's take things step by step. Now, you mentioned the *bassi* of Naples, and you asked me if I thought they could constitute an example of progress. Well, I could reply that the *bassi* of Naples, from the Epicurean standpoint, are models of civilization."

"Have you seen *Filumena Marturano*,† Gennà?" asked Dottor Palluotto. "Do you remember how Filumena *la napoletana* describes her childhood in the *bassi*? Well, do you know what I think? That if Eduardo heard you describe these places as models of civilization, he'd kill you . . . and not with a pistol, Gennaro, with his bare hands!"

"Words are the downfall of humanity! There are billions of sensations, billions of ideas, and only a handful of words to describe them! Sometimes I think that if we had decided to express our thoughts in numbers rather than words we would have found a more precise means of communication."

---

* *I bassi*, purely Neapolitan phenomena, are wretched one-room windowless dwellings opening directly onto the street. Architecturally the basements of the buildings of which they form the lowest floor, they are not, for the most part, below ground level, and the term is therefore not translatable as "basement" or, indeed, any other word.

† Another play by Eduardo De Filippo, about a Neapolitan prostitute.

"Professò, I didn't follow that," said Saverio. "What numbers are you talking about?"

"What I mean, Saverio, dear boy, is that when I use the word 'civilization,' the syllables you hear me utter mean one thing to me, something else to you, and something else again to Dottor Vittorio."

"So what can we do about it?"

"We must have patience and we must talk, and by talking try to reach an understanding, putting aside all our prejudices and preconceptions."

"Very well," said Dottor Vittorio, "I'll listen to what you have to say, but now you must explain what you understand by the word 'civilization.' "

"You see, Vittorio, when people use the word 'civilization,' they immediately think of man's most important achievements, and so they end up confusing civilization with progress. But true civilization, as I understand it, means something more. It means the dimension of the human spirit in things. Take your business in Milan, for example, the environment in which you work. True, I've never been there, but since it's in Milan, I imagine it as very well organized, with splendid offices, secretaries, switchboards, and so on and so forth. But now I ask you to consider, Vittò, whether in your opinion this business is an example of civilization or of progress? Does it possess a human dimension in which you can recognize something of yourself?"

"What do you mean by a human dimension?"

"An ice-cream seller on a bicycle is a very basic example of a business with a human dimension; the bicycle remains in motion only as long as there's a man pedaling it. But perhaps your business is not a bicycle but a gigantic tandem with hundreds of people pushing the pedals, and one day it might occur to you that even if you stopped pedaling, the tandem would go on running, and after a while, if your tandem grows so big that it now takes thousands of people to pedal it, it might occur to you that even if you all dismounted, the machine would still go on running. That is the point at which a business begins to lose its human dimension. And on the day when everyone dismounts, you'll notice that the only riders left on the machine are robots, identical in all respects to the real riders except for their eyes, which are dead. And you'll be struck by the chilling thought that even if the entire human race were to be wiped out by some global catastrophe—a nuclear bomb or whatever—this business of yours would be running still and would go on running until the next pay day, through a silent, corpse-strewn world where the only sound was the hum of electronic machines printing out paychecks, invoices, and past-due notices."

"And just what would be the maximum number of employees that a business could have without losing its human dimension?"

"That depends upon you, upon your capacity for love. If you took the company bus to a conference and could recognize everyone on it by name, that would mean that there was still a human element in the company. But the day you recognize nobody, you too will have lost your identity."

"So would you say, Professò," asked Salvatore, "that big companies ought to split themselves up into lots of little companies? Would that be a good idea?"

"An excellent idea, Salvatò. And sooner or later that's what they will have to do."

"I'm sorry, but you're wrong, Gennaro," objected Dottor Vittorio. "It's a proven fact that only the very largest companies can achieve optimum cost-effectiveness. Today's technology dictates a very heavy investment in research that only very large companies operating on a worldwide scale are able to absorb."

"Yes, I am aware that the present situation is exactly as you say, but the day is not far off when we shall see a change, when we shall enter upon the third industrial phase, the 'phase of love,' and a return to the human dimension will be inevitable."

"What is this 'phase of love,' Professò?" asked Saverio.

"Gentlemen, the driving force of modern commerce is incentive. Until a few years ago this incentive was the stick, and no man would lift a finger without it. If you didn't work, you were fired. This 'stick phase' lasted, more or less, until the sixties, when labor legislation, by giving protection from unfair dismissal and guaranteeing a minimum wage, removed the stick from the hands of the employers. So industry reacted by introducing the 'carrot phase.' If you worked, you were rewarded, you were paid better. But then, during the seventies, came tax reform, affecting employees in particular; this gradually negated the merit system as people realized that contrary to expectation, they couldn't really earn more. What was left? Power! Power with its symbols, its liturgy, and its medals. Power is so important today that a company can reward its favorites just by handing them little snippets of power, and the recipients are happy to shoulder a greater burden of responsibility just for the sake of a job title and without expecting any actual increase in pay. But how long will power retain its charm? And above all, what will happen when businesses exhaust the available supply of power? Because as you draw upon reserves of power, the reserves are depleted. If all you can do is chop up what remains into smaller and smaller portions to keep more and more people happy, the time will come when you are forced to hand out a counterfeit in place of the real thing, and when that happens the second phase, the 'carrot phase,' will be over."

"And what then?"

"And then the third phase will begin, the 'phase of love.' "

"Women?"

"No, love. The love that I can feel for my superior and that he can feel for me. I'll work in order to earn his respect, and he'll work in order to earn mine. But this will only be possible in businesses where the human dimension is present."

"Words, mere words," scoffed Dottor Palluotto. "Fine, inspiring words, perhaps, but the truth is that three things make the world go round—productivity, the cultivation of the mind, and specialization—and that these three things presuppose commitment and responsibility."

"Nonsense!" replied Bellavista. "As far as productivity is concerned, don't be so sure that it makes the world go round; the day may even dawn when productivity itself becomes, in real terms, counterproductive. Just think about the environment and all our terrible ecological problems. Then, with regard to the cultivation of the mind and specialization, let's get our ideas straight. In my book these terms are antithetical. The former, as I see it, implies curiosity about the world in general, while the latter implies curiosity about one thing in particular. You would be correct in assuming that while I have the greatest respect for the first, I am no friend to the second."

"One moment, Gennà," interposed Dottor Vittorio. "You are digressing. Just a few minutes ago you came up with the startling opinion that the Neapolitan *basso* was a model of civilized living, then you dropped the subject. Could we now have the inestimable privilege of hearing from the lips of the esteemed Professor Bellavista some words of wisdom about the social amenities of the *bassi napoletani*?"

"I knew it! Amenities! If by civilization you mean gas, water, and electricity, then we need say no more. The home in the *basso* is uncivilized. But if your definition of home includes love, family, community, friendship, then we find qualities in the *basso* that are much harder to come by in the more genteel environment of the sixth floor."

"But have you ever tried living in the *bassi*?"

"No, but that is totally irrelevant. I know plenty of people who do, and also plenty who live on the sixth floor. I had a friend in Turin who said to me one day, 'Gennà, here I am, wealthy, unmarried, and living in an apartment with two hundred square meters of floor space. Do come visit me; I want to show you what a fine place I've got, and besides, your company would be so welcome. I must confess that partly because I'm lazy and partly because I don't know many people here in Turin, I spend every evening alone, and after watching television, if I'm not sleepy enough to go to bed, I get so depressed you wouldn't believe it.

Gennà,' he said, 'wouldn't it be wonderful if we could all live together, close to each other, in one little *vicolo*,* I in my *basso*, you in the next, then Peppino and Federico and Giovanni, all in a row. But instead of that, fate has landed me in Turin, you in Naples, Peppino in Paris, Federico in Rome, Mimì at La Spezia, and Giovanni in Milan. How can we possibly talk to each other like this!' "

"That's going too far, Professò!" said Salvatore. "What's to stop this friend of yours from making some friends in Turin?"

"If it were only that simple! But it takes nearly a lifetime to make a friend. You have to be poor together, and happy together too. Friendship takes time, and continual moving around the country makes the cementing of affectionate relationships impossible. Companies that transfer their personnel from place to place never think about this. Sometimes even a big city, where it may take an hour and a half just to get from one end to the other, is enough to separate two friends forever. In the *bassi* that sort of thing can't happen. Imagine for a moment that this house is a typical *basso* dwelling: here we are, the door is open, and we can see all the people walking past. All at once a friend walks by: Peppino. Peppì, we say, how's life? Come on in, we've got something funny to tell you. And so we start chatting."

"I know a man, the brother of our mussel-seller, who lives in a *basso* in Vico Pace a Forcella," said Salvatore. "The other day he was telling me how he had the television on for three days without any sound because the speaker had blown, and nobody in the family even noticed. They heard everything from their neighbors' sets!"

"You see?" said the Professor, beaming. "They heard everything from their neighbors' sets! Indeed, the problem of 'what shall I do tonight' never arises in the *bassi*. Social life simply flows in through the open front doors by itself. There's no privacy, but by the same token no one in need is ever neglected. Do you ever

---

*A narrow street typical of the poorer areas of Naples.

think about old age? About what it's like to be old and alone in a sixth-floor apartment in the residential district of a big city? Your communication with the outside world is limited to the telephone, if you're lucky. But in the *bassi* no old person is alone, no child ever without a playmate. In effect it's rather like being on a cruise ship: each has his own cabin, but everyone meets on deck to chat. Just think, in Naples there are at least two hundred thousand people taking a perpetual cruise."

"My dear Gennaro, that's all very amusing, but if I were God, I'd make you live henceforth in a Neapolitan *basso*. Some cruise you'd have! You of all people, who can't even bear the company of your own wife and daughter, I'd really like to see you cope with a crowd wandering in and out of your house all day long."

"I knew you'd say that, Vittorio. Naturally, after spending an entire lifetime in an apartment, I wouldn't be able to rise to the depths, but that in no way detracts from the validity of my remarks about the capacity for love to be found in the *vicolo*. And my point is proved by the fact that the people who live in the *basso* have no desire to move up to the sixth floor. More than once, in fact, the authorities have tried to transfer whole communities from the *bassi* to new low-cost housing developments and have failed because the people refused to leave their beloved caves. And rightly so! The official 'do-gooders' had considered the *bassi* merely as dwellings, but they were wrong. The *bassi* are also shops, consulting rooms, sports clubs, meeting places, churches, the offices of import-export companies, and above all human environments."

"Gennà, you're cheating and you know it! Of course it was only natural that the poor souls should refuse to leave their homes, but why? Because the *bassi* represented their only source of income. What do those people live on? Deals and illegal imports. Toys for the kids and cigarettes for the adults. If the 'do-gooders,' as you call them, had offered them not only a decent apartment but a decent job too, they'd have been out of their caves in no time flat."

"On the contrary, I maintain that they would have accepted the jobs but gone on living in the *bassi* selling contraband toys to children and cigarettes to adults."

"To think that the *bassi* have been criticized since the days of Goethe and Dumas, yet nothing has been done about them in all that time."

"In my view those criticisms were ill considered. Do you realize what a vitally important social role the *bassi* have played over the last few centuries? Has it ever occurred to you that Naples is the only big city in the world that has no poor quarter as such? The ghetto districts you find in the great industrial cities such as Turin and Chicago simply do not exist here and never have. In Naples the *popolino** lived in the *bassi,* the aristocracy on the first floor—the so-called *piano nobile*—and the middle classes on the floors above. This vertical type of social stratification has naturally favored cultural exchanges between the classes, thereby excluding one of the great evils of the class system, the ever growing cultural divide between rich and poor."

"In all honesty I can't say that the Neapolitan *popolino* strikes me as being particularly cultured!"

"Wait, Vittò, when I said 'cultured' I was not referring to the book learning of the Neapolitan proletariat. That's another problem, for which the responsibility falls fairly and squarely on the shoulders of the central government. What I meant was that the Neapolitan laborer, in spite of his ignorance, is nevertheless rich in certain human values that stem, I contend, from the fact that he lives in a mixed environment where a continual rubbing of shoulders between the marquis on the first floor, the lawyer on the second, and the poor jack-of-all-trades in the *basso* underneath has enlarged the horizons of each and every inhabitant of the building regardless of his social status."

"Things have changed now, however. The rich have abandoned the run-down areas of Naples and have created their own ghettos

*The poorer people in general.

along Via Orazio and Via Petrarca, where, coincidentally, there are no *bassi*. The poor people, on the other hand, have remained behind as the sole inhabitants of the *basso* districts, where they may be as happy as you say they are, but where they are most certainly poorer than they used to be."

"Vittò, I wish you could get it into your head that happiness is relative. Every individual has his own concept of happiness that serves him as a standard of measurement, so to find out whether he is happy or not at any given instant, he has to compare his actual state with his ideal of happiness. Let me put the question to Saverio, for example: Savè, what does happiness mean to you?"

"Whatever you say, Professò."

"What kind of a reply is that, Savè? Tell me what in your opinion is meant by happiness," persisted the Professor.

"But I always agree with you, Professò, and whatever you say is okay by me. So you tell me what happiness is, and your devoted Saverio will never dream of contradicting you."

"Savè, listen to me. You once told me that you and all your family revere San Pasquale . . ."

"San Pasquale Bajlonne! A very great saint, a buddy of San Gennaro. I've been devoted to him since I was married, and I must say he's always delivered the goods!"

"What are you talking about!" protested Dottor Vittorio. "You're unemployed, you haven't got a lira to your name, and you say he's delivered the goods! You yourself told me recently that you were worried because the children were growing so fast, especially their feet, and you didn't know how you were going to be able to buy shoes for all three."

"Yes, you're right, Dottò, I'm worried sick about the kids' shoes, but we haven't mentioned shoes to San Pasquale. All we say to him is 'San Pasquale, bless us,' and thanks be to God, we've always been fit as fiddles."

"There!" said the Professor. "That's just what I wanted to hear. I needed to know the greatest blessing Saverio could ask for, because from that I can deduce Saverio's idea of happiness. To put it another way, when we see a dirty, ragged boy playing in the doorway of a *basso* and laughing and singing, we, because we're used to all the comforts of home, naturally feel sorry for him, he arouses our tenderness and sympathy; but the child himself, who knows no other environment, may well be at the apogee of his relative happiness."

"What you term relative happiness I prefer to call crass irresponsibility," retorted Dottor Vittorio. "And I'll tell you why, my dear Gennaro. Though it's true that the importance of some benefits is relative to the person who desires them, the argument is invalid in the case of others. For example, I can see that the pleasure I would derive from the acquisition of a rubber dinghy would be much the same as the pleasure derived by a millionaire's son from the acquisition of a yacht, but there are some benefits in life that are entirely objective and have the same importance for everyone irrespectively. Take the example that Saverio has already cited, health. Saverio's family enjoys the best of health and is content, and I sincerely wish him continued good health for the next hundred years, but what would happen if he needed medical attention, if he needed the services of an efficient hospital? Can you tell me where he would find an efficient hospital in Naples?"

"Dottò," interrupted Saverio, warding off the evil eye with a gesture, "forgive me, but one can't be too careful . . ."

"And efficient hospitals," continued Dottor Vittorio, "do not appear out of thin air, they are the result of hard work and productivity. Without the self-sacrifice and dedication of thousands of scientists and scholars, humanity today would still be living in a state of nature."

"The reason we always disagree, my dear Vittorio, is that you are always so radical in your reasoning. I have never advocated that men should slack off or refuse to improve social conditions. But even you must concede that all men are not equal, that there are some who are supermen and others, far more numerous, who are just normal people. Well, Epicurus devised his behavioral ethic specifically for the ordinary, decent human being. His doctrine of prudence and common sense was designed to guide men away from the false idols by which they are conditioned. Naturally, a man blessed with genius, with the inextinguishable fire of the explorer, the innovator, the seeker, must fulfill his mission in life. Men like Christopher Columbus, Sabin, and Fleming are a race apart. However, it does not follow that every Tom, Dick, and Harry has a right to renounce the affection of his own family merely in order to rise to the position of managing director in some nameless company."

"Permit me to disagree. I see men such as Sabin and Fleming merely as possessing to the highest degree a quality inherent in all men. I am convinced that the considerably more civilized standard of living in Milan as compared to Naples is attributable not to the administration but to the population of Milan as a whole. And don't drag up the whole business of what I mean by 'civilized' and 'uncivilized' yet again. In my book the fact that Pozzuoli holds the record for infant mortality in Italy is uncivilized. An illness like cholera is uncivilized."

"Dottò, remember that you're Neapolitan yourself and you shouldn't say things like that," said Salvatore. "It isn't the people you should be blaming but those who are really responsible for conditions in Naples, such as the city administrators and above all the Italian government. Don't forget that in the nineteenth century Naples was the first capital city to have a railway, and it had more theaters in those days than we have now."

"Salvatò, I say things like that precisely because I am Neapolitan. When I read about Naples in the papers, when I see one of its poor citizens being subjected to the pitiless probing of a television interviewer, it hurts me. At one and the same time I feel affection and shame for my compatriot as he struggles to speak Italian, and who, *abbasta ca vence 'o Napule,** is prepared to sit by and watch his city go to the dogs."

---

* "As long as the Naples team wins."

"Vittò, I understand your feelings, and I love you for them," said the Professor. "I'm only too aware of the hard work that lies ahead of Naples before she can free herself from the traffic congestion and the corruption that are strangling her, but you wouldn't want Naples to become a carbon copy of Milan. In Naples a few dozen people have died of cholera, but in the same space of time many thousands in Milan have died of loneliness. I don't want to buy progress with the coin of love. I'd prefer to try a different road, a road that does not need to be paved with the stones of power and competitiveness. So I put to you once again the all-important question: What is Life?"

"Life is life," replied Dottor Vittorio without hesitation. "And don't dismiss my reply as banal. It means that living is the absolute priority. But for everyone to live as long as possible, everyone must strive to the utmost. Epicurus considered things only in the short term, only analyzing the consequences of a particular choice with reference to the next two or three years. But the scope of the problem is much greater. We work hard today so that our children's children may be happy tomorrow."

"By the logic of that argument, however, not even our children's children will be happy."

"Why not?"

"Because they won't have time. They'll be working so hard to provide for the happiness of their children's children that they'll die without having ever experienced happiness themselves."

"Idle chatter, Gennà, idle chatter! Sadly, that's all we ever achieve, idle chatter. I give up. Still, I comfort myself with the knowledge that you aren't really fooling yourself. I know that when you walk down a street in Naples you are very well aware that the Naples you see is not the Naples you describe, the Naples that only exists inside your head and perhaps has never existed at all."

"Don't be too sure. No one knows what Naples really is. But there are times when I think that even if Naples, the one I mean, does not exist as a real city, it certainly exists as an idea, as an adjective. And then I think that Naples is the most Naples city I know, and that any other place I've been to has always needed a bit of Naples. Luigì, you've been very quiet, but you've also spent some time in Milan, so do me a favor and tell Vittorio what Naples means to us."

"I don't really know what to say. I've been listening to you carefully, and it seems to me that you're both right. Yes, I lived in Milan for a year, and I understand what Dottor Vittorio means when he says that the city functions as a city, and the people aren't as unfriendly as they're sometimes made out to be—in fact, I always found them very courteous. And the metro, for example, is wonderful: clean and extremely fast, and even if you miss a train another one comes along almost immediately. The climate? You get used to the climate. I remember certain days in Via Melchiorre Gioia at eight o'clock in the morning. Cold and fog. The sun did shine sometimes, but you never saw it, you only knew that it was shining because there was one point in the sky where the gray was a shade lighter. At eight o'clock people were going to work, and you never heard a word spoken, just a puff of smoke from their mouths and hurry, hurry, hurry. There, that's what I mainly remember about Milan, that everyone was in a hurry."

XIV

WAKE-UP CALL

"GOOD MORNING, INGEGNÈ!" Salvatore greeted me as I passed him on my way out. "Lovely day, isn't it! You'd never think it was December."

"Really lovely, Salvatò. Almost too warm for an overcoat."

"Well, they say the good Lord spreads sunshine where He sees snow—need, that is."

"That's the least He can do."

"Speaking of need, Ingegnè, I've been talking so much this morning that I almost forgot. Have you got the time?"

"It's five past nine."

"Then I must go wake the young Baron De Filippis up. Why don't you come with me? It'll only take a second."

"To wake the Baron De Filippis up?"

"Yes, but we won't go to his apartment. We'll just pop into the courtyard at the back and call up to his window. He lives on the first floor. You see, he pays me three thousand lire a month to wake him up at nine on the dot every day except Sunday."

"But wouldn't it be simpler for him to use an alarm clock?"

"Oh, no, Ingegnè! An alarm clock wouldn't be the same at all."

"Why not?"

"I'll explain," said Salvatore as we walked toward the court-yard. "The young Baron is studying law at the university, and somebody has to wake him up every morning at nine o'clock so that he can hit the books, otherwise he'll fail his exams."

"But he should be awake at nine o'clock anyway. I could understand it if you'd said six o'clock."

"Of course you're right, but the Baron is unfortunately a bit of an operator, if you know what I mean. He likes the ladies," said Salvatore with a wicked grin. "So he never gets in until two, sometimes even three in the morning, and that's because he goes dancing at the Mela; he's quite a playboy."

By this time we had arrived beneath the window of the room where our man-about-town was presumably still asleep. At this point, Salvatore began in a very low voice, scarcely above a whisper, to go through the motions of shouting:

"Baroncino ... Baroncino De Filippis ... it's nine o'clock. ... Avvocato, wake up ... it's nine o'clock."

"But Salvatò, if you don't shout louder than that, he'll never hear you!"

"Of course not, Ingegnè. If I shout any louder I'll wake him up, and then I'd really be in for it!"

"So what's the point of doing it at all?"

"Oh, Ingegnè, come on, it's not that difficult!" explained Salvatore patiently. "As I told you, he pays me three thousand a month to stand under his window every morning at nine on the dot and try to wake him up, so I do my duty and then I take off. For his part, by arranging for me to come and wake him up every morning at nine, the Baron has shown his good will, so to speak, and his conscience is easy. You were our witness. That way, you see, we're all happy."

XV

THE COMPASS
OF THE SIXTEEN CALLINGS

Your reason and your passion
are the rudder and the sails
of your seafaring soul.

KAHLIL GIBRAN

"IN MY OPINION, every epoch has produced its own philosophers," I said, "and it's impossible for us to share the ideas of a philosopher who lived more than two thousand years ago. Had Epicurus been born in our time, I'm sure his teaching would have been different."

"Wrong, Ingegnere, the philosophy of Epicurus is always up-to-the-minute."

"Oh, come, Professor, you can't say that! Epicurus' dictum that men should only satisfy their primary needs is no longer tenable. The difference, as I see it, lies in the fact that in Epicurus' day, the provision of the basic necessities of food and drink was a real problem . . ."

"It still is, Ingegnè," interrupted Dottor Vittorio, "it still is!"

"Well, let's say that seventy percent of humanity is still starving while thirty percent is on a diet," put in the Professor.

"What I was trying to say," I went on, "is that the standard of living in the West today has risen to such a degree that many of the benefits that Epicurus, in 300 B.C., designated secondary if not even tertiary, such as the arts, meat, education, communication, and so on, are now impossible to do without and therefore of primary importance."

"And so?" the Professor interrupted. "Gentlemen, please, can't we try a little harder? Let's not be so ruthlessly literal! If we only attempt to understand the substance of the Epicurean message, we shall see that the philosophy of Epicurus has perhaps never been more germane than it is today. What was Epicurus actually saying? That pleasures should be evaluated in the light of their inherent naturalness and necessity. By doing this we arrive at a scale of values that enables us to rank pleasures in descending order: at the top of the scale are the primary pleasures, those that are natural and necessary, then the secondary pleasures, natural but not necessary, and last, at the bottom, the vain pleasures, characterized by being neither natural nor necessary. Now along comes our friend and tells me that benefits not considered necessary in Epicurus' day have in our own day become indispensable. Very well, I reply, but that doesn't worry us in the least: it only means that the line that divided the primary from the secondary pleasures, according to Epicurus, has since shifted to accommodate a few more primary pleasures. But that in no way invalidates Epicurus' argument; indeed, I would go so far as to say that it even reinforces his thesis. Epicurus designated food, drink, sleep, and friendship the primary pleasures, so if, as you have said, food, drink, and sleep are relatively easier to come by nowadays, then we must conclude that the importance of Friendship as a primary pleasure has greatly increased. And Friendship, we must never forget, is the antithesis of Power, Power being a competitive pleasure and the single begetter of all the tertiary pleasures."

"Quite honestly, this seems to me a Christian rather than an Epicurean stance."

"Death and damnation, that's because you're always thrown by the term 'Epicurean,' which in fact means something quite different! Forgive me for insisting, but am I or am I not right in saying that the world in which we live today is one big race where everyone is desperately competing for success, that is to say, for a degree of personal power? The stylish car, the right letters after one's name, the seat of honor, and all the thousand and one commodities invented by the consumer society are nothing but steps on a scale of values created by Power in order to force men into producing more and yet more. Go into any office today, whether it houses a political party, a private business, or a government department, and every single thing that your eyes light upon represents some degree of power acquired by the functionary you happen to be visiting. A simple carafe of mineral water or an exotic rubber plant one meter high are not there for their beauty or utility but because they represent very precise grades of power won by years of hard work and daily struggle. In some companies there is even a full-time employee whose sole function is to make sure that nobody furnishes his office with objects that are the prerogative of superior ranks. So now Epicurus plunges into this maelstrom of false values and says, Gentlemen, observe the intrinsic value of things and remember that after health the thing that counts most is Friendship! Don't allow yourselves to be conditioned by false values! Before you choose your objectives, weigh them carefully to insure that they are consonant with your true desires!"

"There's one thing that doesn't quite fit, Gennà. The other day you spent three hours convincing us that liberty and love were antithetical; today you are arguing that love is opposed to power; I therefore deduce that you see liberty and power as the same thing . . ."

"Not so fast, not so fast, you're jumping to conclusions!" interrupted the Professor. "If you'll give me a minute, I'll draw you a diagram that will explain my theory precisely. Savè, this is a request, not an order. Would you please look on the desk and see if you can find a pen and a sheet of squared paper? If you look hard you should find a notebook somewhere there . . ."

"Here you are, Professò, just as you ordered: pen and paper, and now, if I may, I'll go and get another bottle of Lettere, because the matter looks to be complicated and we need something to refresh the old brain cells."

"Good idea, Saverio. So as I was saying, in order to get a clear idea of the theory of love and liberty, we should have before us a graphic representation of the human mind. Let me explain in more detail. Supposing that human nature was composed of only two types of response, one of love and one of liberty, then I would be able to represent the mind by a two-dimensional Cartesian diagram . . ."

"Good night, Professò," said Salvatore. "We'll be going now . . ."

"Be quiet, Salvatò. Just wait a moment and you'll see that it's all quite simple. Look here." And so saying, the Professor drew two straight lines bisecting one another at right angles.

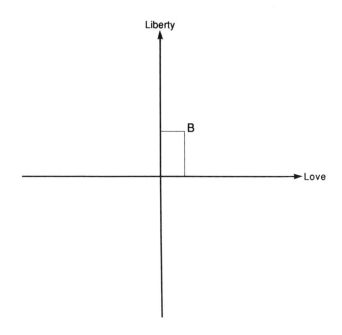

"The horizontal line here represents the axis of love, the vertical line the axis of liberty. Now, where am I, Gennaro Bellavista, on this diagram? I am at point B, which is approximately here." The Professor put a dot on the paper and drew two lines from it, intersecting the other two lines at right angles. "This dot represents me in the sense that it shows me as possessing a certain quantity x of love and a certain quantity y of liberty. It goes without saying, of course, that this point B that identifies me shifts moment by moment according to circumstances. If, for example, I were forced to live in overcrowded conditions, naturally my desire for liberty would increase at the expense of my desire for love, while if I were shipwrecked on a desert island, I would immediately feel a need for love. Think of the difference in attitude between a driver caught in the rush hour and a sailor on the open sea. Coping with the congested road, the first will be ready to quarrel and hurl abuse at his fellow drivers, but the second, surrounded by nothing but water, will hail another boat as soon as he sees it, even if the man who returns his 'Ahoy there' is a perfect stranger."

"True, true."

"However, that's not to say that we don't each occupy a specific point on the diagram, a point that we might call the center of gravity of the area around which we have moved in the course of our lives, determined by the states of mind that have recurred with the greatest frequency."

"And where am I, Professò?" asked Saverio. "If it's not too much trouble, could you put me on the diagram too?"

"This is you, Saverio, point S. Lots of love and very, very little liberty."

"Why am I so short on liberty, Professò?"

"Because when Assuntina and the children went to Procida, instead of thanking the Madonna for a few days of peace and quiet, you were at your wits' end until they came back to Naples."

"You're right, Professò, you're absolutely dead right."

"But let's continue our attempt at graphic analysis. As I said before, the horizontal axis is the axis of love; however, this axis also has its negative part, the part on the left, which represents hate. So we now see that what we have here is an emotional axis, instinctive, all heart and no head."

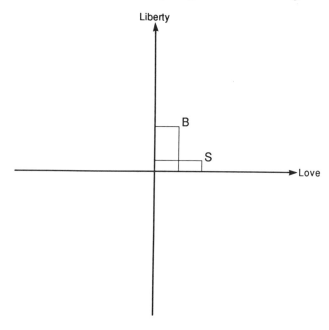

"And the negative part of liberty, Professò, what is that?"

"Slow down, because this is where things get more complex. While we all understood, more or less, what we meant by love, I don't think we can say the same in the case of liberty."

"Liberty is liberty," said Salvatore.

"Unfortunately, Salvatore, it's not quite as simple as that. For some people liberty means democracy, for others it means anarchy, so at this point I shall have to spend a couple of minutes explaining exactly what I mean by liberty."

"Carry on, Professò, we're listening."

"Now, I would define liberty as the simultaneous desire not to be oppressed oneself and not to oppress others. So the opposite of liberty will be the desire to be subjugated and to subjugate others, or in other words, Power."

"As far as I'm concerned, the opposite of liberty is fascism," said Dottor Vittorio.

"Fascism is only the worst manifestation of power. If you

identify power with fascism, you risk excluding from the ranks of the power seekers men who have no pronounced political views yet enjoy ordering other people around, be they members of the family or colleagues at work. No, my friends, when we use the term 'power' in the present context, we are not using it merely in the sense of a coup d'état. It is the desire for power that lies behind the ambition to become head doorkeeper or the ambition to own a 128 in a neighborhood where everyone else has a Fiat 500, not because the 128 is a better car, but simply to arouse the envy of other people. *'Invidia crepa,'** as the slogan reads on handcarts in the poorer *vicoli* of Naples.*"

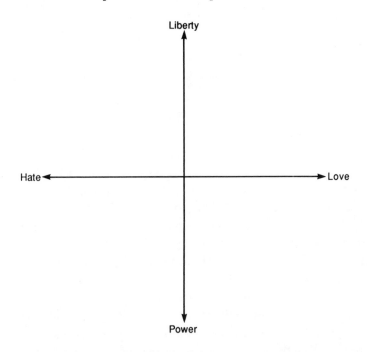

"But Professò, if we can't even buy a 128, what should we do? Should we ignore progress?"

"Not at all, Savè. We can buy a 128, but we must remember

*"Envy and die."

the words of Chuang: 'Use things as things, do not allow things to use you.' In other words, he meant that you must use the 128 as a 128 and not as a status symbol. For example, our friend here, our Ingegnere, was telling us about the splendid motorboat he's just bought. That's fine, but we should now ask him exactly why he bought this motorboat. Was it because he likes the open sea, the clear, unpolluted water? Does he want to get away from the crowds on the beach? Does he want to be alone with his thoughts? If he answers yes, that means he's a man of liberty. But if he bought it because he wants everyone to say, as they see him pulling away from the pier, 'Look what a beautiful motorboat he's bought, heaven knows what he must take home at the end of the month,' then we would have to classify the Ingegnere as a power seeker."

"I think," said Saverio, "that the Ingegnere got himself a motorboat for a little offshore fooling around."

"So can consumerism," I asked, "be envisaged as a search for power?"

"Definitely," the Professor replied. "Consumerism draws on the desire for power that manifests itself as a desire for aggrandizement, and with this in view it sets itself a whole scale of goals: every step is a stage along the way, a medal to be won. Only for the philosopher is consumerism a path that leads down, not up, a path that leads toward the abyss and takes him ever further from the axis of Love."

"But in actual fact," said Salvatore, "we Neapolitans don't consume an awful lot."

"Now let's take another look at our diagram," continued the Professor, "and see if we can give a name to each quadrant. The positive quadrant, here at the top on the right, I would call the Sage's quadrant, and first and foremost in it I would put Gandhi, the Mahatma, or Great Soul, the prophet of nonviolence. One could actually place thousands of other great thinkers in the quadrant of love and liberty, men like Bertrand Russell, Pope John XXIII, and Martin Luther King, for example; however, if we consider them carefully one by one, we notice that Russell tended slightly more toward liberty than love, and that John XXIII was more a man of love than a man of liberty, and the same applies to all the others. To occupy the middle path, the line that actually bisects the quadrant, a man's desire for liberty and his desire for love must be absolutely equal and balanced, and the further he is from the point of origin of the axis, the more worthy he will be of our admiration."

"What about St. Francis?"

"St. Francis is pure love; the problem of liberty doesn't even arise in his case, so we shall find him right on the love axis, very close to Jesus Christ."

"And who shall we put in the other quadrants, Professò?"

"Let's see. This quadrant at the bottom on the left is the quadrant of the Tyrant, the worst type of man that exists. In these circumstances there is only one name that springs to mind: Hitler. Hate and Power."

"A real stinking bastard!"

"At the top on the left we have the quadrant of the Rebel, and that I would dedicate to the fedayeen. Try putting yourselves in his shoes and tell me whether he, poor devil, hasn't got every reason to hate, and to desire liberty at the same time! He's been stripped of practically everything: home, country, and self-respect. The Israelis didn't merely appropriate his land, they spat in his face by proving to all the world that hard work and intelligence could wrest well-being and plenty even from a soil as arid as Palestine's. This, as I see it, is the root cause of the fedayeen's hatred of Israel."

"I really can't understand these fedayeen," said Saverio. "The Israelis arrive with plenty of capital in a country on the verge of starvation, and instead of falling to their knees and thanking the Madonna, they create all this fuss and confusion! Wouldn't it have been more sensible to make the most of the Israelis' desire to work and all reap the benefits together? But not them! They became terrorists. Saints alive, doesn't it make you want to say to them, Look, there you are with Jerusalem, the holiest city in the world, so why not go ahead and build it up into a great center of religious tourism? Sell relics, statuettes of the saints, medallions, and bits of stone you can claim were taken from the Wailing Wall! Learn a lesson or two from the Vatican, go see what they do in Pompeii and Padua, organize a soccer tournament for teams from different religions!"

"Saverio's on to something there," said Salvatore. "With a small investment they could make a fortune! A bit of publicity— say, for instance, some posters with 'One Communion in Jerusalem Is Worth Two Anywhere Else' or 'Get Your Circumcision Now During the Holiday Sale!'—and they'd all be better off, Israelis and Palestinians alike. Isn't that so, Professò?"

"In my opinion," said Dottor Palluotto, laughing, "the Americans should recall Doctor Kissinger and send Saverio and Salvatore to the Middle East instead."

"Laugh if you like, Dottò," said Saverio, "but if all the UN delegates came from Naples you can be sure that there'd never be another war and that all the armament companies in the world would turn out nothing but sparklers and firecrackers for New Year's celebrations."

"Gentlemen, concentrate!" said Professor Bellavista. "Let's return to our subject and try to give a name to the last remaining quadrant, that of love and power. I don't know what you think, but it seems to me that these are precisely the objectives of the Christian Church as an institution, and I therefore propose that we call it the Pope's quadrant."

"But haven't we already put John XXIII in the first quadrant?"

"Indeed. But in speaking of love and power, I'm thinking of the Papacy in the abstract and in its historical function. If we consider the popes individually, John XXIII plainly belongs in the same quadrant as Gandhi, while Alexander VI and Boniface VIII belong with Hitler."

"Which pope shall we put in this quadrant?"

"That I can say without hesitation: Gregory VII, Hildebrand

of Soana. And now that we've defined each quadrant, we can amuse ourselves placing all the historical personages that occur to us. Let's see. Byron we'll put here: a great desire for liberty and a pinch of hate for the whole world . . ."

"But wasn't Byron a love-and-liberty man?" asked Dottor Palluotto.

"Not at all. Plenty of liberty in his makeup, but almost no trace of love. Don't confuse love with romance. Byron was a Calvinist, a cripple, a misanthrope, and a snob. And don't forget that he liked to identify himself with Lucifer, the bright angel who rebelled against God for the sake of liberty. And speaking of rebels, let's put Nietzsche in his rightful place too. My friends, Nietzsche is an extremely difficult person to classify. Undoubtedly he was both a great poet and a great man of liberty, but the question is, do we put him under power or liberty?"

"Nietzsche was Hitler's pet philosopher," said Dottor Vittorio. "Why do you hesitate? Put them side by side and let's go on." "Indeed, no. Zarathustra was not a power seeker. It was Zarathustra who said, 'Rebellion is distinction in the slave.' Perhaps Nietzsche had a bit of everything, liberty and power, love and hate. A moving point darting all over the place. However, if I were forced to nail him down, I'd put him here, in the hate-liberty quadrant, with the rebels rather than with the tyrants. Intelligence, Nietzsche said, can be measured by the amount of solitude a man can bear. But let's proceed and place a few more people. Now, let's see: we'll put Rousseau here, Voltaire here, Albert Schweitzer on the other side, lower down on the right, Napoleon here, and Stalin down there halfway between Hitler and Napoleon; Ezzelino da Romano we'll push more toward hate, John Locke must clearly go somewhere near the middle line, and Timon of Athens, who claimed to hate everybody irrespectively, we can put right on the hate line. And how about Prometheus? Prometheus stole fire from the gods for love of man and was condemned to languish in chains forever, so we'll put him here, in the love-liberty quadrant. Yes, and we must find a place for Marcuse in the hate-liberty quadrant, and one for Marx . . ."

"Marx really belongs in the quadrant of love," said Dottor Vittorio.

"Absolutely not. Nobody could have written what he wrote without a certain capacity for hate. And down here we'll put Judas and Cain, and up here St. Simeon Stylites, right on the axis of liberty; now Landru, Kennedy, Khrushchev, Pericles, Dido, Socrates. Joseph II of Hapsburg, the greatest of all European sovereigns, we shall put in the sector of love and power, and now Abelard, Shylock, Lorenzo the Magnificent, St. Augustine, Lorenzo Bresci . . ."

"This is so intriguing," I said, "that one could even make a game out of it. We could make a list of famous people, ancient and modern, and then see where each of us, working separately, would place them on the diagram."

"As a matter of fact, I once amused myself by devising a kind of formula for just such a game, a formula I later christened 'the compass of the sixteen callings.' "

"The compass of the sixteen callings?"

"I'll show you. Look," said the Professor, taking a fresh sheet of paper and drawing another diagram. "This time we've got sixteen lines, just like the points of the compass, and we ascribe to each one a vocation, a calling in the widest sense. As far as the main axes are concerned, I don't think that after our previous conversation I need go into long explanations. The emotional axis will have the Saint at one extreme and the Devil at the other, while the rational axis, on the side of liberty, will have the Hermit, the man who shuns all relations with his fellows, whether of love or of hate, and on the side of power will be the King, conceived as an abstract idea rather than as an individual of flesh and blood. As we've already talked about each of the quadrants, you can anticipate the definition of the axes that bisect these at an angle of forty-five degrees, so I'll just go over them quickly: the first quadrant is that of the Sage, the second that of the Pope, the third that of the Tyrant, and the fourth that of the Rebel. The sectors in between, however, are even more interesting. In the principal quadrant, for example, we'll put the Poet, more sentiment than logic, and on the other side the Scientist, more intelligence than love. In the second quadrant, by contrast, we find Woman . . ."

"Woman?"

"Yes, Woman seen as a type. A type endowed with a great capacity for affection but also a certain possessiveness, and therefore displaying all the characteristics that such a combination generates: jealousy, passion, protectiveness, a desire to be enslaved, maternal instinct, and so on."

"But I know some women who . . ."

"Yes, yes," said the Professor, cutting me short, "but please remember that my theory is one of generalizations and makes no attempt to classify the people we actually know. So let's continue. In the second quadrant, between the King and the Pope, I put

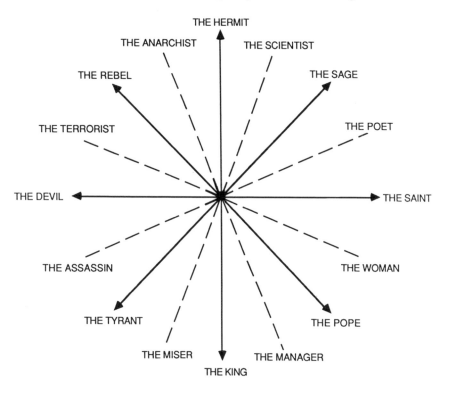

the Manager. Here I'm thinking of a particular type of manager, the kind of businessman who, although he's at the very top of the hierarchy, loves and looks after 'his' workforce. In other words, I'm using the Manager to denote paternalism, benevolence, little presents at Christmas, and all the things that create a bond between the employer as 'father' and his dependents as 'sons.' So the term also includes the Mafia godfather in the old-style romantic sense, the constitutional monarch, the enlightened prince, and so on."

"I see, Professò," said Salvatore, "but one thing's still not clear, and that's where you'd place somebody who's got more than one of these qualities you've described. For example, a woman scientist."

"Give me strength! I've only just explained all that to the Ingegnere! This theory deals with generalities, it only provides a schematic formula."

"Carry on, Professò."

"So now we come to the third quadrant. In this we put the Miser: more power than hate. Indeed, the miser is miserly even with his hate; he hates his neighbor only so far as this hate serves to defend his property. On the other side of the Miser we have the Assassin: a great deal of hate and little power. The true assassin is the one who kills not for honor or theft but for the sake of killing. In the fourth quadrant we find all the various gradations of revolution, from the independent Anarchist, who combines a colossal desire for liberty with hate for his fellow men, to the Terrorist, who takes advantage of the moment of revolution to satisfy his own craving for hate and violence."

"I would like to ask a completely different question," said Luigino. "On this diagram that you've drawn, where do we, the common people, fit in?"

"Luigino, my dear friend, that is perhaps the most important question I have been asked all evening. Where do we fit in? It's all very well to know where to look for Voltaire and Napoleon, but what really matters to us is ourselves, our friends, the people we meet every day. My first instinct, as I try to answer this question, is to gather nearly all the people I know into the love and liberty quadrant, because after all, they are all good people. I don't know a single dictatorial person, nor anyone who spends his time hating his fellows, so by a process of elimination, I see them all huddled together in the first quadrant with modest amounts of love and shreds of freedom. But then, as I think about it, I am struck by the realization of a fundamental truth: that hardly anyone is a man of liberty. Those who like money are men of power. Those who want careers are men of power. Criminals, egoists, jealous lovers, extremists, consumers, all those who chase after status symbols, all are power seekers. So one by one, all my friends and acquaintances are consigned to the lower quadrant, to a zone characterized by a limited need for love and a more urgent need for power."

"You may be right, but I like to imagine that things are different," said Luigino. "I see almost everybody in the quadrant of love and liberty. I see children there, and animals—especially dogs—and I see the trees and plants too; who knows, they might be longing to move and stretch out in the sunshine. Sometimes when I stop and really look at trees, I can almost hear them talking. I'll never forget these lines by Pavese:

> '. . . the earth is covered by plants
> that suffer in the light,
> yet not a sigh is heard.' "

XVI

CONTRORA

THREE O'CLOCK on a summer afternoon. The sun is beating down. Shade is nonexistent, or perhaps that is an optical illusion induced by the fact that I feel no sense of respite even though I'm sitting under a beach umbrella outside a Mergellina café. In Naples this time of day is called *controra*, a "contrary hour." The word shows that this is an hour to be treated like nighttime—stretched out on a bed in a dark room. The eight-hour day is an invention of countries where the sun never shines.

I have with me a colleague from Milan, and we are resting after an excellent meal at Vini e Cucina, the famous trattoria just opposite the station at Mergellina, run by the Signora. The Signora prepared us *una cosa semplice* ("something simple") and harangued my poor companion—guilty of being Milanese and therefore a likely supporter of Inter—throughout the meal. In vain he protested that he had never been to a soccer match in his life; his words fell on deaf ears. The Signora continued relentlessly, commenting on his appearance, on the fact that he didn't roll his *r*'s, and on his presumed lack of virility, an observation then extended to all Milanese males and to Helenio Herrera, ex-coach of Inter, in particular, and finally she launched into a philippic against Garibaldi for having united Italy with the express purpose of preventing Naples from winning the Kingdom of the Two Sicilies cup every year.

We had emerged into a blaze of sunshine with the suicidal intention of walking back to the office, way up on the second steep slope of Via Orazio. We collapsed, quite predictably, near the beach chalets of Mergellina, and as luck would have it, right at the crucial moment we found two vacant swing seats under an umbrella. Lawrence of Arabia himself would not have gone a step further. Responding wordlessly to the waiter's questions with a mere nod or shake of the head, we managed to order two lemonades with crushed ice. Now, after ten minutes of lethargy, the drinks arrive. We swallow them, draining our glasses to the last drop, then relapse into immobility, incapable either of movement or speech. In the complete absence of thought, I gaze in front of me at the orange-colored table, the empty glasses, the thousand-lira bill stuck under the ashtray, and wait for the waiter to return. At this point they appear: *'e guagliune*. About ten boys, all barefoot, in bathing trunks, with rolled-up jeans under their arms. They are returning from one of the many beaches down at lower Posillipo. They pass by, laughing and shouting. One of them, at the tail end of the group, thirteen or fourteen years old, with wet hair, bright eyes, skin black from the sun, stops in front of our table, thinks, looks at me, and says:

"Dottò, if I grabbed that thousand-lira bill and ran away with it, what would you do?"

"What would I do? I'd chase after you and give you a kick in the pants."

"Oh, sure, Dottò! You're sprawled all over that swing seat, and before you got out of it I'd be at the top of the hill there by the church of Sant'Antonio."

"What are you talking about?"

"Nothing. I only wanted you to know that you almost just lost a thousand lire. Let's make a deal. Two hundred and we're even."

At this point my friend is all for giving the kid the whole one thousand lire. I demur, believing that there are certain initiatives that should not be encouraged. We settle for five hundred and a cigarette.

XVII

THE FOURTH SEX

When setting out on a march,
many do not realize
that the enemy is leading the column.
The voice that commands them
is the voice of the enemy.
And he who speaks of the enemy
is himself the enemy.

BERTOLT BRECHT

"SAVÈ, in international terms, you're nobody," said Salvatore. "Get that into your skull: you, as an Italian, count for less than an Abyssinian tribesman! You're a colony, Savè, an American colony. And you can thank the good Lord that the slave trade's a thing of the past, otherwise you'd wind up in Rockefeller Plaza in New York with a price tag around your neck."

"Jesus Christ, I'd go crazy!" replied Saverio. "But if I were President of America, you know what I'd do? I'd say, 'You made your bed, now you lie in it, because from now on I'm going to look out for Number One, and you Italians are free to starve along with the Russians, the Egyptians, the Chinese, the Vietnamese, and any other pain in the ass who wants to join you.'"

"If only America would do that, if only it would! That's just what we're waiting for!"

"Well, there's gratitude for you! Salvatò, let me remind you that at the end of the last world war Italy was one big mess until a certain Marshall, an American Signore came along and said, 'Don't worry, all you nice Italians, Uncle's here to take care of you. Just tell him what you need, don't stand on ceremony!' And some said, 'But how come? Yesterday we were enemies and we'd shoot you as soon as look at you . . .' But he replied, 'Don't give it another thought, it was tit for tat, and please forgive us if we caused a little damage here and there in the heat of the moment, but don't worry, we've got the dough and we'll take care of everything.' And after they literally saved our lives and fed and clothed us, all the thanks they get from us is a chorus of boos and catcalls every time an American president shows up in Italy! Do you call that fair, Salvatò?"

"What I like about you, Savè, is your childlike innocence. You're like a six-year-old kid: if someone gives you a candy, you do anything they ask. You think Marshall spent a little money on Italy because all of a sudden he fell in love with Vesuvius? The American bases, Savè, think of the American bases! Tell me, if he hadn't tossed a few coins in our direction, where would Signor Marshall have put the American military bases? He would have had to stuff them up his own sisters' skirts—to the great delight of the troops but to pretty limited international strategic effect."

"Okay, okay, but it doesn't seem right to criticize America and then crawl to New York begging every time we're short of cash."

"Forget your scruples, Savè. The Americans aren't fools. If they bother to nurse our economy, they do it for a reason. Remember what I said just now: Savè, you're a colony."

"Okay, okay, so I'm a colony. I'm just glad it's them who support us and not us who have to support them."

"Up to a certain point, you're right. It's fine just as long as you do what they want you to do. But try to change the system of government and then see what happens. You're like a Christmas capon tied to a post with a piece of string. As long as you stand still, you can imagine that you're free to go where your fancy takes you, but the minute you move a single meter away, *wham!*— the string tightens around your leg. You're a colony, Savè."

"And I suppose that Hungary and Czechoslovakia are as free and independent as a couple of eagles flying around in the sky! The truth is that Naples has always been a colony, and the only question now is whether it's better to be a Russian colony or an American one."

"Enough, enough, *guagliù!*" exclaimed Professor Bellavista, intervening. "We've had enough talk of politics. It gets us nowhere. The arguments are always the same: you say Chile and I counter with Czechoslovakia, you find fault with America and I find fault with Russia, and at the end of the day we're all left with the same opinions we started out with. The same things have been repeated a million times over. The ruts in this sort of discussion are so deep that we can no longer steer a path along the road of political argument without getting hopelessly stuck."

"But tell us where you stand, Professò."

"There! I knew it! 'Where do you stand?' That's another thing I dislike about all political arguments: labels. What are you, a Fascist? A Communist? A Liberal? If you're none of these, then you must be an Indifferentist. Do you know what I'd like to say sometimes when people ask me what my politics are? 'I'm a man and I like women.' "

"What's that got to do with it?"

"A lot, Savè. For once let's try to confront the question of politics from a completely different standpoint, that of sex. Let's imagine that there are four sexes in the world: males, females, homosexuals, and power seekers. Now we'll try to understand this fourth sex by putting ourselves in their shoes."

"In Naples we say *è meglio cumannà che fottere.*"*

"In fact, Salvatò, that's exactly the attitude of the fourth sex. They get as excited about acquiring power as we do in the vicinity of a pretty girl. The only difference lies in the fact that power cannot satisfy but on the contrary acts like a drug and creates a craving for ever larger doses."

"That's sheer Indifferentism, Gennà!" interrupted Dottor Palluotto.

"See, what did I just tell you? The need for labels. Words

* "Calling the shots beats screwing."

wielded like blunt instruments. One man puts forward a point of view, the other disagrees, but he doesn't give a reasoned reply explaining why, in his opinion, the facts appear to be different. No, sir; the rules of political argument presuppose labels: I don't agree with you, so I call you an Indifferentist, like the Sicilian who, whenever he lost an argument with his friend, cut the discussion short by saying, 'All right, but you're still a cuckold.' The idea is to make your opponent feel inferior. To call someone an Indifferentist is like calling him a cuckold. Who knows, by the end of our discussion, I might surprise even myself by agreeing with Mao about the theory of permanent revolution, but my friend Vittorio has already labeled me an Indifferentist because he knows that by so doing he has undermined the theory, debasing the idea even though it may be shared by everyone. Nobody likes to be called a cuckold."

"*Madonna mia,* Gennà, what a mountain out of a molehill!" exclaimed Dottor Palluotto. "I can see I'd better hold my tongue. But at least have the courtesy to refrain from calling this a political discussion."

"How come you two, with all your learning, can't say two words without jumping down each other's throats?" said Salvatore. "I'd understand it if you were like me and this other illiterate, Saverio, who's always voted Monarchist as if he were a prince of the House of Savoy."

"So what? I didn't vote Monarchist because of any political idea but because the superintendent said he'd see that my brother Vincenzino got a job with the Sanitation Department, which he got anyway because my brother's fiancée, who is now my sister-in-law, was housekeeper to the superintendent, the Honorable Abbondanza, and one day when they were all out together my brother saved the child's life, that is, the superintendent's son, when he was about to get run over, actually the boy has always denied this, but anyway the superintendent got my brother the job with the Sanitation Department all the same, and Vincenzino doesn't have to clean the streets because his job is just to make sure that the others clean them."

"A political discussion in Naples always ends up like this," said Dottor Vittorio. "As farce. Gennà, forgive us for having interrupted you. Do continue with your interesting parallel between sex and power."

"You've expressed it well: sex and power. That's exactly how I see power, as a violent craving that seizes and dominates people, an uncontrollable urge that overrides all moral inhibitions, a blind force stronger than friendship or honor or pity for those weaker than ourselves, and therefore a compulsion that comprehends even treason, that justifies torture. But what does Power really mean? Who is this *femme fatale,* irresistible and capricious because the passion she arouses is, like all true passions, absolute? How can she be conquered when she is one and is desired by many? We realize eventually that it will take an army to conquer her, and we start looking for a banner behind which to muster our troops. And so the great ideals are born, the great 'historical pretexts.' "

"Historical pretexts?"

"Yes. Freud referred to the phenomenon as 'identification.' If I want an army to follow me, the first thing I must do is find a pretext, that is, a standard to march under. My men must be provided with uniforms so that they can recognize each other in battle, and they must also have slogans, battle hymns, and above all, ideals. But in order to select the best ideals, I must carefully sound the human soul and find which chords to touch, which sentiments my young soldiers cherish in their hearts. Thus I discover that there are in fact three ideals that inspire the soul of man: Religion, Patriotism, and Justice. All the great empires in history have used one of these three as a binding agent. When the priests of ancient Egypt declared, 'Osiris is with us,' they were in fact proclaiming a well-known principle of power. Other successful specialists in the use of Religion followed them, namely the Mohammedans and the Christian Church. The former used Allah as a propellant for the invasion of Africa and Europe, and just as a modern American manager would have done, Islam produced a scale of incentives: the Koran. If you killed an infidel you went to Paradise, if you died for Allah you spent eternity in bed with the Prophet's houris. Nor was the Christian Church to be outdone: having scooped the exclusive rights to Jesus Christ in the Western Hemisphere, it used them as a means of domination for about fifteen centuries. Anything went as long as it helped maintain power. They discovered that God was the best extortionist in the world, because nothing could be hidden from Him. And since nothing could be hidden, everyone was obliged to pay ten percent of his income to God's representative on earth, the Pope. It was even possible to commit the most terrible sins and then bargain your way out of years in Purgatory with cash, coupons, and the purchase of indulgences. What a pity computers hadn't been invented at the time."

"But this is ancient history."

"Not quite. In Northern Ireland they still go on merrily planting bombs under each other's asses in the name of Christ, even though they are all Christians. But let's continue with our historical overview. The ideal most widely used in the past for the purposes of power was undoubtedly Patriotism. Patriotic sentiment derives naturally from family sentiment. Who does not love his own children and his own parents? Who does not feel a sense of solidarity with his own friends and fellow citizens? Between rooting for one's own soccer team and fighting a foreign nation there is but a short step. Language, race, and custom are already a uniform in themselves. All you have to do is exaggerate the differences a little and you find yourself with an army. That's how the Roman Empire came into being, when the title *cives romanus* was the highest honor the world had to offer. That's how Napoleon, Hitler, and Mussolini all came to power. The ideal of Justice, on the other hand, only began to be chosen as a motive force toward the end of the eighteenth century. Until then, the Christian Church had operated a truly ingenious system by which all the victims of oppression and deprivation were persuaded that Justice was not to be looked for in this world, that accounts would only be settled in the world to come. But once the idea of Justice had gained a foothold, it soon leapfrogged ahead of the ideals of Patriotism and Religion. Marx was the Messiah, Lenin the Strategist, Stalin the Dictator. Once again we have started out with Christ and ended up with Boniface VIII. Power is the monster that invariably insinuates itself into the ranks of the pure in heart and then pops up at the head of the column, by which time everyone has spontaneously fallen into step behind it."

"Forgive me for interrupting, Gennà, but are you saying that we should not have ideals because there will always be people who twist them to their own ends?"

"Yes, to a point. I wish men were cooler and reasoned more with their heads and less with their hearts. It's not a coincidence that in Italy, which is part of the world of love, the political parties that have the greatest mass appeal are those that have chosen as their rallying cry one of the three basic ideals: Religion, Patriotism, and Justice. The masses are emotional and therefore vote for the Christian Democrats, the MSI on the extreme right, or the Communists—the parties of love—while the Liberals, Republicans, and Socialists, who appeal to the head, can count on far fewer votes."

"I wanted to vote Republican in the last election," said Saverio, "but then I thought they'd come in last and I changed my mind."

"But Republicans and Socialists also have an ideal of Justice."

"Yes, but they're not so aggressive about it. You see, when you evaluate a political ideology, it's never the ultimate objectives that have to be considered, only the means by which they are to be achieved. I'll try to make it clearer. Imagine that you are coming out of a side street onto a major road and the first decision you are asked to make is which way you want to turn. If you turn to the right you're a conservative, you like things as they are, and all in all you see no point in risking what you already have for the mere possibility of improvement. But if you turn to the left you're an innovator, someone who likes to change things in the hope of improving them. Now, I would guess that all of us in this room would more or less agree that things as they are at present in Italy

are not perfect. None of us could honestly declare himself completely satisfied with our hospitals, schools, our pensions, and
the whole mess we continually see around us. So I imagine we
would all turn to the left and set off on the famous road paved
with ideals, that is, toward innovation. But we are immediately
confronted by another and to my mind more important decision:
How fast do we want to travel? We know that the ideal society,
Utopia, lies at the end of the road, and so it's only human that we
should want to get there as quickly as possible. But there are
many curves along the way, and we have no control over these;
they are obstacles that exist independent of our will, and we have
to negotiate them or we'll land in the ditch. I'll give you an
example. There was a time in Italy when it was thought that to
speculate in people's health was immoral and that all workers
should therefore have the right to free medical attention. So a
scheme of state-assisted medical insurance was introduced. The
idea itself was absolutely perfect and worthy of its great objective.
But its application was catastrophic. And why? Because people
abused their rights by claiming much more medication than they
actually required, and many doctors thought only of increasing
the quantity of visits at the expense of their quality, and at the
end of the day the only ones to gain were the pharmaceutical
companies and the dishonest doctors. So now we must ask ourselves what went wrong. And the answer is simple. We had
forgotten that along our road, the road of progress, there was a
curve. We had forgotten the fact that the Italian people, at
present, have a rather slender social conscience. All we needed to
do, only marginally, was to reduce the speed of social reform. It
would have been quite sufficient, for example, if the legislators
had established a deduction of, say, one hundred lire for each
medicine, payable by the recipient, and we would never have
seen those heaps of almost unused medicines discarded in the
trash. The consumption of medicine in Italy would have been the
same as in other countries, and the state coffers would have been
many billions the richer. But this would have meant some form of
agreement with the demagogues. And what Italian politician

would willingly take such a risk today? Only La Malfa, perhaps, but not many people vote for him, and he hasn't got the right kind of face for television. To sum up, then, every time there's a choice to be made, it's no use simply thinking about the ideal solution; we must also take account of the facts as they stand. In the political climate of Italy today, riddled as it is with shady deals and favoritism and bureaucracy, I for one would hesitate to trust any single party, even the Communists, with all the levers of power, the centers of industry and commerce, the police force, and the channels of information. Is there any Communist among us here who believes deep down in his heart that the Italian people would rise worthily to such a challenge?"

"There's a lot of truth in what you say, Gennaro," replied Dottor Palluotto. "However, harking back to your illustration of the street, you forgot to mention those who turn to the right, the reactionaries. Now, this blessed bunch doesn't simply stand by and twiddle its thumbs; it also acts as a brake, and we have to take that into account. It means, in effect, that we always have to accelerate a little bit more to compensate for the fact that there's someone on the other side surreptitiously putting a foot on the brake. Take the student riots, for example. Nothing could have been more muddled and chaotic, yet their effect was simply enormous. Without this hefty kick in the backside, the government would never have even addressed the problem of the schools. The point I'm making is that the government of the country does not depend solely upon the moderate parties; extremists too have a very definite role to play."

"Which is fine as long as they never get into power."

"We have to admit that Professor Bellavista is consistent," said Luigino. "He observes the same moderation in his political thinking as he does in the search for pleasure. One wonders why this kind of moderation seems to appeal to so few people."

"There's a reason for that, and it's quite simple. The driving force of a society, to all intents and purposes, is its young people and artists. As far as the young people are concerned, may I remind you of Longanesi's dictum: 'We are born incendiaries and we die firemen.' And as for artists, obviously, moderation is a dirty word. But remember that events over the last few centuries have taught us that in the end it is always the middle class that makes the decisions, and the middle class can be more dangerous sometimes than the student revolutionaries. If the middle class were ever to notice that communism, if misapplied, could become a new form of fascism, all would be lost. The desire for law and order, for the return of capital punishment, for making strikes illegal, is too prevalent for us to be able to discount such a possibility."

"Forgive the interruption," said Saverio, "but there's one thing about communism that puzzles me. They say that in a communist society we'll all be equal and all earn the same pay. Maybe, but that's none of my business. What worries me is this: the shit, who's going to clean up the shit?"

"What?"

"The shit that piles up everywhere, who's going to clean it up? Somebody's got to deal with the shit. Now, I'm just wondering, will everybody take turns, or will some people be employed specially to clean up the shit? As far as I can tell, democracy or communism, I'm always going to have to clean up the shit."

"But there'll be machines to do things like that."

"Right, machines! And what do you do with a sick old man? Clean him up with a machine? No, sir, the truth is that some people have it easy and some don't, and it's the good Lord who decides that even before we're born. It's the good Lord who says, This one I'll call Saverio, and he'll have to shovel shit."

"Yes, indeed, Saverio's right," said Luigino. "But the good Lord also says, And I'll make this Saverio fall in love with Assuntina Del Vecchio, and I'll send them three children, and these children will all be beautiful, and they will always love one another."

"True, Luigì," said Saverio. "And I'll tell you something else. You get used to shit, and after a few days you don't even notice the smell."

XVIII

A BUSINESS LUNCH

ARRANGE A BUSINESS LUNCH in Naples? Impossible! The city isn't organized for it. There are no restaurants to cater to such specialized requirements, the menus are all carbohydrate-based, waiters and customers allow one no privacy at all, and lastly, the strolling singers persist in their belief that anyone eating in a restaurant must be a tourist eager for a rendering of " 'O Surdato 'Nammurato."

All this does not imply, however, that to do business over a meal in Naples is impossible. It is merely different, and one has to be prepared to adapt accordingly. I remember, for instance, a so-called business lunch involving myself and a customer that occurred while I was still working in Naples. I had decided against Ciro a Santa Brigida, where the food was certainly excellent but where, with equal certainty, there would have been too many people, and had opted for a trattoria in Santa Lucia, right opposite the cinema, which according to my calculations would be quiet at that time as the clientele tended to eat around two o'clock. Everything went according to plan: an almost deserted room, spaghetti with clam sauce, then the all-important choice: fish or meat. However, we managed to cope, for good or ill, with the formalities of ordering, and I had just begun to broach the subject on my mind when there he was: the inevitable, fatalistic, emaciated, smiling *posteggiatore*. Clad, as the role demands, with dignified poverty and appropriate bohemian touches, armed with a spectacular guitar, he entered the nearly empty restaurant and took up a position about three meters away from our table. I waited with patient resignation for our minstrel to launch into a moving interpretation of *"Tu si 'a canaria, ca pure quanno more canta canzone nove,"* but contrary to all expectations, he remained silent, watching us respectfully.

As I continued to talk business I had the impression that the singer was waiting for us to finish our discussion, but during a pause in the conversation he approached the table discreetly, gave a slight bow, and handed us a card printed with the words "I REFRAIN FROM PLAYING TO AVOID DISTURBING YOU, THANK YOU."

We gave him five hundred lire, and he left.

When Gaetano, the waiter, came to bring us the bill, he said, *"È pate 'e figlie.* The poor man's got a family to support, and he can't play a note!"

XIX

Bellavista's Politics

Free me from the paths of death
that I may walk with liberty at my side
toward lands unknown.

RABINDRANATH TAGORE, *Balaka*

"FORGIVE ME, Gennaro, but you talk and talk, and at the end of
the day you still haven't said anything," said Dottor Palluotto.

"What do you mean, I haven't said anything?"

"I mean that after this whole political dissertation you still
haven't told us in so many words what your own political ideas
are."

"Perhaps Dottor Palluotto wants to know who you voted for,"
suggested Saverio.

"And I realize that. You all want to pigeonhole me willy-nilly
because, so you believe, no one can discuss politics if he doesn't
know beforehand whether the person he's talking to is a Fascist
or a Communist. Isn't that so, Vittò?"

"It's got nothing to do with it," retorted Dottor Palluotto. "I
don't give a single, solitary damn how you voted. I only wanted, in
all humility, to point out that in your remarks about politics just
now, you made two fairly weighty observations. You said that
power, whatever its ideological basis, was nothing but the desire
of a minority to impose its will upon the mass of the people; then
you damned all revolutionary initiatives opposed to power by
preaching a policy of moderation. Now, it seems to me, but
correct me if I'm wrong, that to advise disengagement from
politics insofar as politics is power-motivated, and at the same

time to urge a slowdown on all attempts to redress injustice, is the equivalent, when you come to think of it, of a counsel of Indifferentism, and in the present state of affairs, that plays straight into the hands of the powers that be. So at this point, Professor Bellavista, I'm going to ask you to come clean and tell us where you stand. What are your real political convictions?"

"What would you say if I told you that I, Gennaro Bellavista, had no political convictions? If I told you, my dear Vittorio, that sometimes the only political idea that occurs to me is to shut myself up at home and think? Would you believe me?"

"No, I wouldn't."

"And perhaps you would be right. However, I'd like to make a suggestion. Seeing that we have both the time and the inclination for a discussion, let's try to construct, by mutual agreement, a political ideal that will work for the common good."

"I don't think we'll ever succeed."

"Maybe not, but at least we will have tried. Let's see what happens. We'll start with a question. What, according to you, should be the ultimate objective of a political system?"

"No two ways about it," replied Dottor Vittorio. "The ultimate objective must be social justice. What, after all, is the State if not an institution owing its very existence to the fact that men are still bastards at heart? *'Homo homini lupus,'* as Hobbes said. Thus, if the State has come into being as the result of man's egoism, clearly its first objective must be the control of this egoism, in other words, the attainment of social justice."

"I agree absolutely with the Doctor about the importance of social justice," I said, "but we mustn't forget that there are other objectives the State should take into account. As you will have guessed, I'm referring to personal liberty. The word 'liberty' has unfortunately become somewhat vague as a result of being constantly bandied about by all and sundry, but if we consider it in relation to what Dottor Vittorio has just said about the origins of the State, we see that the State is *ipso facto* coercive, that its first objective is, in fact, the restriction of individual free will . . ."

"Yes, but only in order to control the predatory impulses, that is, to prevent some people from taking unfair advantage of others."

"I agree, but since the moral evaluation of such issues is left to the State, and since the State is invariably made up of the very human beings Hobbes defined as wolves, it follows that the importance of personal liberty cannot be overestimated . . ."

"I observe with pleasure," said Bellavista, "that you have gone straight to the heart of the problem: justice and liberty, public good and personal freedom."

"But why can't we simply say that we want both justice and liberty, and that's that?" proposed Saverio.

"Because it would seem, Savè, that we can't have both," replied Salvatore. "We have to make a decision. Do we want to eat in silence, or do we want the freedom to starve?"

"As I see it," said Luigino, "it depends on the character of the individual. If I were an antelope, for example, and had to choose between living in a jungle full of lions and snakes or in a zoo where I'd be fed daily by the keeper, I wouldn't hesitate. I'd choose the jungle."

"That's great, Luigì," broke in Saverio, "but remember that in Naples nearly everyone's unemployed, and the authorities—our keepers—have said that with twenty-five thousand dependents already, they can't take on any more. This means that every morning we all have to forage together in the jungle. And there's an awful lot of us, Luigì. You know what I think? That a bit of the zoo treatment now and then wouldn't be such a bad thing."

"Gentlemen, may I have your attention, please!" said Bellavista. "I should like you to hear what a very great contemporary thinker, Bertrand Russell, had to say about this. The grand old man maintained that there are two kinds of goods, material and spiritual, and two kinds of corresponding impulses, possessive and creative. Material goods are characterized by being finite in quantity. In other words, according to Russell, if I drink all the wine in this bottle, you're left with your tongues hanging out, so wine is a material good."

"You can say that again," said Saverio.

"Spiritual goods, on the other hand, are characterized by being infinite or unlimited in quantity. If I enjoy Beethoven, I can feast on his music from morning till night without depriving any of you of the opportunity of enjoying it for yourselves. Indeed, the more I listen to the music of Beethoven, the more chances you have of hearing it. Having thus shown the qualitative superiority of spiritual over material goods, Russell immediately goes on to make an observation that is extremely important for the purposes of our present discussion: it is impossible for a man to respond to any creative impulse unless and until he has satisfied his basic material needs."

"If I'm not mistaken, Professò," Saverio chimed in, "your friend was saying that you can't enjoy Beethoven on an empty stomach."

"Precisely. But unfortunately the matter is more complicated than one would suspect. What do we actually mean by 'basic material needs'? How do we decide what goods each individual is entitled to? In a society where everyone owns a car, the poor devil who hasn't got one will justifiably feel deprived. So when we talk about a just distribution of material goods, we must not take simple survival as our frame of reference, but rather the average social conditions prevailing at that moment in time. All in all it would seem, my friends, that man is capable of spiritual development only after he has achieved what he considers a basic level of material well-being. Now, the last few hundred years have seen the rise of two principal forms of sociopolitical organization, capitalism and Communism. It would be interesting to analyze the limitations of these systems in light of what we have just been saying. Capitalism, invented by a certain Adam Smith, is a system of growth based upon a free economy and having, on the debit side, two fundamental flaws. In the first place, it offers no guarantee of social justice, and in the second, it distracts humanity from the search for spiritual goods. The driving force behind capitalism is egoism, the only really universal source of energy at the present time. In the absence of a sense of civic duty or Christian charity, capitalism feeds on man's natural greed and turns the profit motive into a religion. The canons of this creed are simple enough: people identify themselves with their bank accounts, and their worth is measured in terms of power and cash. Consumerism is now in full flood. Every man is obliged to produce more and more so that he can afford to buy his own excess production. There's no letup, no time to pause, no chance to seek spiritual enrichment. The creative impulse cannot be developed for the sole reason that men are too busy earning the money required for their next vacation. And what is the result? How is it that we were happier before when we had less? The answer is simple: consumerism has raised its prices. The minimal level of well-being is higher than it was. And tomorrow it will be higher still, tomorrow it will be a severe privation not to possess a color television."

"You're telling me, Professò!" exclaimed Saverio. "I can't even get Channel Two, and when they show the Wednesday movie, I have to drop in on my sister-in-law who lives in the next street."

"And now we come to Communism," continued Professor Bellavista, refusing to be sidetracked. "Here we see a system that in order to achieve the very objective for which it was designed has up to now been obliged to resort to force, that is, to the so-called dictatorship of the proletariat. And like every example of absolute power, whether in politics or industry, it demands total conformity on the part of the underlings. My friends, let's not delude ourselves. Where power is absolute, the individual ceases to exist, and therefore liberty, too, ceases to exist."

"However," said Dottor Vittorio, "in my opinion we should first establish the meaning of the word 'liberty.'"

"Vittò, let me quote you, as nearly as I can remember them, some words of Russell's. The prime objective of any political system must be the sanctity of the individual. The politician must not conceive of the people as a uniform mass but as so many distinct human beings, men, women and children, people who think and from the diversity of whose thoughts the idea of the future is born. Individualism signifies life, uniformity death. Those in power, however, know that the greater the uniformity of the mass, the easier it is to command. If the mass is homogeneous, it is predictable. Thus, while social injustice produces an imperfect distribution of material wealth, the lack of individual liberty constricts the human mind into a smaller and smaller space, a process Russell compares with the ancient Chinese custom of binding women's feet to prevent their natural growth. Conclusion: even under Communism, the creative impulse is given short shrift, though for entirely different reasons than those that obtain in the Western world."

"Forgive me, Gennaro, but I think you're being grossly unfair. The Eastern bloc has always placed enormous stress on spiritual values, as is demonstrated by the energy with which the Communist countries have tackled the problem of education from the outset, and also by the fact that incentives, in both the factory and the office, are exclusively moral ones. It isn't greed for higher and higher wages that motivates the Communist worker to increase his productivity but the knowledge that he is serving the community. This is the true miracle of Communism."

"My dear Vittorio, leaving aside the fact that I wouldn't care to wager my shirt on your so-called miracles, I think we have a case of misunderstanding here. The liberty I'm talking about is primarily freedom of thought, and until I find proof to the contrary, I shall continue to believe that it can only be found, however imperfectly, in the parliamentary democracies."

"With their capitalist economies."

"All right, but dear God in heaven, what's to stop us from trying to achieve a democratic regime that's based on a multiparty system and that controls capitalist cynicism by sane legislation while at the same time encouraging people by all the means of information at its disposal—the press, the movies, and television—to strive after spiritual goods?"

"Once they've got their material goods, right, Professò?"

"Obviously men are more receptive to the creative impulse when they are no longer in thrall to material necessity."

"I'd go along with everything you've said so far," said Dottor Palluotto, "but I'd still like to know why you insist on thinking of Communism as a dictatorial regime. Or rather, I know why you do: because you identify Communism with Russia. Admit it, Gennà. But why won't you try to imagine a different sort of Communism, an Italian Communism?"

"Apart from the fact that I have every reason to view Communism as a dictatorial regime, all I said was that I prefer a democratic system to any kind of totalitarianism."

"And why do you rule out the possibility of a Communist government in Italy remaining democratic?"

"It might, but in that case, can you tell me how such a Communist party would differ from a Social Democratic one? No, Vittò, I repeat that as long as I can, I want to go out and buy myself three papers a day, and I shall feel free as long as these three papers report the same fact in three different ways."

"Your three papers, however, only differ from each other on the front page, my dear Gennaro, that is, in the political columns. The inside pages are identical, and it's there, where you least suspect it, that the danger lurks."

"What are you getting at?"

"I'll explain. Every communications medium, whether it consists of pictures on the television screen or words on the printed page, has one common feature, and this common feature is advertising, in other words, capitalist propaganda. You may fantasize about a world in which spiritual values take pride of place, but you're tilting at windmills as long as advertising is brainwashing the more susceptible and seducing them with luxury goods."

"I agree with you absolutely, and that's why I say that we have no choice but to fight modern capitalism."

"But you can't fight capitalism by yourself, it requires a considerable political shake-up, and that, translated into practical terms, means acting through a political party that can count on public support. Now, as far as I'm aware, Bertrand Russell never founded any political party in Italy, so you can only defeat capitalism with the help of the Italian Communist Party."

"Why should we leave the job to the Communists? Why shouldn't we all put our shoulders to the wheel and push together?"

"All I can say is don't count on me to do any pushing," said Saverio. "I haven't got what it takes. First give me a decent job and a two-room apartment just for me and my family, and then I'll help you push. You're a lucky man, Professò, to be able to read three papers every day. It's not the time I envy you, because that I've got—to tell the truth, time's something I definitely do not lack—but what I do envy you, from the bottom of my heart, is the four hundred and fifty lire you fork out every morning to buy the papers. Now, don't be mad. Let me pour you another little glass of wine. Your health, Professò, and may you live to be a hundred. I admit I don't know a thing about politics. Salvatore's better off because his cousin belongs to one of those extraparliamentary opposition groups, but as for me, when I go to vote I feel like a donkey in a concert hall, and I always end up voting as a favor to a friend. One day I find myself voting for the extreme right, and the next day for the Communists. I remember, for instance, that when we had the referendum on divorce, I made a deal with Ferdinando because he wanted to vote yes and I wanted to vote no so we agreed that neither one of us would vote, and instead we toasted the referendum with a liter of Gragnano in the porter's lodge, and to make sure that neither of us pulled a fast one by voting the next day, we flushed our ballot papers down the toilet, if you'll forgive the expression. Look, Professò, you can't blame me. How can you expect me to take a stand on divorce when I can't even get a separation from the Percuocos."

"The Percuocos? Who are the Percuocos?"

"The Percuoco family, father, mother, deaf sister-in-law, and four fedayeen that Signora Percuoco insists on referring to as 'my poor little babies.' "

"And what has the Percuoco family got to do with divorce?"

"Well you see, Don Ernesto Percuoco's a nice enough guy who gets by as a knower . . ."

"A knower?"

"A knower is someone who knows people. For example, if your car gets smashed up, you can go to Don Ernesto, and he'll take you to a man he knows who's a mechanic and introduce you as a friend of his, so you get a discount and Don Ernesto pockets a small fee for the introduction."

"And what kinds of people does Don Ernesto know?"

"All kinds: tilers, plumbers, tailors, undertakers, restaurant owners, electricians, and so on."

"But did I understand you to say that this Percuoco lives in your apartment?" I asked.

"He sure does," replied Saverio. "And the reason is that I got to know Ernesto Percuoco when we were both doing our military service at Fortezza, and later, in Naples, we'd meet from time to time at the billiard hall in Mezzocannone to play a few hands of *scopa,* and you know how these things go: 'My, what a nice place you've got! But what on earth do you want with a place this big! Why don't you sublet one room to me and my wife, and another little one to my sister-in-law who'll only be with us for a few days because she's getting married to a schoolteacher. My wife and I are such quiet people you won't even know we're there. We've been married for five years, and no children. It was not the will of the Lord.' How could I know that as soon as the Percuocos set foot in my house the Lord would change His mind? Four children in five years! Signora Percuoco got pregnant with the next one almost before she gave birth to the one before! The youngest is now eight. A few days ago he tried to set fire to the newsstand in Piazza Sant'Anna because the owner, Don Eugenio, had squashed his soccer ball. Amelia, the sister-in-law, became deaf, and her fiancé became a priest, which was another reason why he decided not to marry her. Just try for a second to imagine what it's like in my house. The four Percuoco kids and our own three make a grand total of seven criminal lunatics trying to murder each other every other minute, and when they stop trying to murder each other, they get together to try to murder someone else. My wife spends her time arguing with Signora Percuoco, who, being the daughter of a retired coach driver, has inherited a vocabulary that has to be heard to be believed. To put it in a nutshell, compared to my home, the Middle East's a debating society. I keep trying to talk to Ernesto: 'Ernè,' I say, 'find yourself a place to live! One of these days someone's going to be carried out of this house feet first. We can't go on like this, we must separate!' It's no good. He claims that he's a legal tenant and that wild horses wouldn't drag him from the house. So what's all this got to do with divorce, you say? Everything! If it's not even possible to get separated from the Percuocos, how could a man possibly get rid of a wife and find the money to run two different homes?"

"Right, Savè, but tell me, suppose you were unhappily married and your wife was unfaithful to you. If you couldn't divorce her, what would you do?"

"What would I do? In the first place, I'd kill her without thinking twice about it, and then, while I was at it, I'd kill Signora Percuoco, and all her brats too."

XX

THE NEWSBOY

THIS AFTERNOON I bumped into an old school friend, De Renzi. I was standing at a bus stop, and he was in his car right in front of me, trapped in a solid line of cars and trucks.

The zero velocity of the traffic made it possible for us to recognize each other and initiate a regular old-boys' reunion along the lines of: "I wonder what happened to Bottazzi," "Do you remember Professor Avallone?" and "What was the name of that girl in 1-E?" And all while I remained standing at the bus stop and he remained sitting at the wheel of a red Fiat 127 with a Catania registration. At a certain point De Renzi asked me:

"By the way, where are you going?"

"A place near Piazza Nazionale."

"Jump in, then, I'll give you a lift."

And so, more to continue the trip down memory lane than to speed up the trip across town, I got in and sat beside him.

"De Renzi, tell me, what are you doing now? Where do you work?"

"I'm the manager of the Catania branch of SAMAP-ITALIA, involved in plastic goods for the building trade. Nothing to brag about, but things aren't too bad. I'm spending Christmas in Naples. Naturally I still miss Naples in some ways, even though I've been away for more than seven years. I married a girl from Catania, and we've got a couple of children, one five and one seven. That's how it goes. We've got our own circle of friends, and thank God, we're all healthy. But what are you doing now?"

I was just about to reply when a newsboy selling the *Corriere di Napoli* came along shouting at the top of his lungs, "Disaster in Catania! Read all about it! Disaster in Catania!" Somewhat alarmed, De Renzi immediately bought a copy of the *Corriere* and began to leaf quickly through the pages. Nothing in the headlines or in the late additions made any reference to a disaster in Catania, however, and we were still searching for the item when the newsboy came up to the car again and said, "Don't worry, Dottò, it can't be serious. If the paper doesn't say anything about it, nothing much can have happened."

And he headed in the direction of a car with Caserta license plates.

XXI

Permanent Struggle

While I sit silently with folded hands,
spring comes, grass grows without my intervention,
blue mountains need no help to be blue mountains,
white clouds no guiding hand to be white clouds.

TOYO EICHO, *Zenrin Kushu*

"SAVÈ, what you don't seem to be able to get through your head is
that it's no longer enough just to be a Communist," said Salvatore. "It doesn't mean anything anymore!"

"What are you talking about? You've always been a Communist
yourself!"

"Not any longer. I've moved to the left."

"Further left than the Communists?"

"You bet. My cousin Tonino, who's a mechanic at Sesto San
Giovanni, knows all about these things. The last time I saw him,
he went to great lengths to explain why, at the present moment in
time, the only real Communists are the *extraparlamentari.*"

"People in Sesto San Giovanni know what they're talking
about. Here in Naples we're always a little behind."

"Figure it out, Savè. The present Italian Communist Party is
really the old Socialist Party, while the present Socialist Party is
nothing but a rehash of the old Christian Democrat Party."

"Is it? And what's the present Christian Democrat Party?"

"You might say it's the same thing as the Monarchist Party
immediately after the war."

144

"*Gesù,* what a mix-up! When did all this happen?"

"What happened is that the Italian electorate has shifted to the left while the parties have shifted to the right, so we're back where we started."

"And you got all this from your cousin Tonino?"

"Yes, but the Professor agrees. Don't you remember him telling us a few days ago that the real danger at the moment is that the bourgeoisie has started to vote Communist?"

"Salvatò, there's something I've been meaning to ask you for a long time. What is this bourgeoisie we're always hearing about? I keep hearing things like 'The proletariat must defend itself from the bourgeoisie!' and 'Up with the workers, down with the bourgeoisie!' Salvatò, I wish you'd tell me just who these bourgeois are. People who don't work? Well, I haven't got a job, so what am I? A worker or a bourgeois?"

"Look, Savè, in plain words a bourgeois is a conservative, someone who's happy with the way things are and only wants to hang on to whatever money he's managed to make. Your bourgeois works, but he's still the most worthless member of the community because he makes no effort to improve things. When there's a strike, he prefers to go on working just the same, and when we had the referendum on divorce, he was the one who voted against it because it was something new. Now do you understand, Savè?"

"Oh, yes, but what did the Professor say? That the bourgeoisie had begun to vote for the Communist Party? You think he was pulling our legs?"

"No, not at all. In fact, there's a lot of truth in what he said. The Professor would argue like this: What is it the bourgeoisie wants? Law and order. So now that the Communist countries have apparently got law and order, Communism has become attractive to them. But then someone else says, Okay, they may have law and order, but under a Communist government you won't be allowed to have any political ideas of your own. And the bourgeois, who only thinks of himself, replies, I don't give a damn about political ideas. But they'll take away your property!

Mine? replies the bourgeois. Not mine, they won't. They'll take away Lauro's and Agnelli's, but not mine, because I haven't got any worth mentioning. So bit by bit we arrive at the point where the bourgeoisie votes Communist, but with one small difference—that the Communism they want isn't the same Communism we want."

"So we need two different Communist Parties."

"Bravo, Saverio. Now you see what I'm getting at. Two Communist Parties, one for the bourgeoisie and one for the real Communists like you and me."

"But what would this second Communist Party be called?"

"Lotta Continua. Permanent Struggle. And I've already joined it. Now I want you to come join too."

"Join Lotta Continua?"

"Right."

"But tell me one thing, Salvatò. Does the struggle really have to be permanent?"

XXII

THE POWDER

"I've had it! It's impossible to go on like this any longer. This country is shit, Dottò! Excuse my language, but there are times when it's necessary. What? Some wretched woman gets her handbag snatched in the street? Okay, we say, these things happen. They rob a bank? So what, it doesn't matter, the banks can afford it. They kidnap a millionaire's son? Well, Daddy can come up with the money. The boy who helps me in the shop goes off in the evening with the best cuts of meat in his pocket? Never mind, I keep my mouth shut, because if he runs to his union telling tales about my national insurance contributions, he could put me out of business. In short, what I'm saying is that in Italy we put up with a certain level of petty crime. We're used to it, it's not news anymore. But there are occasions when something really gets to you and you think, Jesus, Saint Anna, Mary, and Joseph, can't I trust anybody in this world?"

"This sounds serious, Don Ernè. What happened?"

"I'll tell you. As you probably know, all of us in the butcher trade make our meat look a little bit redder by using what we call 'the powder.' After all, presentation is important. But now, God alone knows why, this powder has been banned. The scientists have declared it an 'adulteration,' so from time to time the Department of Public Health sends out inspectors to do checks. So the other day one of these inspectors came here, and I said politely, 'Inspector, I've taken the liberty of putting aside a piece of steak for you that's out of this world! It'll make a superb Genovese.' 'No, thank you,' he replied. 'Today's

Friday, and we don't eat meat.' And with that he immediately found a minute quantity, the merest trace, of powder on a piece of fillet sitting in the fridge. Dottò, this bastard slapped a fine on me, but the sort of fine that makes you think that one of these days you're going to close up shop, run across the street, raid the branch of the Bank of Naples that's sitting there, get your hands on a couple of hundred million, and retire."

"You're joking, Don Ernè. With this shop of yours you earn more than any bank robber."

"So, as I was saying, I'd hardly gotten over the shock of this damn fine when I heard that the Public Health people had also paid a visit to my brother Giggino, who's got the butcher's shop up at Villanova, and who, of course, puts as much powder on his meat as the rest of us. And they took away samples of meat, they had them analyzed, and they didn't fine him!"

"Perhaps they had some kind of agreement with your brother."

"Agreement nothing, Dottò! Someone sold him phony powder!"

XXIII

PIEDIGROTTA

We are angels
who have but a single wing
and we can only fly
if we cling to one another.

L. D. C.

"Do you remember the festival of Piedigrotta in its heyday?"
asked the Professor. "It's not the same anymore. It comes and
goes, and you hardly notice it. It used to be different, a festival
that one enjoyed, that one looked forward to. People who had
balconies overlooking the streets where the procession passed,
along Via Roma and Via Partenope or down by the Riviera, invited
their friends up. The children ran around the streets in little
groups with confetti, tin trumpets, and rubber bats, laughing
and hitting each other over the head. When I was a boy, my
mother was too frightened to let me out on the street, so she
always bought me *o cuppulone,* a kind of large bucket made out of
colored cardboard that I tied to the balcony with a piece of string
and held upside down, and then as soon as a likely subject passed
underneath, a lady in some ridiculous getup or an odd-looking
man, I could drop it as quick as lightning, *woomph!* right over
their heads!"

"As far as I can remember," said Dottor Vittorio, "it was always
a festival in the worst possible taste. Noise and violence, that was
Piedigrotta. That we should now, at a distance of so many years,
remember Piedigrotta as an amusing festival is something I can
quite understand, but I suggest that the enchantment with

which we now view it is entirely due to our own impressionable adolescence and owes nothing to the festival itself, which was never an edifying occasion."

"There," said the Professor, "now Vittorio's managed to turn even my memory of Piedigrotta into so much crap!"

"Oh, come on, let's not be foolish. Do we or do we not concede that all this folksy rubbish has been the death of Naples? All of us here remember how we avoided the streets where all the fuss was going on during Piedigrotta, so let's be honest and admit that Piedigrotta wasn't really any fun at all."

"No fun, Dottò!" exclaimed Saverio. "I know I was only little, but I still remember the floats. There was the float with the *maschere,* Harlequin and Columbine and all the other characters, and then there was the seafood float with the girls waving their legs around from inside the shells, and the Vesuvius float with real smoke coming out of it, and the funicular all lit up and people singing '*Iamme, Iamme, Iamme Iamme Ià.*' Piedigrotta was beautiful, Dottò. Papà once bought me a little tin trumpet and made me a *bersagliere*'s cap out of cardboard painted all over with black ink, and then he got some string and a pot of glue and decorated it with feathers from the chicken we'd eaten the Sunday before. One of those real chickens we used to raise in the house and then eat on special occasions."

"And do you remember the fireworks? The fireworks out in the bay?"

"Yes, but wasn't it boring waiting for them to begin! We used to sit around half the night, I remember, wishing they'd get started! They'd set off one, then there'd be a two-hour wait before the next, so I nearly always went to sleep wherever I happened to be, curled up in an armchair or on the sofa under the window."

"We always used to go to my grandmother's house to see the fireworks," said Luigino. "My grandmother, my father's mother, lived in Corso Vittorio Emanuele and had a roof terrace from which you could see the whole of the Gulf of Naples from the Castello dell'Ovo to Punta di Pietra Salata. It was a lovely house, and on the evening of Piedigrotta it was always full of people. Grandmother gave a dinner, the sort of dinner you associate with Christmas, and all the aunts and uncles and cousins came, and there was one table for the children and another for the grownups. You wouldn't believe the racket we kids made in Grandmother's house on the evening of Piedigrotta. We'd start out throwing confetti and end up throwing punches."

"Luigì, to tell the truth, I can't imagine you punching anybody."

"Why not? Even I was a child once. But I remember that there was always a moment, after we'd been running around all over the place, when the little ones would collapse, exhausted, on the beds and we boys would join the grownups to wait for the fireworks to begin. There was no point in everyone getting cold, so one of us would stay outside and shout, 'Fireworks, fireworks' as soon as the first one appeared, and then everyone ran out on the terrace. Papà would shout, 'Bring Mother here!' and my youngest uncles would lift her up, armchair and all, and carry her out to the front of the terrace. Someone would yell, 'There they are, look!' and then everyone would exclaim, 'Ah, how beautiful!' And I remember the evening when I was standing behind the others with my little cousin Annuccia beside me. Annuccia was a year younger than me, and I was head-over-heels in love with her. I used to write poems for her, and they always sat us next to each other at the table and called us the lovebirds. And I remember as clearly as if it were only yesterday that as we watched the fireworks that evening, I took her hand in mine. Annuccia's hand was like ice. At first she tried to get it away from me, but then, gradually, she began to squeeze back. My heart was thumping as if it were about to jump out of my chest. Then I remember turning to look at her and seeing a pale, frightened little face and eyes that wouldn't look at me, a little face that turned red and white by turns, partly with shyness and partly with the reflection of the fireworks. I wonder where Annuccia is now."

XXIV

GENNARINO THE KAMIKAZE

"INGEGNÈ, if you'd gotten here ten minutes earlier, I could have introduced you to Gennarino *'o kamikazze.*"

"Gennarino who?"

"Gennarino *'o kamikazze,*" repeats Salvatore. "Gennarino's a friend of mine and Saverio's, and he's also a famous Neapolitan character, and all the major Italian insurance companies know him."

"And what does he do, this Gennarino?"

"He gets himself run over so that he can make insurance claims."

"What nice friends you've got, Salvatò!"

"Ingegnè, wait a minute," Salvatore protests in an injured tone. "Gennarino's got to earn a living like anybody else. And if you think about it, it's his own life he's playing with. Heaven knows how many ribs he's broken on the job."

"All I know is that because my car's still registered in Naples I have to pay twice the normal insurance premium on account of people like your Gennarino. Does that seem right to you?"

"I can see I'll have to tell you all about Gennarino. Gennarino started out as a glove maker, like his father, grandfather, great-grandfather, et cetera, et cetera. Then the fashion changed and no one wore gloves anymore except murderers who didn't want to leave fingerprints, so poor Gennarino, who married at eighteen and had kids to support, had to do the best he could. For a while he specialized in stealing the brass grilles from train lavatories. He would get on the train, pry the grille up from the floor, and throw it into some field where he could pick it up later at his own convenience. But again fashion went against him. The Italian National Railway decided to change the design of their lavatories, and poor Gennarino had to change jobs yet again. He decided to take up a career more in line with the times, so to speak, and went in for the insurance business, which has at least insured him, if you'll forgive the pun, of a reasonable livelihood."

"Excuse me, but do the insurance companies know that the accidents are faked?"

"Faked? They're not faked at all, Ingegnè. He really does get himself run over!"

"Without getting killed?"

"No, no, he's an artist! Gennarino's got split-second timing: he can judge the speed of a car, the reflexes of the driver, the make of the car, and the bank balance of its owner all in the twinkling of an eye. Just imagine, if he made the slightest mistake, Gennarino could really wind up dead, or he could risk being run over by one of those yahoos with no sense of honesty or public responsibility, people who are so tight with every last lira that they don't even carry insurance."

"But the poor man must get seriously hurt from time to time."

"That can't be avoided. Day after day, a bump here, a fall there, and Gennarino's no longer a young man. But at least he's managed to save a little. And just think, he himself told me that the Italian insurance companies recently held a special conference all because of him, and they apparently offered him some sort of lump sum on the condition that he doesn't get himself run over again. A kind of pension, I suppose."

"Great! Now he won't have to risk his neck anymore."

"But now Gennarino doesn't want a steady job! They should have offered him that years ago! Today, by the grace of God, Gennarino's famous, and he's gone wholesale."

"What do you mean, wholesale?"

"I mean he doesn't just deal in his own injuries now. He buys them, so to speak, from other people. If anybody in the neighborhood injures himself—I don't know, let's say by falling down the stairs and breaking a leg—well, instead of going straight to the doctor, he calls Gennarino, who immediately organizes a fake accident involving the car of some friend with a clean driving record, and then, and only then, the person's taken to the hospital."

"And do you approve of this?"

"Absolutely, because as you can imagine, it works out very conveniently for the person with the broken leg, who gets first-class legal and medical advice from Gennarino as well as damages from the insurance company. Gennarino is a real expert when it comes to forensic medicine. Sometimes he only has to hear the injured person moan to know exactly what kind of fracture he's got, the number of days he's going to be in the hospital, and the damages to be claimed. You know, Ingegnè, I bet Gennarino could be a consultant in the emergency room at Capodimonte. They should award him—what is it now?—an honorary degree!"

XXV

CRIME

In a church I heard a wretch praying
that God would ask St. Gennaro
to give him a win in the lottery.

ALEXANDRE DUMAS, *Le Corricolo*

" 'YOUNG WOMAN RAVISHED by Four Youths at Centocelle,' "
announced Saverio, reading aloud from a copy of *Roma*. "Professò, what do they mean by 'ravished'?"

"It means they all had sex with her."

"But when I, as we say, have intimate relations with my wife,
am I ravishing her?"

"No, indeed, Savè. Those men, the four youths, got what they
wanted by violence."

"Well, then, Professò, last summer I ravished a German girl
who, I swear, was almost two meters tall! But I still ravished her
all on my own, in broad daylight—keeping my eyes peeled, of
course—behind the ATAN bus station in Capodimonte. She was a
schoolteacher, and she'd come to Naples to see the Capodimonte
Museum, so she asked me where the entrance was and I pretended to take her there and sweet-talked her and got what I
wanted. Professò, believe me, after I'd ravished her, so to speak,
she was so happy that she wanted to tear up her plane ticket and
stay in Naples for the rest of her life. She really fell for me, as
they say! So I had to explain that I had a wife and family already,
and she became more reasonable and said, '*Maine libbe Saverio,
ich zuriuc kommen da te,*' which in the German language means,

'My darling Saverio, you are a wonderful lover, and I will return to Naples as soon as I can to make love with you again.' "

"Okay, Saverio, but that wasn't really ravishing her," said Salvatore. "It was one against one, and if she hadn't been willing she'd have beaten you up, and in that case you'd have been the one who was ravished. But at Centocelle it was four against one."

"The bastards!"

"Unfortunately there's nothing anyone can do about it," observed the Professor. "Violence is something we have to live with."

"Violence, as I see it, is built into the system," said Dottor Vittorio. "And Moravia said the same thing in no uncertain terms after the incident in Circeo. A society that makes the tyranny of the strong over the weak one of its guiding principles naturally produces assassins!"

"Indeed, we laid ourselves open to violence," said Bellavista, "by throwing out all the nineteenth-century ideals—religious faith, love of one's country, the sense of family—with no thought of putting anything else in their place. Let's be honest: in this day and age, the only idealists still at large in Italy are the genuine Communists and the soccer fans! Now, it seems obvious to me that men cannot survive without ideals. It's always some ideal that draws men toward either love or liberty, the choice depending on faith versus desire for independence. Absence of motivating ideals allows a man to fall into the hate-power syndrome where he is forced to choose, as a substitute ideal, between a BMW and heroin. In short, if you have children and you realize that they haven't been blessed with faith or with any special skill or talent, then push them into sports as soon as you can or enroll them in the Communist Party while they're still in the cradle, and that way you may avoid having drug addicts or criminals in the family."

"That's just fine, Professò," said Saverio, "but then we're stuck with our children being Communists forever."

"I doubt it. No, not forever. Haven't you heard the saying 'He who is not a Communist at twenty has no heart, and he who is still a Communist at forty has no head'?"

"But seriously, Professò, what do you think should be done about all this violence?"

"Ah, in the first place, the origin of violence is a somewhat complicated matter. Everyone has a different theory, and strangely enough, everyone may be right. Some talk about a natural disposition for violence, others blame the present shortage of wars to satisfy it. Some blame unbridled hedonism, others the sudden collapse of religious faith. Some blame a permissive society, and others go so far as to blame a political program of subversion."

"Do you mean the Fascists, Professò?"

"Yes, but at the same time we should remember something Pasolini said a few days before he was killed. Pasolini said that it was very convenient to blame violence on an external cause, to imagine, for instance, a Fascist group plotting away in the cellar to destroy us, while the truth, unhappily, is that violence is within us all, possibly not innate, but certainly encouraged by the system."

"Professò, forgive me, but wasn't Pasolini, may he rest in peace, a bit of a queer?"

"He was an extremely intelligent man, and like all great non-conformists, he often did and said things that annoyed other people. And as you know, where a celebrity is concerned, people sometimes pay more attention to what he does than to what he thinks. There's an extremely clever saying that goes, 'When a finger points at the moon, idiots watch the finger.'"

"But still . . ."

"Pasolini, in that period of illumination that sometimes comes shortly before death, was the first to predict the arrival of the monsters. He warned us, he tried to sound the alarm, but no one believed him. 'Attention!' he cried. 'Turn off your televisions! Beware, the light from the screen feeds the monsters! They grow fat upon it!' But no one listened, and the psychologists went on talking about the innate goodness of man and refusing to admit the existence of the Devil. The monsters, however, knew that Pasolini had sounded the alarm, and they did away with him."

"But what monsters do you mean, Professò? Pasolini was murdered by that little queer Pino the Frog!"

"I'm talking about the monsters of consumerism! *Gesù!* Tell me, if you expose some poor devil with no culture and no moral principles to images of blithe consumerism day in day out, what can you expect? Will he be content to resign himself to a second-class existence just because he was born on the wrong side of the tracks?"

"Then are you saying, Professò, that everyone should help themselves to whatever they want?" asked Saverio. "That's anarchy! We all know that some are born rich and others poor, but we get used to it and eventually it doesn't matter too much."

"Saverio, my dear friend, it may not matter much to you perhaps because you're more Neapolitan than you think. But if consumerism continually raises the basic standard of living, and if you are a man with no interest in the things of the spirit—in short, if you have no inbuilt resistance to the conditioning effect of advertising—what do you do? You grab a machine gun and shoot the first well-to-do man you see in a dark alley."

"Easier said than done! Machine guns don't grow on trees, Professò!"

"Gennà, in general I agree with you that consumerism is one of the root causes of crime," said Dottor Palluotto. "However, you will have noticed that in the majority of cases the criminal is predefined by circumstances. Here in Italy a man who is employed, who has a job to go to, has usually come to terms with his social status and is unlikely, in the normal course of events, to go around killing people. But God knows, when the State can look at a city like Naples, with a population of a million and a half, knowing that it has an unemployment figure of two hundred thousand but not giving a damn and refusing to provide the preconditions for a really sound program of industrialization, then the State has to accept the sole responsibility for crime. It's no longer a case of a Manichean opposition between right and wrong, it's not a question of lack of ideals, it's simply the result of bad social planning."

"Watch out for that word 'industrialization,'" said the Professor. "Lauro, Gava, and the chimera of industrialization have ruined Naples between them. Lauro ran the city like the last of the Bourbons, Gava was even worse, but neither of them did as much damage to Naples as those who believed they could solve its problems by industrialization. Imagine a Naples with no smoking factories, a Naples where the Bagnoli Plain, instead of being blighted by Italsider, was an uninterrupted vista of hotels, vacation homes, villas, and casinos. Look at Positano, Amalfi, Ischia, Capri, Procida, Baia, Lake of Avernus, Pompeii, Herculaneum, Vietri, Cumae, Faito, Vesuvius, all the islands, cliffs, mountains, volcanoes, and lakes. This could be the very Mecca of tourism! The European Las Vegas! Paradise on earth! Think of the Castello dell'Ovo, for example, a wonderful medieval castle with vast halls, winding passages, and impressive workshops, and imagine how much money Naples could have made for itself with a castle in the middle of the sea renovated as a conference center, its halls equipped with facilities for simultaneous translation, and shorefront hotels and restaurants within a stone's throw! And then, I ask you, look at the Neapolitans and tell me whether in your opinion they're the kind of people more naturally suited to heavy industry or to the tourist trade. What, after all, are the prerequisites of a great tourist center? Some help from the good Lord in providing the beauties of nature, and an efficient Office of Tourism to take care of the business end. The good Lord has done all that was required of Him. The Office of Tourism has not!"

"And how many people would have found jobs with the tourists?"

"Nearly everybody. Between the hotels, the shops, the boating, and all the rest, a million and a half could easily have been absorbed. Naples already had all the principal attractions: the open sky, the sea, the climate, beautiful islands, thermal springs, friendly natives, and archeological sites. Foreigners would have flocked from all corners of the globe bearing hard currency, and we would never have had to build up disfiguring industries like Alfa Sud."

"That's all very well, but what has it got to do with crime?"

"Everything, because even if a few men are born criminals, there are many more who are driven to crime by necessity. And whereas crime used to operate on the rather picturesque level of the pickpockets and con artists, in today's world of consumerism it has become better organized and better equipped. Firearms are used so casually nowadays that one often wonders if the criminal's real objective is the take or simply violence for its own sake."

"There's still a kind of appealing side to crime in Naples," put in Salvatore. "A week ago, for example, I read that five kilometers of copper wire were stolen from the Cumae railway and the train had to stop in the open countryside."

"And I was reading," added Saverio, "that two brand-new pumps, installed in Via Caracciolo to bring up drain water and take it to Cumae, had been swiped. Incidentally, Professò, what on earth will they do with two pumps?"

"Let's hope they sell them back to the city at half price. But to return to our discussion of crime, the first thing we should do is arrive at a basic classification of crimes and distinguish between honest theft, dishonest theft, and violent crime. Then we should insist that the State provide different prisons and different sentences for each category of criminal."

"Honest theft?"

"Indeed. Honest theft is theft motivated by social necessity and serving to restore the equilibrium in certain cases of economic imbalance."

"Come again, Professò?"

"Savè," explained Salvatore, "the Professor means that while we're waiting for the Communists to get into power and bring in equal pay for all, you have every right to expropriate the odd thousand lire from someone else's pocket to reduce the present difference in income between you and the person expropriated."

"Actually, that wasn't exactly what I meant, but Salvatore has clarified one of the philosophical goals of honest theft. If we treat theft as a competitive game having, like any other game, a strict set of rules, we can say that if a thief abides by the rules, then his victim has no right to redress and the theft qualifies as 'honest.' "

"And what would these rules be?"

"Rule number one: To steal only the amount strictly necessary for one's own and one's family's survival."

"So thieves with large families have the right to steal more?"

"Epicuristically, yes, if it's a question of necessity. Rule number two: To steal only what the victim has in superfluity, and then only when the victim has shown himself unworthy of it."

"What do you mean?"

"Imagine a wealthy tourist coming to Naples and leaving an expensive camera unguarded on a car seat. Who is the more guilty, the Neapolitan thief or the foreigner who has provoked him?"

"I'd arrest the tourist for incitement to crime!" said Salvatore. "Professò, would it be true to say that if the victim is an American, the theft becomes a little more honest?"

"Certainly. In fact, the victim must be either American or Swiss."

"Why so?" I asked.

"Because in that case minor local thefts make up for the major market thefts committed, for example, by the giant multinational banks."

"And what other rules are there?"

"There's the 'touch of class.' "

"What's that?"

"A touch of class attaches to any exercise of the imagination that raises a theft to the realm of art. As always, it's much easier to explain by examples. For instance, a petty thief disguised as a ticket collector boards a bus in the station and sells tickets to all the waiting passengers, pocketing eight hundred lire. Or a busboy armed with a tray full of coffee cups collides with a wealthy passerby looking in the other direction and tearfully provokes a passing of the hat; he repeats the same gambit until all the china from the original cups has been utterly pulverized. Again, intrepid thieves disguised as carabinieri arrest a wealthy fence and after confiscating all his valuables scrupulously compile an inventory in duplicate and deliver the fence himself to the court jail at Poggioreale, where, it is later revealed, the victim spends two months awaiting a hearing on his case. As you see, in this form of honest theft, what is stolen is immaterial. It's an expression of artistry, showmanship, inventive flair!"

"In my opinion, Professò, the first two examples you mentioned don't cut the mustard, they're not artistic thefts at all," said Salvatore. "The poor guys were only scrounging around to see if they could scrape together the price of a meal. I know a man who does a different job every day. One day he's a *gettonaro*, meaning that he goes to the station and checks all the phone booths to see if anyone's left any *gettoni** lying around, and he says that sometimes he'll pick up as many as twenty or twenty-five. Another day he's a *mollicaro*, and he gets the pastrycooks to give him all their crumbs and broken pastries and then sells these *molliche* in paper cups outside the primary schools. Sometimes he'll jump on a train as soon as it arrives, gather up all the papers and magazines left on the seats, and sell them at half price outside the station. All in all, he manages to make ends meet. It's a shame, though, because when he was a boy everyone thought he was going to be a great inventor. He designed the Eros stove, which was a sort of portable oil heater to keep prostitutes warm while they waited around in the streets. He had a market all right, but no financial backing. To get the thing off the ground he needed a poster campaign at least!"

---

*Tokens used instead of money to make a call from a public phone.

"It's always the same in this house," complained Dottor Palluotto. "One begins a serious discussion, and it ends up in wild eccentricity. I wouldn't like our friend to return to Rome with the idea that Naples is the only Italian city uncontaminated by the tide of violence. I assure you, my esteemed Ingegnere, that in this respect we Neapolitans are in no way lagging behind our Milanese cousins. The largest local industry is smuggling, with a workforce of around forty thousand—not bad. It would seem that in 1975 we led the mugging league. Where the car industry is concerned, we compete fairly favorably with Turin. They have the great Fiat factories building cars, but here we have the international center for stolen cars and spare parts. Add the odd kidnapping, a few armed robberies, some unsolved murders, the armed bands of left-wing extremists, and you have the general picture. If you find all this hard to believe, just pick up a copy of *Il Mattino* every day and turn to the local news pages."

"Quite honestly, I can't agree with you about the value of the information you get from the press," said Luigino. "The general picture sketched by Dottor Palluotto is neither true nor just. If you only read the papers, you end up believing that the human race is beyond all redemption. Fathers killing their children, children killing their fathers, babies being kidnapped! Life's not really like that: people, by and large, are much nicer, but the papers never say anything about all the nice people because what they do is not News. The problem is that there are thousands of nice people—no, nonsense, there are millions of them! Imagine how wonderful it would be if they published a paper with only this sort of item in it: 'Signor Esposito, a bank clerk, celebrated a pay raise of twenty-two thousand lire by taking his wife to see *Cries and Whispers,* the new release now showing at the Delle Palme cinema.' 'Sports page: Playing *scopa* the other evening, Cavaliere Cacace beat Brigadiere Dacunto by winning ten hands out of ten. Brigadiere Dacunto remarked that Cavaliere Cacace is so lucky at cards that he'll have to watch his step.' 'Signorina Angela Calcagni has been hired as a stewardess by Alitalia.

Angela's mother presented her with a little heart-shaped diamond locket containing the image of St. Anthony that she will wear pinned to her new uniform.' 'Yesterday evening Signor Pasquale Tuccillo went to meet his daughter after school. As soon as she saw her father, the little girl ran up to him shouting, Papà!' "

XXVI

RIDDLES AND MYSTERIES

IT WAS TWO O'CLOCK on a sunny afternoon, and I was sitting with Pasquale Amoroso and his signora in a wayside tavern on the outskirts of Terzigno.

The road we had just traveled had taken us through practically every town of the Vesuvian hinterland—Sant'-Anastasia, Somma, Ottaviano, San Giuseppe Vesuviano, and Terzigno—before circling around the shoulders of Vesuvius to emerge once more on the Autostrada del Sole at Torre Annunziata. Throughout the trip Amoroso's unbridled passion for the lottery—a passion obviously not shared by his lady—had been the subject of repeated arguments, and having made a few attempts at keeping the peace, I had eventually found my attention wholly absorbed in contemplation of the other side of Vesuvius, the spent crater providing a spectacle for which I had been totally unprepared.

The little tavern, with its paper napkins, marble-topped tables, and adolescent chickens pecking around one's feet, had all the required characteristics of a trattoria in a poor inland village. We settled for spaghetti *aglio 'e 'uoglio** and began to soothe the pangs of hunger with slabs of black bread, butter, anchovies, and Boscotrecase salami washed down with a Gragnano as fresh and sharp as a black grape straight from the vine.

This outing with Signor and Signora Amoroso had come about through a customer of mine who, aware of my interest in

*With olive oil and garlic.

Naples and certain Neapolitan traditions, had said, "Ingegnè, if you want to learn all about the lottery and the *assistiti** you must have a word with one of our doormen, a certain Amoroso, who, if he takes a liking to you, might even accompany you to Croce del Carmine to speak to the *Santone*."†

During our first conversation, back in Naples, Amoroso had explained that this *Santone* was different from all the ordinary *assistiti* in that instead of divulging the numbers clearly, he wrapped them up in riddles, or *misteri*. To be precise, Amoroso had said, "You see, Ingegnè, the *Santone* cannot reveal the actual numbers, and there are two reasons for this. In the first place, he's been forbidden to . . ."

"Forbidden? Who has forbidden him?"

"Those up there!"—pointing skyward—"They have forbidden him! That's what they're like, Ingegnè. If the *assistito* isn't careful and gives away too many numbers, they might stop helping him from one moment to the next, if you follow me."

"Ah, I see. And the other reason?"

"The government itself was getting suspicious. The Department of Finance interviewed him twice about that time when eighteen came up on the third draw after he'd gotten half of Naples to bet on it. In those days the *Santone* was still revealing the actual numbers, and what happened was that one evening in the cantina he said, 'Next Saturday the third number that's drawn will be seventeen, and the following week number eighteen will come up on the same draw.' I don't have to tell you that when number seventeen came up exactly as he had predicted, the entire population rushed to bet on number eighteen the week after. People were pawning everything they could lay their hands on in order to back such a safe

---

Assistiti (literally, "guided ones") are people who claim, or are held by other people to possess, inside knowledge from some supernatural source about the numbers that will turn up in the lottery.

†*Santone* (or *Santo*) and *Monaco* are both accepted courtesy titles for *assistiti,* deriving from the fact that saints and monks are presumed to have a hotline to vital inside information from on high.

bet—gold, silver, household items, the works. Anyway, on the day of the draw—which, as you know, takes place in San Biagio dei Librai—immediately after the first two numbers had been drawn and while the lottery official was turning the barrel with the rest of the numbers in it, someone in the crowd shouted, 'Turn and shake the barrel as often as you like, the third number must be eighteen!' And sure enough, up it came. So the government, having had to pay out a fortune, immediately ordered the Department of Finance and the carabinieri to find out how the man in the crowd had known that eighteen would come up. And their investigation eventually led them to the *Santone,* which is why he has never, from that day to this, revealed the actual numbers. He became secretive and began to speak in riddles."

"And what are these riddles?"

"They're little stories, ever so simple, which you can either interpret for yourself or have interpreted for you by someone who does it for a living. I know a wonderful interpreter in Villanova who's been doing it for so many years that he hardly ever gets it wrong."

"Why don't you tell me one of the riddles the *Santone* has told you?"

"Of course. I'll choose a very simple one so that you can follow it easily. Have you got a pen handy? Fine! Now write this down: Salvatore means six, so write down 'six'; Gennaro means nineteen, so write down 'nineteen'; but now Gennaro calls out to Salvatore, and calling equals fifty-two, so write down 'fifty-two.' Gennaro says, 'Salvatò, come here.' What does it mean?"

"What does it mean?"

"It means that Gennaro's *cadenza,** nine, wants Salvatore's *figura,†* six, near him. Now, what numbers have digits totaling six?"

"What numbers?"

*Last digit.
†A number whose digits add up to a given sum.

"Six, fifteen, twenty-four, thirty-three . . ."

"Forty-two, fifty-one . . ."

"Well done, Ingegnere! Got it in one try! However, we now have to discover among these numbers one with a *figura* of six that also has nine as its *cadenza*. Which is it?"

"Which is it?"

"Sixty-nine."

"Why sixty-nine?"

"Because six plus nine equals fifteen and fifteen equals six because one plus five equals six. Now, since Gennaro, who equals nineteen, wants to be near Salvatore, whose *figura* is six, we have two possible courses to choose between. We can play twenty-five and seventy-seven or sixty-nine and seventy-seven."

"Amorò, you've lost me. Where do twenty-five and seventy-seven come from?"

"Follow carefully, Ingegnere. If Gennaro and Salvatore are, so to speak, united, obviously one has to play twenty-five because six plus nineteen equals twenty-five. If I were to say, 'Rosa has taken Giovanni's arm,' what number would you play?"

"?"

"You'd play fifty-four, because Rosa equals thirty and Giovanni twenty-four and thirty plus twenty-four equals fifty-four! If, on the other hand, Gennaro and Salvatore are simply standing next to each other but not touching, then we work out the configurations as I explained before and play sixty-nine."

"But where does seventy-seven come from?"

"*Gesù*, a child could do it. Calling is fifty-two, Gennaro six, and Salvatore nineteen; so the grand total, when you add together all the numbers in the riddle, is seventy-seven. Fifty-two plus six plus nineteen."

"Oh."

"As you can see, one has to be careful not to miss a single word when the *Santone* is speaking, otherwise it's a waste of time and money. He once told me this riddle: Antonio watches

Pasquale, who is coming down the stairs, but as soon as Pasquale gets to the bottom, Antonio turns around and attacks Giuseppe. I put my money on eight . . ."

"Why eight?"

"Because Pasquale is seventeen, add the digits and you get eight, and since Pasquale had come all the way down to the bottom of the stairs, I chose the smallest number possible whose digits add up to eight, which is eight itself."

"Ah, I see."

"And then I bet on thirty-two, reasoning that because Antonio is thirteen and Giuseppe nineteen and Antonio attacked Giuseppe, thirteen plus nineteen equals thirty-two. The riddle seemed simple, so I staked quite a bit on eight and thirty-two: ten thousand lire for a straight double on the Naples draw. If my numbers had come up I would have won a million and a half! But what do they draw?"

"What do they draw?"

"Eight and fifty. Ingegnè, Antonio turned around! Thirteen had become thirty-one. You see, when Antonio attacked Giuseppe, he had already turned around, so thirty-one plus nineteen equaled fifty. Thirty-two was wrong!"

"I'll be damned! You were right about the importance of not missing a single word!"

"Not a single word, Ingegnè! Not one!"

"Are there other *assistiti* besides the *Santone*?"

"There certainly are. As a matter of fact, we should have seventy-two of them in Naples."

"Seventy-two?"

"Right. And in the past they all knew each other, and so people got to know them too, but nowadays you get *assistiti* who have become lawyers, doctors—people of a certain standing, in short—and because they've gone up in the world, so to speak, they don't exercise their profession openly anymore, if you see what I mean. However, there have been some very great Neapolitan *assistiti* in the past: the famous *Cagli*

Cagli, Buttiglione, 'o Servitore, 'o Monaco sapunaro, 'o Monaco 'e San Marco . . . many, many of them. Once, when they wanted to force *Cagli Cagli* to reveal the numbers, they hung him up by his heels. But he still refused to speak. All he said was 'You can kill me, but you can't make me tell you the numbers.' Those people could be tough bastards when they wanted to be. For example, I'll tell you one really strange story . . ." And Amoroso got up and came to sit near me. This story was apparently not for the ears of his signora. "When a woman went to *'o Monaco sapunaro* to ask for the numbers, do you know what that dirty old man did? He wrote them very small, with an indelible pencil, in her most intimate parts, if you follow me, so that the wretched woman couldn't read them for herself even with the help of a mirror."

"Then how did she manage to play them?"

"She had no choice but to get someone else to read them for her. Which of course made it clear that she had committed, so to speak, an infraction, to wit, hanky-panky."

"This was *'o Monaco sapunaro*?"

"Yes. Then there was *'o Monaco 'e San Marco*, who was once commanded by those up there to reveal an *ambo** to a man who was his worst enemy. Let's say he was being asked for a proof of humility. So what did this son of a bitch do? Since the numbers of the *ambo* he'd been commanded to reveal were three and fifty-nine, he threw a saucepan of boiling water over the poor devil's leg. In case you haven't quite followed, Ingegnè, it was like saying, 'Here you are, three and fifty-nine—three for the boiling water and fifty-nine for the leg.' "

"Dreadful!"

"Yes, but to be fair, the *assistiti* themselves get beaten up too, at night."

"Beaten up? And who beats them up?"

"Supernatural beings. You didn't think only living people

---

*Pair of numbers drawn in a lottery.

could be violent, did you? My interpreter, Don Antonio, the one who lives up at Villanova, used to act as secretary to a great *assistito*—now dead, God rest his soul—and he told me how they, the *assistiti*, get beaten black and blue: they're hit and punched and kicked in the head something awful. So you see, Ingegnè, even they have their cross to bear."

"Signora, do you believe in all this?"

"Not a word of it!" the signora replied. "I don't mean that my husband's a liar, but I cannot understand how grown men—air force colonels, engineers (no reference to present company), in a nutshell, all kinds of educated men old enough to know better—can possibly believe in this sort of rubbish! I know that even among the aristocracy you can find people who are, shall we say, weak-minded, but what I say to my husband is this: Being, by the grace of the Lord, in a decent, respectable job, why do you lower yourself to listen to that peasant at Terzigno and all his stupid stories? 'Gennaro goes into the church . . . Aitano calls Gennaro . . .' And their language sometimes! Listen, you've been gambling with a good job and a decent income for ten years, no less; why can't you see that it's all just so much hot air? That those . . ."

"Don't mind her, Ingegnè! Keep quiet, woman, there are things that you as a female can't be expected to understand. It's not true that I've never won. I've had an *ambo* several times, and several placings too."

"Ah, yes, you made at least enough for a box of matches!"

"What my wife can't understand is that a man gambles because he sees it as a chance, maybe his only chance, of not dying as he was born, starving in the gutter. Great God almighty . . ."

"May His name be praised! Don't you dare blaspheme or you'll call down His wrath, do you hear! Starving in the gutter, indeed! Ingegnè, it's true we're not rich, but we've got everything we need, which isn't to say we wouldn't be better off if my husband didn't gamble away ten or even twelve thousand lire a week! I'll tell you what my father says, he says he's won five million in the lottery because he's won all the money he never gambled!"

"That's the craziest argument I ever heard . . ."

"And you're not crazy, I suppose, when you let yourself be taken for a ride by 'o Santone!"

"Gesù, but I've got proof, Ingegnè! Once it was snowing in Naples, but I simply had to go see 'o Santone in Croce del Carmine. I didn't have a car in those days, so I went on the Vespa, and believe me, Ingegnè, when I got there, 'o Santone had to thaw me out before he recognized me. Anyway, to cut a long story short, he was so sorry for me that he said, 'Pascà, I want to give you a present. Play twenty-four to come up first.' "

"And did you?"

"Indeed I did."

"And did it come up?"

"No, what came up was three and seventeen: three for the present and seventeen for 'Pasquale.' "

"Don't pay any attention to him, Ingegnè, he's lost every time."

"Keep quiet! Another time he said, 'The Gypsy throws himself at the Gypsy woman.' A Gypsy is fifteen, a Gypsy woman sixty-four, so I backed seventy-nine to come up first and I lost. The next week he said, 'Gaetano goes into the house,' meaning seven goes into nine. Obviously I should have stuck with seventy-nine, and I would have if my wife hadn't arranged a trip to Ischia and I couldn't bet at all because I didn't know until we got there that the lottery offices in the islands are shut on Saturday morning, but I turned on the radio at five o'clock, and presto! There it was, seventy-nine!"

After a lot of this sort of chatter about numbers, figure, and cadenze, we eventually arrived at Croce del Carmine. It hardly deserved the name of a village, consisting of one street with a dozen houses, a church, and a bar that was both cantina and supermarket. "Have you seen Don Gaetano?" Amoroso asked.

"He was in the piazza a minute ago" was the reply. I had no opportunity of discovering to what piazza our informant might be referring, however, because we came face to face with Don Gaetano as soon as we left the bar. He was a middle-aged man, nearer fifty than forty, with deeply tanned skin, an unshaven face sprouting long white whiskers here and there, and a scar on his chin. He had apparently lived in America as a young man. He was wearing a threadbare black suit with a fawn woolen winter vest in place of a shirt. He sported a hat.

"How are you, Don Gaetà?" asked Amoroso, all smiles. "I want you to meet this friend of mine, another great lottery enthusiast."

"Good, good," the *Santone* replied. "Let's go sit down. I'm a bit hungry, and I want to eat something first."

The three of us walked through the bar and into a little dark room at the far end furnished with four chairs and a soccer machine. The signora had stayed in the car—to spare her nerves, she said. The *Santone* ordered a beer and a roll with mozzarella, and as he ate he took a sheet of ruled paper apparently torn from a child's notebook and drew two parallel lines on it. Then, after a pause for thought, he said:

"This is a ditch. Antonio stands close to the ditch waiting for Pasquale because they've arranged to meet. Antonio, close to Pasquale, says, 'Pascà, I've been waiting for you so long!' " Then to us, looking up: "Take care of yourselves; you can go now."

Amoroso got up and put five hundred lire in the *Santone*'s pocket (apparently he wasn't permitted to touch money), and I paid for the beer and roll.

"We'll talk when we're in the car," said Amoroso very solemnly as we came out of the bar.

And in fact, as soon as we had left the village behind us, he launched into an interpretation of the riddle.

"Now, Antonio is thirteen, but because he's standing beside the ditch, which is sixty-five, the first number we should back is obviously seventy-eight, because otherwise why would Antonio be standing so close to the ditch? Our problems start with the second number, because here we've got a choice: we could play seventeen, Pasquale, or forty-three, the meeting, or a number with the *figura* of eight and meaning lateness."

"Why?"

"Because if you remember, the *Santone* said that Antonio had been waiting a long time for Pasquale. Now we need to know what number with the *figura* of eight has the most lateness attached to it, and that we can only get if we pop in to see the interpreter at Villanova. He knows everything, and he even works through the night when he has a riddle to decipher. But I was just thinking, I wonder whether we should play thirty-one for the roll and eighty-four for the beer?"

"Amorò, forgive me, but it seems to me that the *Santone* gives too many numbers all at once!"

"I know, I know. Still, if one pays attention, one can always work out when he really means it and when he doesn't. Incidentally, Ingegnè, did you notice the mark on his chin?"

"Yes, a kind of scar."

"Well, do you remember the precise moment when the *Santone* touched his scar? Was it while he was talking about the ditch or the meeting, or when he ordered the beer and the roll?"

"I can't honestly say that I noticed."

"And damn it all, I wasn't paying attention! You see, when the *Santone* is about to reveal an absolute certainty, at that precise moment he always touches his scar."

Thus it came about that in the end we played twenty-six, forty-three, and seventy-eight. None of these numbers came up, but Amoroso said, "Don't be so easily discouraged, Ingegnè! You must play this combination for at least three weeks running. Give it a chance, at least!"

My sternest critic, however, was Ingegnere Carloni, manager of the electronics division of the company for which Amoroso worked as a doorman.

"What!" said Carloni. "You went to the *Santone* at Croce del Carmine with Amoroso? You, an IBM engineer, a space-age technologist! I'm surprised at you being led astray by all that talk of riddles and saints! I really shouldn't need to remind you, of all people, that this is the age of positivism, the age of the computer . . ."

"I know, but I . . ."

"Ingegnè, for heaven's sake, if you're really interested in the lottery, come with me to the computer center for a couple of minutes and I'll show you something that I believe, in all modesty, to be truly interesting. Two years ago a small group of programmers, of which I was one, put together a statistical package that extracts, with the help of an IBM 370, the numbers that have the highest probability of being drawn in the Naples Lottery every Saturday."

"No!"

"The method's called 'the chromatic dispersion system,' and I'll explain why. Supposing that next Saturday a certain combination of five numbers comes up, the question is, after how many weeks will this combination of five begin to disperse?"

"Disperse?"

"Yes, that is, we need to know after how many weeks, based on a calculation of probability, any one of the numbers contained in this combination of five is likely to recur. When it does, we say that the combination of five has begun to disperse, because now the series of five has become a series of four. Eventually the series of four becomes a series of three, the series of three becomes a series of two, and so on. Now, if we allocate a different color to each series of five and its respective dispersions, we get a color diagram, the diagram of the chromatic dispersions, that allows us to perceive the predominant color of the next series of five. Do you follow me?"

"Only up to a certain point, to tell the truth."

"It's not difficult, Ingegnè. We've stored the lottery draws for the last ninety years in the computer's memory, and we've discovered that apart from the famous twenty-eight chronically recalcitrant numbers that recur so infrequently we decided to disregard them once and for all, the maximum period for a series of five to begin to disperse is six weeks, and it will finish dispersing at the latest within eleven weeks."

"Is that so?"

"Absolutely. And now the FTP program . . ."

"FTP?"

"Fortune, Technology, and Perseverance. The FTP spits out a series of probable numbers for us to bet on every Saturday."

"Have you ever won anything?"

"Not yet, but we will. Because the longer the program runs, the higher the level of probability. And we are now about to combine chromatic dispersion with another system designed by Ingegnere Scarola, called 'obsessive persistence.' Just a moment, I have an idea. I'll get him to come over, and we can all go and have coffee together, and then Scarola can tell you all about his system as we go."

The obsessive persistences were too complicated to be even minimally comprehensible as far as I was concerned. Ingegnere Scarola talked at great length about asymptotic curves and laws pertaining to very large numbers, but I had reached saturation point and preferred to abandon myself to the pleasure of a cup of espresso perfectly made, as blunt and as powerful as a karate chop.

When the time came to pay the bill, there was a problem, as there always is these days, of finding the right change. Every Italian city resolves this problem in its own way: Turin was the first to print bank drafts for one hundred lire, in Milan they give you tickets for the metro, in Naples our cashier produced a card bearing the numbers one to ninety and inquired:

"Would you like to choose one, Dottò? We pay six thousand lire for the first number drawn on Saturday."

XXVII

Neapolitan Power

If a man wished to study the principal reasons why friendships are destroyed and enemies made, he need look no further than the *polis*. Observe the envy generated by those who wish to excel within it. Observe the rivalry inevitably aroused among competitors.

PHILODEMUS OF GADARA, *Volumina Rhetorica II*, 158

"POWER MEANS programming the future," said the Professor. "Naples, however, depends on fantasy and therefore improvisation. But here is our Ingegnere at last! Ingegnè, what happened to you this evening? We've been expecting you for the past hour!"

"I know, and I'm truly sorry, but I got caught in traffic halfway down Corso Vittorio Emanuele, and there was nothing I could do about it."

"The same thing happened to me a few days ago," said Salvatore. "I'd driven Dottor Passalacqua to the courthouse for a perjury case, and on our way back, coming up the Salvator Rosa hill, we were held up for an hour, and I really mean one solid hour by the clock, bumper to bumper! Eventually we'd been waiting there for so long that a *scugnizzo** came by and sold us two mortadella rolls, and later, since we still hadn't moved, he came back and offered to go and phone our families—for two hundred lire including the cost of the call—to tell them we were okay."

"They think of everything!" said Saverio.

*Neapolitan street boy.

177

"I've never seen the traffic as bad as it was this evening, though!" I said, still trying to excuse my late arrival. "It's because the normal volume of traffic is so swollen at this time of year by people coming in from all over the province to do their Christmas shopping. And as if that weren't enough, the road apparently caved in again in Via Tasso this evening, and Vomero's been cut off for the umpteenth time."

"One must be patient," sighed the Professor. "As you may know, my dear Ingegnere, Naples was built over a whole network of underground vaults. No, I'm serious. Just under the surface of the city of Naples there are innumerable caverns of tufa and thousands upon thousands of columns, and if the rainwater seeps in or the drains overflow, all these caverns fill with water, and every so often one of the columns collapses, hence the cave-in of which you complain. And because Naples is built on a slope, like an amphitheater, the tragedy is that one of these days it's going to float out to sea like a ship."

"In any case, Professor, I have the impression that my arrival interrupted you in the middle of a philosophical discussion."

"You're right," said Saverio. "The Professor was talking about contempt for power."

"Well, almost, but I was more concerned with indifference to power than with contempt for it. I believe that your typical Neapolitan considers power more trouble than it's worth, a hard taskmaster undeserving of a lifetime's dedication. And power is indeed a hard taskmaster that will not accept the halfhearted approach, the compromises, the part-time attitude, shall we say, that the Neapolitan is prepared to offer, so at the end of the day we find our man delegating responsibility, stepping aside, and coming out with all those apathetic expressions like 'Who cares?' and 'Life's too short' that earn him such a bad name."

"But Professò, you must agree that life really is short," said Saverio. "And if someone goes in for politics, tell me, how does he find the time to earn a living? Now, if every party offered a small retainer to all its members . . ."

"This apathy where power is concerned," interrupted the Professor, "is the reason why Naples has never, and I mean never throughout its history, played an imperialistic role. If you think about it, every other Italian city can boast its moment of glory, of historical importance. Leaving aside Rome, which is almost synonymous with empire, take, for instance, Venice, Genoa, Milan, Florence, Turin, and their like, all cities that for a longer or shorter period fought by land and sea and succeeded in subjugating neighboring states. Not Naples! During the Roman expansion in Italy, for example, Naples was never heard of: not only were we a nonaggressive people but we didn't resist the aggression of others. In fact, somebody reading the history of Rome might well imagine that Naples didn't even exist at the time! That was not, however, the case: Naples was already a flourishing city with a large population, but its inhabitants occupied themselves almost exclusively with tourism, fishing, farming, and theatrical displays. Naples had been colonized by the Greeks—obviously of Athenian rather than Spartan origin—and they catered to the taste of the indigenous citizens by building only amphitheaters, stadiums, and country homes. So there were no great generals like Camillus or Mark Antony among the population, only skilled comic actors who earned their living playing the roles of the famous Atellan characters, Maccus, Pappus, Bucco, and Dossenus, for the delight of the imperial audiences. Despite their easygoing nature, however, the people of Naples still had trouble with their more bloodthirsty neighbors, because every so often they were caught between the devil and the deep blue sea. For example, when Marius the conqueror arrived, the people of Naples welcomed him with open arms, but then came Sulla, Marius' enemy, who punished them with great brutality. Along came Pompey, more celebrations, and immediately afterward Julius Caesar showed up and gave them hell for having welcomed Pompey."

"*Gesù!* But what on earth did Pompey and Caesar want with the Neapolitans?"

"Sulla, Caesar, and Pompey were all men of power and therefore unable to understand the concept of neutrality. As far as
they were concerned, the slightest hint of preference was enough
to classify a people as friend or foe. But let's return to our
Neapolitans and their disinclination for war, and consider for a
moment how strange it is that Naples, a coastal city, should never
have had a real navy. Historically, over the last three thousand
years, the Mediterranean has been dominated by the Turks, the
Genoese, the Phoenicians, the Saracens, the Venetians, the
Pisans, the Carthaginians, the people of Amalfi, et cetera, et
cetera, et cetera, but never by the Neapolitans. Us, we fished in
the bay, and that was that."

"But what about Admiral Caracciolo?"

"An excellent man, but more able as a navigator than as a
commander!"

"I've got a theory about all this," said Salvatore. "It seems to
me that the worse the climate of their own country, the more
imperialistic people tend to be. It only seems sensible that men
won't want to go off and occupy someone else's country if they're
happy where they are. And that would explain why the Neapolitans have always been better at being conquered than at
conquering."

"To show you how much truth there is in Salvatore's thesis,"
said the Professor, "I should like to give you a quick rundown of
the history of the city of Naples from its inception to the present
day . . ."

"For heaven's sake, Professò!" exclaimed Saverio, interrupting
him. "There's a movie on television tonight, and you want to go
into the whole history of Naples!"

"My dear Saverio, the history of Naples, believe me, is
remarkably brief. The entire history of the city can in fact be
condensed into just three episodes: subjection to a random vari-
ety of foreign powers, Masaniello, and the Parthenopean Republic."

"How many foreign conquerors has Naples had, Professò?"

"I'd say about a dozen. Without putting them into chronological order, those that come to mind are the Greeks, the Romans, the Goths, the Lombards, the Byzantines, the Normans, the Saracens, the Swabians, the Angevins, the Aragonese, the Spanish in general, the French, the Austrians, and the Piedmontese. And that's not counting the more recent Allied invasion by the Americans, Canadians, English, Moroccans, et cetera, et cetera."

"*Gesù!* Is there anyone who hasn't come to Naples?"

"Only the Russians—so far—have refrained from doing us the honor."

"They may yet, Professò. The twentieth century's not over."

"The fact is that during the first centuries of her existence, Naples' proximity to Rome meant that she was completely under Rome's thumb, so while the provinces that were farther away took advantage of the fact to create a certain autonomy, Naples elected to become a holiday resort for the Roman emperors. Later, during the Dark Ages, the great European dynasties amused themselves by tossing the responsibility for the Kingdom of Naples from one to the other, so that the Neapolitans might well go to bed under the rule of Spain and wake up the next morning under the rule of France. For four or five centuries there was quite a game going among the reigning dynasties to divide Europe up like a Monopoly board: you give me the Kingdom of the Two Sicilies, and I'll give you Lorraine and the Duchies of Parma and Piacenza. Unfortunately, the Neapolitans invariably found themselves cast as pawns rather than players in this game. On the other hand, thank God, our ancestors never resented their conquerors but quite happily extended a big warm welcome to each and every one. Certainly some kings were more popular than others, such as the Bourbon Ferdinand I, who was a man of the people, lazy and fun-loving, whereas Alfonso of Aragon, because of his efficiency and mania for getting things done, aroused a certain degree of suspicion and dislike. All of them, however, became Neapolitanized sooner or later and so lost the instinct for power that would have enabled them to defend the Kingdom against the next invader."

"Professò, excuse me," said Salvatore. "It's not that I doubt your word or anything, but now that Dottor Palluotto has returned to Milan and you've lost—how should I put it?—your sparring partner . . . What I'm trying to say is that neither I nor Saverio nor even Luigino, if it comes to that, knows much about history, and the Ingegnere, as you've seen already, is too polite to take liberties with people he doesn't know very well, so he wouldn't dream of contradicting you. So what I would like to know is how come Naples has always counted for less than nothing in the world at large?!"

"I never said that the Kingdom of Naples was totally lacking in importance, simply that the instinct for power has never been part of the Neapolitan mentality. Indeed, it will interest you to know that between the twelfth and thirteenth centuries the Kingdom of Naples was one of the most important and most advanced countries in the whole of Europe. Under the Norman king Roger II, and especially under Frederick II of Hohenstaufen, Naples had a political and administrative structure of the highest quality, a great state university, and a legal system in no way inferior to the Roman. However, the people who promoted and maintained all these benefits were not the Neapolitans but Frederick's Germans, so when the Germans departed, the structure went with them."

"But what about Masaniello, Professò?" asked Saverio. "Masaniello was Neapolitan!"

"He certainly wasn't," replied Salvatore. "Masaniello came from Amalfi, didn't he, Professò?"

"Masaniello was more Neapolitan than either you or I," stated the Professor categorically. "Masaniello, or, to give him his full name, Tommaso Aniello, was born and raised in Vico Rotto al Mercato. But it's not biographical data like this that made him Neapolitan. Of all the famous historical, theatrical, political, and artistic people born in Naples, Masaniello was the truest embodiment of the Neapolitan spirit. He expressed all the contradictions, the loving instincts, the inability to exercise power, the generosity and the ignorance of his race. Masaniello is love and disorder. Yet Naples has never, down to the present day, seen fit to honor this most representative of her sons by naming any notable street or piazza after him."

"Was Masaniello a kind of Che Guevara, then, Professò?"

"Not at all. It is impossible to compare Masaniello with any other revolutionary we know. To understand Masaniello we have to see his revolution as a piece of theater above all. A great tragedy, both epic and comic."

"Tell us, Professò, tell us the story of this tragedy."

"There are many versions of the so-called Masaniello revolution, and they frequently contradict one another. If you read Benedetto Croce, the man himself is treated almost dismissively and the entire revolutionary movement is attributed to the plots hatched by Giulio Genoino, while Alexandre Dumas, that inveterate teller of tall tales, puts the young fisherman on such a pedestal that he becomes a dashing figure like D'Artagnan. What we can be sure of, however, is that our hero was immensely famous throughout the civilized world. Even Croce, who, as I mentioned, was no fan, tells us that medals were coined in Europe bearing Masaniello's likeness on one side and Cromwell's on the other, and that two centuries later the Belgian revolution was actually sparked off by the production of Auber's opera *La Muette de Portici,* based on the story of Masaniello. Anyway, if you want to go into the matter more deeply, all you have to do is read the books that have been written about him by Michelangelo Schipa, Carlo Botta, and Capecelatro, or the more modern and therefore more authoritative accounts by Antonio Ghirelli or Indro Montanelli."

"Did you hear, Savè?" said Salvatore with the utmost seriousness. "You must go to the Minerva bookshop by Ponte di Tappia tomorrow and buy all those books the Professor mentioned."

"No way," replied Saverio. "The Professor's word is good

enough for me, and I learn all I need to know from him. Professò, just ignore Salvatore and finish the story of Masaniello."

"Well, Masaniello's revolution began, like any reputable piece of theater, with rehearsals. Yes, indeed, with rehearsals. One month previously, Masaniello, annoyed because his wife had been arrested for smuggling flour, set fire to the customs post in Piazza del Mercato. The week before, on the pretext of celebrating the festival of the Madonna del Carmine, he armed two hundred *lazzaroni*,* the so-called *alarbi,* with long sticks, disguised them as Turks, and paraded them in front of the royal palace. When they were right in front of the royal family and the whole court, Masaniello's *alarbi* ranged themselves in a line, and instead of giving the clenched-fist salute as our modern malcontents would have done, they turned around and laid their bamboo sticks on the ground, deliberately exposing their backsides to the Viceroy and all the Spanish grandees gathered on the balcony."

"That was brilliant, Professò!"

"One week later, on July 7, 1647, the revolution itself began. As all of you know already, the revolution was caused simply and solely by the tax on fruit that the Duke of Arcos had imposed a few months before with the consent of the Neapolitan nobility, so it is hardly surprising that it began not with the throwing of stones, which is how all proper revolutions have always begun— at least until Molotov enlightened us as to the use of bottles—but with the throwing of figs. Yes, my friends, figs and curses put the Spanish troops to flight, and the Neapolitan people, shouting, 'Long live the King of Spain, long live San Gennaro, long live Masaniello, and down with taxes,' stormed the palace."

"And was the tax on fruit abolished?"

"The very same day. But that was no longer enough to satisfy Masaniello, at least in part because he was now being egged on by the crafty Genoino, ex–secretary of state to the Duke of Ossuna, who was masterminding the revolution because it gave him an

---

*Name given by the Spanish rulers of Naples to the followers of Masaniello, hence the poor of Naples.

excuse to indulge his own political whims, which were half liberalism and half hardening of the arteries (Genoino was over eighty at the time). But to resume. The revolution continued with a series of invitations to the palace—another new element in the history of revolution! Dressed in a tunic of white wool trimmed with silver, a plumed hat on his head, Masaniello was received by the Viceroy and promptly fainted at his feet in precisely the same way as Paolo Villaggio playing Fracchia on TV. When he came to he professed his allegiance to the Spanish King, like a true Neapolitan revolutionary, and promised a tribute of over a million ducats. (Where on earth did he think they would come from?) The Viceroy for his part presented Masaniello with a gold chain worth three thousand ducats, which Masaniello first refused and finally accepted. Anyway, they appeared together on the balcony, and the enthusiastic crowd greeted them ecstatically with cheers for the King, Masaniello, and the Madonna. A few days later the Viceroy's wife, the Countess of Arcos, presented Masaniello's wife, Donna Bernardina, with three dresses and invited them both to the palace once again for a private dinner. That was when the mysterious incident of the lemonade occurred."

"The lemonade?"

"That's right, the lemonade. The drama of Masaniello, my friends, is a drama in two acts, and the curtain falls on the first act at the moment when Masaniello drinks that lemonade at the palace. History is unclear about what happened, but there are three theories: either the lemonade was poisoned, or someone deliberately started the rumor that Masaniello was mad, or power went to his head. Whatever the reason, we know that Masaniello was never the same again once he had drunk that lemonade. He went, as we say, off his rocker and began to do the most extraordinary things. He kissed the Duke of Arcos' feet, he kicked the Count of Maddaloni, he delayed the Viceroy's cortege, which was accompanying him to the Cathedral, to take a leak behind a fountain, he proclaimed himself 'Generalissimo of the Most

Serene Republic of Naples,' and in short, he made a complete fool of himself. This second act of the drama lasted, like the first, for exactly five days and eventually went down in the history books as 'the five mad days of Masaniello.' My own interpretation is very simple. Just as an Earthling could never survive on another planet without an oxygen tank, so Masaniello, as a Neapolitan through and through, was unable to breathe on a planet totally unfamiliar to him, the planet Power."

"Poor Masaniello!"

"The strange thing was that Masaniello, in the midst of all this uproar and in the space of only ten days, was also able to dispense rather energetically a kind of justice. He eliminated many brigands that the Spanish viceroys had never managed to lay their hands on and emptied the prisons by either granting amnesties or dealing out death sentences with a ruthlessness that Draco himself might have envied. Of course, no appeals were allowed. But the madness brought on by the unfamiliar exercise of power was already snapping at his heels. Eventually everyone turned against him, the Spaniards, the *lazzaroni,* even his erstwhile companions of the barricades. He was imprisoned, but he escaped and took refuge in the Church of the Carmine, and here he astonished everyone by taking the pulpit and making this final address to his followers: 'My friends, my people, everyone! You think I'm mad, and you may be right: I really am mad. But it's not my fault, it's others who have made me mad! All I have done I did because I loved you, and perhaps this is the madness that has unsettled my brain. You were garbage, and now you are free. But how long will your freedom last? One day? Two days? Not more, for you have grown sleepy and you all want to go to bed. And you're right! A man can't live with a gun in his hand. Do like Masaniello: go mad, laugh, and roll on the ground. You are fathers of children! But if you want to stay free, then stay awake! Hold on to your guns! Look! Can't you see? They have given me poison, and now they want to kill me too. And they are right to say that a fisherman cannot become a generalissimo from one moment to the next. But I never meant any harm, and I don't want anything. If anyone truly loves me, let him offer just one prayer for me, just a requiem when I die. For the rest, I repeat: I want nothing. I came into the world naked, and I will die naked! Look!' And so saying, he took off all his clothes. The women shrieked, the men laughed, and Masaniello began to weep. His speech had not, in effect, been directed to the people at all, but to God. They chased him and shot him in one of the vaults under the church. He was twenty-six years old. They cut off his head and threw his body into a ditch. After a few days, when the Viceroy raised the price of bread, the people began to understand what Masaniello had meant to them. His body was recovered, and the head stitched back in place. One hundred and twenty thousand Neapolitans carried his body in procession, clothed in white linen and resting on a pall of black velvet."

"What a lovely story, Professò," said Saverio, "so beautiful and moving. And you told it just as though you'd been there yourself."

"Was that the only revolution the Neapolitans ever had?"

"The only one of a truly popular nature. In point of fact, the history of the so-called 'most faithful city of Naples' includes something like forty instances of revolt and sedition, but every one, apart from Masaniello's, was of aristocratic origin. Look, for example, at the barons' conspiracy, the revolt of the Prince of Macchia, or the revolutions of 1799, 1821, and 1848. All these share the common feature of a clear division of forces: the nobles or the intellectuals on the one side, the king and the masses on the other."

"And the Republic of Naples?"

"Ah, now, that was the third significant episode I wanted to say something about."

"Okay, Professò, but hurry, because the TV movie will be starting soon," urged Saverio.

"Listen, Professò, no one cares a damn about movies on TV!" Salvatore interrupted impatiently. "Leave television to the ignorant. You say what you want to say, and don't worry about things like that."

"So, the Republic of Naples!" Bellavista continued without

waiting for a second invitation. "The Republic of Naples, which I mentioned before by the name given to it by the revolutionaries of 1799, was the natural daughter of the more famous French Revolution, but it is immediately obvious that in this case mother and daughter have precious little in common. By a quite incredible misreading of the script, it was the aristocrats and intellectuals who manned the barricades in the Neapolitan revolution, and the *sans-culottes* who defended the monarchy!"

"Professò, I couldn't follow that at all!"

"I was saying, Savè, that in Naples the people, instead of revolting against the monarchy as they did in Paris, all took the side of the King."

"But why?"

"Because nobody had ever taken the trouble to explain to the Neapolitans what the word 'republic' actually meant. But to return to what we were saying, it all began in 1798 when the King and Queen of Naples, misled by Nelson's victory over Napoleon in the battle of the Nile, decided to send an army to Rome to chase out the French. To tell the truth, such an enterprise was totally out of character for Ferdinand, who, if for no better reason than the risk of having to forgo a few days' hunting, would never have declared war on anybody. But unfortunately our poor Ferdinand had his wife to contend with, the formidable Maria Carolina of Austria, who, since she hated the poor, her husband, the Neapolitans, and Napoleon, bullied him into attacking the French. It occurs to me that had Maria Carolina been born a hundred and fifty years later, she would have made the ideal wife for Adolf Hitler. Anyway, war had hardly been declared before forty thousand Neapolitans, under the command of a ridiculous Austrian general called Mack, invaded Rome."

"Like Lazio-Napoli, Professò," said Saverio.

"What?"

"Like when there's a match between Lazio and Napoli and 'forty thousand Neapolitans invade Rome!'"

"Savè, my friend, don't confuse me!" protested the Professor.

"Now, as I was saying, Mack invaded with his army of forty thousand and was almost immediately confronted by the right flank of the French army commanded by General Macdonald, who, with a force of only eight thousand fighting men, still gave the Neapolitans a ferocious drubbing. Then, on the outskirts of Otricoli, Mack had the misfortune to come up against the French commander in chief, Championnet, with the rest of the French army, and the rout began to achieve the proportions of an authentic disaster. Ferdinand, who had been prepared to make his escape ever since the first downturn in the fortunes of war, hesitated no longer. Disguised as a gentleman, so to speak, he went to Naples and collected his children, Maria Carolina, Marshal Acton, the Hamiltons, the crown jewels and the treasure of San Gennaro, a few valuable antiquities from Herculaneum, and everything in the palace that was both valuable and portable, and boarded the first ship bound for Sicily, leaving as his substitute the poor, peace-loving Prince Pignatelli. One can imagine him saying, 'Ciccì, do as you like: resist if you want to resist, make a truce if you want to make a truce, but excuse me because I'm in a slight hurry.' "

"Some king!" said Saverio.

"As a certain poet of the period said, 'He came, he saw, he fled,' " continued the Professor. "Now, at that point the situation seemed hopeless, but then, completely unexpectedly, came the first *coup de théâtre*. The people of Naples, with no Bourbon general to lead them, without prompting and quite uncharacteristically, rebelled against the liberating forces, and poor Championnet, instead of being ushered into Naples along roads lined with cheering throngs, found himself facing an amazing army of guerrillas who had to be fought street by street and alleyway by alleyway. And what happened? Well, quite simply, the people of Naples—whom Ferdinand considered a race of cowards and Maria Carolina held to be less than the dust beneath her feet—to cries of 'Long live the King and San Gennaro,' did nothing less than stop the invincible army of Napoleon! Pignatelli, who hadn't a clue about what was going on, signed an armistice with Championnet that in effect recognized the existence of a Republic of Naples, at the same time agreeing to pay over large sums of money to the French army. Meanwhile, the Neapolitan intellectuals began to draw up the guidelines for the new Republic. You will look in vain for typical surnames like Cacace and Esposito among these Jacobins. The roll call of the first martyrs of Neapolitan democracy contains only aristocratic names: Carafa, Filomarino, Pimentel-Fonseca, Serra, Sanfelice, Caracciolo, Ruvo, and so on and so forth. Of the common people there are none. The only such name I remember is that of a certain Michele, who, because he sided with the Republicans, went down in history as Michele the Mad."

"And what happened next?"

"As it turned out, our first Republicans were too much poets and too little statesmen to be able to set a new Republic on its feet, which is why one could probably say that the only real Italian gifted with both democratic spirit and practical know-how was the French general Championnet. But unfortunately the Parthenopean Republic lost even this single able defender. Jealousy among the generals, the shortsightedness of the Directorate, and gossip spread by a singularly unpleasant individual called Faypoult all resulted in Championnet's being recalled to France and eventually put on trial. Meanwhile, at Punta del Pezzo, near Reggio Calabria, a certain Cardinal Ruffo landed in the name of the King with a tiny band of about ten men. This Ruffo was a great soldier, clever and courageous, a gifted orator, and a brilliant horseman—he was everything, in fact, except a cardinal. By the exercise of these gifts he managed to assemble a vast army under the standard of the Holy Faith, and having allied himself with the greatest brigands of the age, he attacked the French from the north and south simultaneously. Lo Sciarpa, Michele Pezza (known as Fra Diavolo), Pronio, and the terrible Gaetano Mammone put down the poor weak Jacobins with the most appalling brutality, and Macdonald, who had taken over command from Championnet, was doomed to disappointment when he drafted San Gennaro, or rather Cardinal Zurlo, into the army to perform the Miracle post-haste in hopes of winning the sympathy of the *lazzaroni;* by this time the Parthenopean Republic was a lost cause. I should mention, with regard to San Gennaro, that because of the Miracle performed in the presence of the French, the Neapolitans deposed him as their patron saint and replaced him with Sant'Antonio. Benedetto Croce tells the story about the Neapolitans being so disgusted with San Gennaro that they exhibited a picture of him in Rua Catalana being whipped by Sant'Antonio. But they were incapable of staying angry with him for long, and the first minor eruption of Vesuvius was enough to make them reinstate him as their patron saint."

"And what happened to the Republic?"

"It came to a very bad end! Cardinal Ruffo occupied Naples and laid siege to the fortress of Sant'Elmo and the Castello dell'Ovo, where the last of the patriots had taken refuge—the French having already fled at the first hint of danger. Ruffo, who was on the whole a man of honor, promised safe conduct to all the revolutionaries, but the ss monster Maria Carolina and her worthy companion Lady Emma Hamilton, described as an ex-prostitute by Colletta, persuaded Nelson to tear up the safe conducts and to destroy the flower of the city's intelligentsia without pity."

"Poor bastards!"

"Now, I chose these three episodes from the history of Naples because I believe that the conduct of the Neapolitan people in these circumstances provides a key to the Neapolitan soul itself. Three different situations, one pattern of behavior. Whether they are dealing with subjugation by a foreign power, popular revolution, or intellectual revolt, in each case we find them rejecting the option of power. Subjected to foreign domination, they submit passively; presented with the unexpected gift of power, they decline it; and when the intellectuals provoke a social upheaval, they refuse to jump on the ready-made bandwagon.

The only battles they will fight are in defense of the essentials of life or for the love of King and Church. So the question we should now ask ourselves is this: Are we a people of love, or are we just plain ignorant? The two hypotheses are so interwoven that we will never be sure."

"Don't you think, Professò, that it could be the climate that makes a Neapolitan indifferent to power? Or even that the water we drink, from the Serino, maybe—I don't know—refrigerates our insides? I mean, look, just imagine someone working himself up into such a state that he's ready to smash everything in sight, and suddenly he realizes he's thirsty, so he drinks a glass of water, and immediately, as if by magic, his rage vanishes like snow in the midday sun. Don't you think that could be, Professò?"

"Would to God, Salvatò, that Naples had a source of water with such miraculous properties! We could bottle it and sell it all over the world!"

"Then we'd be a manufacturing country too, Professò!"

"Whatever it is, there must be something in the air that restrains us, that makes us less ambitious, otherwise it would be impossible to explain what happened to Hannibal, Celestino V, and Renato Carosone."

"Hannibal and Carosone?"

"Hannibal trekked halfway across Europe to destroy Rome, crossed the Alps with all those elephants, won the most tremendous battles, and then, when Rome was within his grasp, decided to stop at Capua, saying that at the moment what he really wanted was a few months' vacation. Celestino V was actually in Naples when he decided to make the 'great renunciation,' and do you realize that what he renounced was the Papacy itself, the most prestigious office that existed in his time? And finally Carosone, who at the height of his fame abandoned all artistic activity with the excuse that he had already earned enough."

"As I see it, Professò," said Saverio, "Neapolitans are ambitious without overdoing it. A limited partnership as far as ambition's concerned, if you see what I mean."

"What Saverio's saying," said the Professor, "is that in his view a Neapolitan acts as though he had a psychostatic fuse in his brain, a trip switch thrown automatically whenever the pressure of responsibility and its concomitant worry reaches a certain level."

"What do you mean, trip switch?"

"Savè, you know how an immersion heater works. The water gets hotter and hotter, and when it reaches a certain temperature, a simple thermostat activates a switch that turns the heater off. The principle's exactly the same."

"Ah, now I see," said Saverio. "What you're saying is that a Neapolitan heats up like an immersion heater, but only to a certain point, because then this inside switch gets triggered off and says, 'Hey there, do you really give a shit?' "

"In my opinion, however, it's all a matter of order and disorder," said Luigino. "Order generates power, and disorder generates love. Suppose, for instance, that Hitler had been born in Naples and that Naples had been his starting point for conquering the world. To begin with, he would never have found enough Eichmanns prepared to follow his orders without question, and then, let's face it, his famous 'final solution' required the sort of organization that we Neapolitans would never have been able to supply."

"When you think about it, the slaughter of five or six million Jews must have been a fairly complicated business!"

"There would have been some amazing scenarios," Luigino continued. "Let's imagine, for example, Hitler giving orders for a truckload of Jews to be transported from a camp, say, at Frattamaggiore to the gas ovens at Agnano. On the journey, the Neapolitan SS driver naturally starts up a conversation with the Jew sitting nearest to him. He might say, 'Wasn't it kind of a mistake to have been born a Jew? Take my advice, get yourself baptized!' And the other man says, 'But I can hardly help being a Jew. My parents are Jews, my children are Jews, we're all Jews together.' 'Oh, then you're a family man?' 'Yes, indeed, I've got three little ones.' 'What? *Gesù, Gesù, è pate 'e figlie!* There must be some way I can help this poor man! I know, when we turn off the main road and no one's looking, I'll stop and let him out.' End of Italian Nazi Party."

"Luigino's right. It's all a question of order and disorder," said Salvatore. "And that's why, when I get up in the morning and see pieces of paper and bags of trash still lying around all over the place, I always breathe a sigh of relief and say to myself, 'Relax, Salvatò, it's just another day!' "

XXVIII

THE THIEF

"WHAT HAPPENED?"

"I don't know, I just got here."

"But what's all the fuss about?"

"I'm not sure, but I think someone caught a thief."

"No, no! They nearly caught him, but he got away!"

"*Gesù!* You can't feel safe for a second with all these thieves around!"

A vast crowd. At least a hundred people gathered outside a toy shop in Piazza Mercato. I was late already and would really have liked to get home quickly, but my Neapolitan soul rebelled at the thought of passing an incident without discovering the whys and wherefores. I at least had to find out the nature of the disturbance.

"Excuse me, do you know what happened?"

"My dear sir, that's the second time you've asked me, and surely you can see that I'm doing my best to find out! Just be patient, and in a few seconds I'll tell you all you want to know!"

Only those in the very center of the crowd could really know the details of what had happened, while I and the gentleman I had questioned, being on the fringe, had to depend on the reports of people who in turn had heard about it not from the principals themselves but from secondary sources, that is, from those who claimed to have been the first to hear the particulars from the real actors in the drama. The disparity between the versions (some of which were probably the work of mythomaniacs, made up out of whole cloth) was such that we felt obliged to force our way through the intervening satellite groups and infiltrate the focal point of the disturbance. This turned out to be a short, bespectacled man with red hair and a red face who was shouting and trying to explain his grievance to anyone who would listen, all the while tenaciously clutching a soccer ball under one arm.

"I'm telling you, if I'd managed to catch him I'd have killed him, I really would!"

"What happened?" asked a new arrival.

"What's the use! This isn't Naples anymore, it's the Wild West! We're going to have to carry guns on our belts like Gary Cooper! I'll tell you what happened. I just popped into the shop for a minute to buy a soccer ball for my nephew Filuccio for Christmas, and I left my car unlocked for a second . . ."

"That was really asking for it. I mean, how can you complain about thieves in Naples if you leave your car open?"

"So what? I only went in for a second, and because I knew the car was unlocked I watched it the whole time. I had one eye on the toys and the other on the car."

"Maybe, but an unlocked car's always a provocation," insisted the man who had spoken before.

"In Sweden they don't even have locks," volunteered another man. "And nothing is ever stolen. The prisons are empty."

"As I was saying, I popped into Minale's for a toy, and knowing that I had left the car unlocked, I kept one eye on it while I looked for a soccer ball for my nephew Filuccio with the other—and to prove it, I even asked this lady here, who was one ahead of me in the line, to change places with me because I'd left my car open. That's right, isn't it, Signora?"

"Why, yes," said the lady called as witness. "He asked me if he could pay first, and I let him through."

"But while I was paying, when I was actually standing there with the money in one hand and the soccer ball in the other, what do I see but this damn scoundrel getting into my car! I saw red, I pushed past the lady . . ."

"You certainly did! You pushed me right over!" said the woman, now established in the role of principal witness. "If it hadn't been for this nice boy . . ."

". . . I pushed past the lady, dropped the ball, and rushed to my car to catch the bastard. But he was like an eel! I grabbed him by one foot, but he was jerking like an epileptic and kicking me in the face and I couldn't hang on to the stinking, slimy son of a bitch; he slipped out of my hands. In one door and out the other!"

"That's exactly what happened," said one of the bystanders. "The villain disappeared down a side street while the gentleman was still sprawled over the seats of the car."

"I wish I'd gotten my hands on him! *Madonna mia,* if only I'd gotten my hands on him! What I'd have done to him would've been nobody's business! I've had my radio stolen five times! Five times! The insurance company hates me! They're fed up with my claims! The last time they made no bones about it. They told me not to put a radio in the car again because they'd refuse to pay up if it was stolen. I can't even enjoy a little music in the car now! Believe me, I've only got one ambition, to get my hands on one of those thieving bastards and give him such a walloping that he'll be lucky to get away alive!"

"You're absolutely right. As long as the State won't impose the death penalty, we have to take the law into our own hands."

"Hey, come on! The death penalty for petty theft?"

"Signora Santojanni, an old widow of seventy, was mugged yesterday evening right in front of the church," said another man. "They kicked the poor old woman around like a rag doll!"

"What I want to know is what the police were doing! They're never there when they're needed!"

"Naturally! All they're good for is slapping on fines for parking violations, but if they ever see someone stealing, they look the other way."

"That's not quite true, Signora. They catch them, they catch them all right, but it's the courts in Italy that are to blame. As soon as they get hold of them, they turn them loose."

"What happened?" asked another new arrival.

"They were about to steal this gentleman's car."

"Who does this child belong to?"

"Pasqualino, Mamma's little angel, what are you up to?"

"Signora, please hold on to your child and tell him not to touch the toys."

"So did they catch the guy?"

"No, the gentleman let him get away."

"What happened?" asked another man.

The bespectacled gentleman at whom the question was directed, still clutching his soccer ball, paused for a second or two for dramatic effect and then replied:

"I went to buy this soccer ball for my nephew Filuccio, leaving my car unlocked in front of the shop . . ."

"I don't believe it! You left your car unlocked in Piazza Mercato?"

"For heaven's sake, I wasn't far away! I had my eye on it all the time! And I even asked this lady here, who was one ahead of me in line, if she would be kind enough to allow me to pay first because I had left my car unlocked."

"That's just what he said," the woman agreed. "And while he was paying he spotted the car thief."

"As soon as I saw him I rushed out. I pushed past the signora . . ."

"You certainly did! You pushed me right over! If it hadn't been for this nice boy who put out a hand . . ."

". . . I pushed past the signora, dropped the ball, and threw myself at the villain, managing to grab him by the foot. But the son of a bitch was like an eel, wriggling and twisting all over the place . . ."

While the gentleman was involved in the umpteenth account of the incident, a sudden and complete silence fell upon the crowd, which parted to make way for a boy of about fourteen—the "car thief"—and a tall, strapping man who propelled him forward with a hand on his shoulder.

"Dottò," the man said with all the calm assurance of the established *guappo*, "during the incident that took place a few minutes ago, the gold chain the boy was wearing around his neck dropped off in your car. It was a memento of his dear departed mother. Is your car unlocked, Dottò?"

"It is," the man replied.

"Ciccì, go and get your chain. The *dottore* won't mind."

XXIX

THE MIDDLE WAY

Stasira li cimi di l'arbuli
chi movinu la testa e li vrazza
parlano d'amuri a la terra
e io li sentu.

Sunnu li paroli di sempri
chi vui scurdastivu
cumpagni di viaggiu
nudi e pilusi
in transitu dintra gaggi di ferru. *

IGNAZIO BUTTITTA, 1968

"SO THE HOLIDAYS ARE OVER," the Professor said to me. "I don't know whether you feel the same, Ingegnere, but here it seems that no sooner have we begun to enjoy the prospect of Christmas than we find ourselves in the New Year. It's as if the days themselves were not what they used to be, all equal, all twenty-four hours long. Every day seems shorter than its predecessor, maybe only by the merest fraction of a second, but shorter nonetheless. The theory of the acceleration of time is not mine. It was propounded by a certain de Sitter, a Dutch astronomer who said that the days are getting shorter because the universe is contracting, not expanding as most of the other scientists say. De Sitter also maintains that as a result of this quickening of the pulse rate and this contraction, one day the universe will vanish

*"This evening the tree tops/as they wave their heads and arms/are speaking of love to the earth/and I can hear them./These are the eternal words/which you have forgotten/travelers/naked and hairy/traveling in your metal cages."

altogether. As for us, we're contracting too. A few days ago Dottor Vittorio vanished, and tomorrow you're returning to Rome, so it will be only myself, Luigino, Saverio, and Salvatore left behind in Naples, as usual. By the way, Ingegnere, anytime you feel that I'm talking too much, do me a favor and stop me. I know it's my greatest weakness to talk and talk and never let anybody else get a word in edgewise. The trouble is that even after talking at length I worry about not having made myself clear or having confused my listeners, so then I go on talking in order to summarize . . . to clarify . . . Take the discourse on love and liberty, for example, or my condemnation of power—all subjects that are open to misinterpretation. If, as often happens, the person listening to me fails to pigeonhole me comfortably according to his own preconceived notions, that can have most unfortunate consequences for me. I can find myself represented as the nostalgic minstrel of an imaginary Naples, a quaint, picturesque Naples that has never existed except on picture postcards . . . or as a speculator, a dishonest seeker after power, an advocate of apathy. It never seems to occur to anyone that there might be, deep down, a message for humanity! But this is the crux of the matter. If we truly want to live our lives to the full, we must try to use our heads and our hearts and set out upon the middle way. All things considered, the recipe is simple enough to remember: equal measures of love and liberty. In fact, my diagram, as I'm sure you will remember, demonstrated that the middle way could only be achieved by a perfect equilibrium between the desire for love and the desire for liberty. There are times when I ask myself, Am I free or do I only think I am free? Do I perhaps speak, think, and act only in response to the way others expect me to speak, think, and act? Power generally has the upper hand, whether imposed overtly in the form of a dictatorship or subtly by means of conditioning. But freedom means being sure of having reasoned things out in one's own mind without allowing oneself to be influenced by propaganda. And that is not easy! Still, if men will only begin to distrust mass opinion . . . if they will refuse to swell the chorus of marchers chanting any cheap slogan that hap-

pens to rhyme . . . if they could get into the habit of asking themselves every time they buy something, Do I really want this, or
am I being duped by the interests of power into thinking I want
it? . . . then, perhaps, we stand a chance of finding the road to
freedom.

"But who or what is this thing called power? Some identify it
with Capital, others with America, but in both cases there is an
error of scale. The CIA and the multinationals are only little
concentrations of power, not Power itself. The truth is that we
ourselves are the begetters of power. We ourselves, with our
ambition to command, generate millions and millions of mole-
cules of power and end up creating an abstract monster, amoral
and immeasurable, that takes on a life of its own. How can we
control it? How can we defend ourselves? It's not easy, because
power begins its work of subversion when we are still children, so
that by the time we realize what's happening, we wake up to find
ourselves sitting in a moving train, the train of habit. The week-
end break, the car, the things we have bought and must now
protect against theft—in short, all those things that go to make
up our standard of living—now make it difficult for us to get off
the train. And many of us are not alone on the train, we have
wives and children . . . and how can we possibly jump off a
moving train with the whole family? What can you do, for example, if your wife claims that she really must have a vacation on the
Costa Smeralda, or your daughter has set her heart on a moped?
Either you abandon them to their fate and jump off the train
alone, or you work overtime to satisfy their demands. So to
preempt this dilemma, what is needed is a gradual war against
power, the Kissinger 'step-by-step' approach. Without making a
fuss about it, we can refuse a promotion one day, an award the
next, and thus, millimeter by millimeter, we can haul ourselves
up the axis of liberty. Is the television showing commercials?
Turn away and refuse to watch it. Is it a sunny day? Leave the car
at home and walk to work. To put it simply, because the conditioning effects of power are always aimed at the masses, it's not

difficult to see what we have to avoid: the masses, or rather, mass habits. I'm not advocating elitism, because if your desire for liberty leads you to shun the masses, your desire for love will draw you toward them. Never toward the masses as a uniform body, mind, but as an entity made up of individuals, individuals who are all different from each other. You see, depending upon whether you are looking at it from the perspective of power or from the love-liberty point of view, the mass can obviously be regarded either as a single body with a million heads or as a million individuals. Left and Right define only partially: when I have dealings with a man, the only thing I need to know about him is whether or not he is an individualist. That is important. There are those, for example, who believe that all men are evil. Thomas Hobbes is their prophet, and they love dictatorship. Others want democracy because they are convinced, with Rousseau, that men are born naturally good and are only corrupted by the system. Well, my own view is that the majority of men are, as it were, basically good, and that hate is the dominant factor only in the case of a few hardened criminals. One day perhaps we shall all agree with Lorenz that violence has its origins in an organic secretion, and then we shall solve the whole problem by taking down the signs saying 'Prison' and replacing them with ones saying 'Hospital.' But at the present time I believe that our major concern is not the treatment of criminals, from whom society must always defend itself by putting them either in hospitals or in prisons, but the cultivation of the seeds of goodness in the majority. In short, I see men not as evil creatures but not as very good ones either—merely as small. Small because mediocre. Small because they almost always lack faith. In spite of which, however, man has an enormous latent capacity for faith. Never have astrologers, fortune-tellers, and palm readers done such a roaring business as now! Anyone who wishes to dress himself up as a seer will find himself inundated with swarms of men and women, especially women, educated and illiterate alike, all desperate to know about the future. The Church never recognized the existence of this reservoir of faith, or perhaps one should say, rather, never succeeded in tapping it and diverting these millions of cubic meters of faith to its own arid plains. Still, the Church has always managed to survive even the most difficult periods throughout history, always finding the apposite saint for the purpose. But today, despite the efforts of John XXIII, the theologians continue to sit around tables discussing the acceptability or otherwise of masturbation and seem not to realize that a little gesture of love or humility would suffice to draw into the Church millions of despairing souls who ask nothing better than to believe. But God in heaven, how can any intelligent man, in this day and age, be expected to identify with a medieval bishop who tells him that he should copulate only to procreate? Do you realize that when our generation has passed away, the only people who'll still be talking about sex will probably be the priests? It's time to grow up and to remember when we talk about Christ that we are talking above all about compassionate love. Pascal said that all that was necessary for faith was to desire ardently that God exist, and he was right. But Pascal loved only God, mystically, immeasurably, but only God. Pascal had no love for men! Belief in God, Faith, can represent an enormous personal resource, but only love for our neighbor is capable of solving our existential problems, not in the sense of promising a reward in the afterlife, but in giving a meaning to our existence itself.

"My mother, for example, coped serenely with all the problems of a protracted old age because she was upheld by her faith and her love for others. She was eighty, and she had erected a sort of tiny altar in her room—actually a small marble-topped table and a *prie-dieu*. On the wall above she stuck pictures of all her favorite saints, the beloved Sacred Heart of Jesus, and photographs of those she called 'my dear departed.' Every day she recited hundreds of requiems for the souls of the dead. Every dead person had his own picture and his own allotted quota of her prayers. Over the last year or so before she died, the list of her dear departed grew enormously, because my mother didn't restrict herself to deaths in our immediate family circle but would add a name to her roll call whenever anyone died who had the smallest claim on her affection. I remember she even had photographs of Mario Riva and Marilyn Monroe. 'Poor dear,' she said, 'what a terrible way to die!' Until the very last years of her life, she was in the habit of going to church every morning to make her communion, and sometimes I would stand on the balcony and watch her getting smaller and smaller as she got farther and farther away. And the strangest thing was that my mother really did get smaller, she physically shrank, as if all the time she spent at prayer was drawing her day by day and bit by bit into that minuscule paradise of saintly figurines and dead strangers. There are times when I think that my mother never died like all other mortals but simply got smaller and smaller until she disappeared.

"I talk about love, about God, about my neighbor, and then I realize that I am a man of liberty. That's how consistent I am! Yet I want to love. My wife and daughter can't understand me. They regard me as a Martian or an exotic animal in the zoo. They probably think that old age has completely addled my brains, and they put up with me as one would put up with an invalid in the family. They seem to possess a kind of complacency stemming from their conviction that everything in life can be resolved by trotting out one precise rule: one does this, one doesn't do that, one must do the other, because otherwise 'it doesn't look good.' That is the dreadful phrase that governs most of our lives: 'It doesn't look good.' The problem of free will simply disappears in the face of that sentence, 'It doesn't look good.' The obligatory presents, the wearing of mourning, the woman who *must* marry, the tie, the good wishes, the note of sympathy, the kind regards, eating chicken with a knife and fork, but not fish, the wife who is *expected* to become pregnant . . . 'otherwise it doesn't look good.' According to my wife, I should never invite Salvatore and Saverio to my house, and Luigino only rarely, 'otherwise it doesn't look good.' I can invite you and Dottor Palluotto, however, because you are university-educated men. My wife has read *The Leopard, The Godfather,* and *Jaws,* she confuses Chopin and Schopenhauer, goes to exercise classes to stay slim and to the film club to save money. When she sees a falling star, the first wish that comes into her head is to learn to play bridge, because as everyone knows, it's such a genteel game. My daughter, on the other hand, claims to be agnostic, feminist, and rational, but whenever she meets a boy she likes, the first question she asks him is what sign he was born under, and if he answers Leo she says, 'Leo? I knew it!' I gave my daughter a beautiful name, Aspasia, the name of Pericles' hetaera, one of the most beautiful and intelligent women in history, but she didn't like the name. 'Poor child,' her mother said, 'what has she done to you to deserve such a name?' And now she calls herself Patrizia, like a few hundred thousand other girls her age. Yesterday Patrizia bought herself a Fendi canvas bag. 'See all these F's, Papà?' she said. 'It's signed all over, that's why it costs so much more.' These are all links in a chain of events whose logical result is universal uniformity.

"Let's imagine now that Christ decided to return to Earth. How do you think He would try to reach men's hearts? What would the apostles do to spread the Word? Would they stand at intersections distributing leaflets like the Jehovah's Witnesses? Not a chance. In the overcrowded, bustling world of today, there is only one way Jesus could make Himself heard—by appearing on prime-time television any day of the week. It would not even be necessary to perform any great miracles; all He'd need would be a reasonably powerful pirate station and a couple of good technicians. Besides, with the present advanced state of television technology, no one would be in a position to distinguish a miracle from a special effect. But given this opportunity, what would Jesus say? He might begin with the words of the Gospel, 'I am the Light of the World . . . verily I say unto you. . .' Then He would stop and look sadly at all the television viewers sitting in their armchairs, and He would murmur, 'Blessed are they that have not seen, and yet have believed . . .' People would think it was a publicity stunt or something devised, perhaps, by Luca Ronconi."